TEMPTED BY BEAUTY

Brides of Northumbria #3

CATE MELVILLE

www.catemelvilleauthor.com

***Tempted by Beauty*/Cate Melville/1st edition**

Published by Threepwood Press

ISBN: 978-0-473-64823-7

Cover Design: https://gmbookcoversdesign.com

*"Darkness must pass
A new day will come
And when the sun shines
It will shine out the clearer."*

—*JRR Tolkien*

Chapter One

BARMOOR CASTLE, NORTHUMBRIA
Late May 1156

IT TOOK two days for Gilbret to ensure Barmoor Castle was securely under his control. Now he had to find a wife. How, in God's name, he would manage that feat was a mystery.

Heaving a resigned sigh he mounted his courser and rode through the gates. Olivier, his squire, and five men at arms accompanied Gilbret on the fifty-mile journey back to Beauforde. They arrived late, but Ranulf was there to meet them.

"Come, I have viands and wine for you." Ranulf didn't try to hide his curiosity. He was like a wasp's nest about to burst. It reminded Gilbret of when they had been boys. Both outcasts and in need of each other's friendship. Gilbret handed Maigemor's reins to Olivier and watched him lead the horse towards the stables.

"Joss will see to Olivier and your things." Gilbret turned to see Ranulf's young squire slap Olivier on the back as they met. His life at Beauforde was over. In the space of a week Gilbret's future had irrevocably changed and like a piece of flotsam carried along by the river's current he was forced to wait and see where Fortuna led him. Could he have refused? Possibly, but what of his mother and sister? No. He was no victim. He had signed the charter and had accepted his father's edict.

Gilbret turned away and followed Ranulf into the hall and into the small chamber behind the dais that served as Ranulf's small solar. "As you are no longer my seneschal this chamber is yours for as long as you need." Ranulf hit him hard on the back making Gilbret's head jerk painfully. "Now sit and eat. Then tell me what your arsewipe of a father has done."

Gilbret took a deep drink of wine and dipped his hands in the bowl of water that Gefroi, Ranulf's page, offered him. After washing his hands Gilbret used his fingers to pull at the joint of meat before him as he ordered his thoughts into some semblance of order.

"I'm to inherit the barony."

"What?" Ranulf spluttered. "Your missive said that you were to stay at Barmoor but not that you were its new lord."

His friend's incredulity was to be expected. After all, Gilbret had been a bastard with little hope of inheriting anything when he left several months ago to travel to London to secure grain for Ranulf's estates.

With the scratch of a quill he was not only legitimate but also the new Baron Wooler.

"My clever mother persuaded the "arsewipe" to marry her and legitimize me as he lay dying on his bed."

Ranulf placed his cup of wine on the table and stared at Gilbret. "Why would he agree to that?"

Gilbret huffed a mirthless laugh. "Because the same illness that robbed my father of his life also claimed the life of Giles and his young son." Gilbret had had two half-brothers. John, the younger of the two, had died years ago leaving the eldest son, Giles, as the only heir. Although he couldn't bring himself to mourn Giles he had not wished him dead. The years of torment at the hands of his brothers were all but a distant memory. Growing up at Barmoor he had been "the bastard," the son of his father's mistress and an ideal punching bag for his older and more entitled brothers. In a perverse way Gilbret took pleasure in the irony of the situation. He imagined his sire and two brothers would be spinning in their graves to know that the "bastard" had inherited the prize.

Ranulf blew air through his teeth as he digested Gilbret's news. "When will you leave?" The note of regret in Ranulf's voice echoed Gilbret's own sorrow at leaving his friend. Ranulf had been like a brother to Gilbret and he would miss his friendship and his counsel.

Gilbret swallowed the food in his mouth as he considered his response. "I can't leave Barmoor unprotected for long but there is a complication that demands my attention first."

Ranulf raised his eyebrows in silent question.

"I have to find a wife before Lammas."

"God's bones, man, you have less than two months until it's Lammas."

It wasn't in Ranulf's nature to be so obtuse, which indicated that Gilbret's predicament had him shaken to the core.

"Thank you for the reminder," he said sourly.

Ranulf was inured to Gilbret's sarcasm and continued to think out loud. Which Gilbret didn't find at all helpful. It had never occurred to him that his own tendency to think aloud could be so bloody annoying.

But that was how Ranulf tackled a problem so Gilbret waited quietly for his friend to find a solution. Where did one find a wife, and at such short notice? What a godawful mess.

It took several more glasses of wine before Ranulf hit on a remedy.

"Marry Beatrice."

Gilbret spluttered his wine all over his surcoat. He wiped at his chest with the linen towel Ranulf handed him. Gilbret glanced at Ranulf. "Have you lost your mind?"

"Well, I see you are thinking about it." Ranulf eyed him as he continued to sip his wine.

"She's a wet nurse." Admittedly Gilbret was no great catch but even so, marrying a wet nurse was unthinkable.

"She isn't any longer." Ranulf watched Gilbret over the rim of his wine glass. Gilbret recognized that look.

He had been away for several months on business in the south for Ranulf but surely Beatrice's circumstances could not have changed that quickly? "Tell me."

"It seems my wife has taken great pains to care for Beatrice. When Cicele came last year, the relationship between the three of them changed. But it wasn't until Cicele married and left to live with Guyon at Alnwick that Beatrice and Isabeau became inseparable."

"Your wife has not confided in you regarding Beatrice?" That was extraordinary. Isabeau and Ranulf were devoted to each other and Gilbret had believed they had no secrets from each other.

"My wife, it seems, has been sworn to secrecy where Beatrice is concerned, but I suspect Mistress Beatrice is not whom she claims to be."

Well, that was no surprise to Gilbret. From the very first day he had clapped eyes on the beauty he had suspected she was no miller's widow.

"Who is she then?"

"I don't know but she is now my wife's closest companion."

Extraordinary. Gilbret deliberated while he drained his goblet. If Beatrice was no longer a wet nurse for Elizabet had something happened to her boys? "What of the twins?"

"Elizabet had no need of a wet nurse once they started to eat gruel. That's when Isabeau took Beatrice as her companion."

What did Isabeau know of Beatrice? He had his own suspicions that her tale of being a miller's widow were false. She possessed a dignity that belied her lowly status. Given Isabeau's favor, Beatrice might prove to be his salvation. God knows he didn't want to spend the next two months traversing the countryside searching for a wife.

Beatrice was a beauty. And although he was sure she hid her true identity she was a woman who had impressed him with her diligence and quiet manners. If Isabeau trusted her then he could do no less.

Fate might just be in his favor.

Chapter Two

A NAGGING SENSE OF DREAD HUNG ABOUT HER AS SHE OPENED HER eyes. Another terrifying dream where she was falling but never reached the bottom. That was the third time in as many days. It was a harbinger. But of what?

Her heart raced and her pulse thundered in her ears. Edward! Terrified something was wrong with her little son it took all her resolve not to panic. Slowly Beatrice turned her head on her pillow. "Oh, saints be praised." She gently drew Edward's sleeping form towards her. His little snuffling noises were a balm to her anxious heart.

It had been almost two years since she had fled her husband's wrath and found safety at St. Leonard's, where she had given birth to Edward, and over a year since she had arrived at Beauforde castle. Those two years had been the happiest and safest of her life but the nagging sense of dread warned her that her reprieve was at an end. Her husband, curse his blighted soul, was dead but his brother and her father would not be happy until they saw her shut away in a nunnery and little Edward eliminated.

Gently she stroked her sleeping son's downy head. "We are not safe, my darling," she cooed as she kissed his crown. What options did she have? A quick inventory of possibilities darted through her mind. Each was less and less palatable as she sifted through her options. Even marriage was not an option. And besides, who would marry her?

Faces of the men who had shown her kindness while here at Beauforde danced before her eyes. But it was the seneschal who had caught Beatrice's attention the very first day she arrived. Gilbret de la Haye had been away from the castle for over three months and had returned last evening. Just the thought of him brought a rush of awareness that had her breathing a little quicker. It was an impossible and dangerous desire. Once, a lifetime ago it seemed now, he would have been far below her in status and quite possibly she would not have even noticed him. That was a lie. Gilbret de la Haye was a man no woman would be able to ignore.

But two years had changed her and she was now so far beneath him she would need a siege engine to fling her up and over the barriers that stood in her way. The church was clear on its ruling concerning repudiated women and no man, especially the handsome Sir Gilbret, would risk being excommunicated to marry her.

Even now her cheeks burned as she remembered the first time she had seen him. Although her body responded to his casual glances she had never been one to believe in the impossible. To his mind she was a servant only marginally above a peasant.

Sometimes she was aware of his eyes as they traveled over her face. The intensity of his gaze making her pulse race but he never made advances. For that she was grateful. Her traitorous body might long for the comfort Gilbret de la Haye could give but her mind refused to dwell on the impossible.

Edward's babbling interrupted her thoughts.

"Good morn, my sweet boy."

A toothy smile and a chubby hand greeted her as she bent her head and kissed him on his tiny nose.

Edward, fed and washed, crawled around her feet as Beatrice readied herself for the new day.

Her thoughts once again turned to Sir Gilbret. Why had he returned? There were always rumors about the seneschal but Isabeau seldom mentioned her husband's friend. Three months ago, he had ridden out with his squire and had not returned until last night. It was intriguing but Sir Gilbret was also none of her business.

"Don't delude yourself, Sir Gilbret will turn out to be another Walter—all charm and manners on the outside but blackness and rot underneath," she chided herself as she finished dressing.

A sharp knock on her door made her start.

"Who is it?"

"'Tis Olivier, Mistress Beatrice."

Olivier? What was Sir Gilbret's squire doing knocking on her door?

Beatrice ran her hands down her worn kirtle and checked that her veil was in place before she opened the door. A gangly lad with a winsome smile greeted her.

"Good morn, Mistress, Sir Gilbret requests your presence in his chamber."

"Now?"

"Yes, I am to take you to him."

His smile didn't waver but the lad's eyes warned that he would not be dissuaded.

"Very well, but first I must take Edward to the nursery." She turned and challenged Olivier, "That will be acceptable to your master, I am sure?"

She might be a servant but she would not be cowed by a mere lad.

Edward had crawled over to meet Olivier and was clinging to his leg. Beatrice moved to pick Edward up but Olivier had hoisted him onto his shoulder.

"I shall escort you and Master Edward," he said casually as he tickled Edward.

Beatrice watched in stunned silence as Edward grabbed Olivier's hair, squealed and almost toppled off the lad's shoulder. Olivier had a firm hold of Edward's legs as though Olivier had experience with small children. Squires didn't play nursemaid but this squire seemed at ease with a wriggling child perched precariously on his shoulder.

It was time to reclaim her son and leave but Edward seemed content to stay perched on Olivier's shoulder so she turned to fetch her cloak.

What did Gilbret want with her? And why did he send Olivier to fetch her? Was she under arrest? Had Gilbret returned because he had found out who she was? A visceral terror gripped her, snatching the air from her lungs. She reached out to steady herself.

"Are you well, Mistress?" Olivier's worried tone didn't help; it only made it worse.

"I can't breathe," she gasped as she tried desperately to gather air into her lungs.

"Here, let me help you." Olivier, still holding Edward with his left hand, led her to a chair by the hearth. He poured her some wine from the jug on the table and, crouching before her, he offered her the cup. "Take slow breaths," he counseled in a quiet calming voice.

Beatrice obeyed. When her breathing was a little steadier, he handed her the cup. "Take small sips."

Edward reached for her but Olivier stalled him. "You, young sir, are a wriggling trout." And with that pronouncement hauled Edward upside-down, although Olivier never took his eyes off Beatrice.

She did as bid, aware that his sharp green eyes took note of her face.

"You have nothing to fear, Mistress."

It was thoughtful to offer her this morsel of encouragement but Beatrice would not delude herself. If Sir Gilbret knew who she was then her father knew where she was and her life here at Beauforde was over.

Grief so sharp and all-consuming gripped her. Incapable of controlling the tears that obscured her vision she fingered the cup in her lap and gave herself up to an overwhelming sense of despair.

GILBRET PACED the small solar as he waited for Beatrice to arrive. He was nervous. What if she refused? He had learned in his thirty years of life that nothing was guaranteed merely because one wanted it. His future and that of his mother and sister depended on the outcome of this meeting.

All night he had lain awake trying to puzzle out the reason why Beatrice would lie about her identity. From what Ranulf had told him, Isabeau trusted Beatrice and it stood to reason that she knew some of Beatrice's history. Was he willing to gamble his future and the safety of his mother and sister on a woman whom he knew nothing about? Yes, he was because he was desperate.

She was no miller's wife, of that he was sure, but more likely to be a merchant's daughter fleeing an unwelcome marriage. She had the air of a woman who knew her worth although she tried to hide it.

Since that first day Gilbret had watched the young widow as she went about her business as Elizabet's wet nurse. In truth, he had seldom been able to take his eyes from her. Mistress Beatrice exuded a vulnerability that called to Gilbret's sense of honor. "You are a clodpate," Gilbret chided himself but it was no use lying to himself. He had wanted the woman since he first laid eyes on her. Regardless of her past, he would offer her his name and she would ensure his family's safety.

Olivier entered the solar with Beatrice on his heels. "Mistress Beatrice, my lord."

"Welcome, please sit."

She had a haunted look about her this morning. "Please, there is no need to fear," he said as she sat on a chair. "May I offer you some wine?"

"Why am I here?"

He liked that. No preamble. The woman was forthright, if a little lacking in manners. Still, his mother could help with any deficiencies in that regard. As would a wardrobe more befitting a "lady." Her kirtle was shabby but clean, although it didn't detract from her beauty.

Get on with it, man. He was stalling. Taking a fortifying sip of his wine he took the plunge.

"I apologize if my summons has caused you concern. It was not my intention"

She glanced at him then and their eyes locked. He couldn't breathe. His head swam as though he were plunged under the water. As a boy, he had almost drowned when his brothers held his head under the water when they found him in the river. It was only the fortuitous arrival of his father's steward that had saved Gilbret's life.

Almost immediately she looked back to her hands, breaking their silent contact and thus releasing Gilbret. A wave of regret crashed over him.

Pulling himself together he fought for control over his reaction to her nearness. Being this close to her addled his brain.

Clearing his throat of the stone that seemed to be lodged there he blurted the first thing that came into his head.

"I find that I am in need of a wife." What in God's name was wrong with him?

The silence was one thing but the expression on Beatrice's face told him all he needed to know. She was horrified.

"Excuse me; that was poorly done."

She must have taken pity on him because she gave him a small smile.

"Am I to understand that you are offering marriage?" she asked cautiously.

"Yes." To his acute embarrassment, it came out more of a squeak. "I have just recently been informed that in order to save my mother and sister from destitution I must marry," he announced as he moved his cup of wine several times around the table while avoiding her eyes. Bollocks. Thank God Olivier was not present to witness Gilbret's witless attempt at proposing marriage. He would never live this down.

"I thank you for your offer, Sir Gilbret, but I cannot marry you." It was said quietly but firmly.

Gilbret looked up and caught a fleeting expression of regret before she had a chance to arrange her face in a mask of indifference.

Her refusal had shocked him into thinking clearly. "I am aware that you are in need of protection."

She was about to interrupt but he raised his hand to silence her. "No, please let me finish. I have suspected that you are not whom you claim to be." He gave her a small smile. "You are no more a miller's wife than I am the King of England."

She didn't reply but merely watched him.

"Perhaps a merchant's daughter who has fallen from grace?" He studied her face for any outward sign that he had guessed correctly but she held herself completely still.

"Or perhaps a woman who fled a violent marriage? He twirled the stem of his wine cup between his thumb and forefinger as he waited for her to reply but she remained silent.

Time to push a little harder. "Are you in truth a widow?"

That got a reaction.

"I am a widow." Her indignant tone coupled with her raised eyebrows convinced him that she spoke truthfully.

"If you are in need of protection then I can help." A sudden unwanted thought occurred to him. "Unless you have a secret lover whom you hope to marry?"

There was something rather magnificent about the way she raised her chin to a haughty angle and glared at him in outrage. "I do not."

Gilbret continued to hold her gaze but softened his expression lest she think him angry. "A marriage of convenience would suit us both: I am in need of a wife and you might benefit from a husband's protection."

She tilted her head to the side and considered him much the way a shrewd steward would appraise the silver on the dais.

His skin prickled and he shifted on his seat but he did not avert his gaze.

"Would you not be advised to seek a woman of your own class? I am not of noble birth."

Somehow that statement didn't ring true but Gilbret decided to ignore it and instead answered her question. "I am the bastard son of Baron Wooler. He died and his will stipulated that I marry before Lammas if I have any hope of saving my mother and sister from ruin." He took a breath to steady his racing heart. "In short, Mistress Beatrice, I do not have the option of wooing a woman of noble birth between now and Lammas."

She gave him a disarming smile. "I see." Her gaze traveled over his face before she lowered her gaze and looked at her hands.

Gilbret couldn't drag his eyes away from her lips—she was nibbling at the corner of her mouth in concentration. All the blood drained from his brain and pooled in his groin. It was agony but he forced himself not to shift in his seat.

Another small sympathetic smile creased the corners of her mouth. *She is going to refuse me.* Gilbret couldn't breathe.

"I am sorry, Sir Gilbret, but I can't marry you …"

"Can't or won't?" Now he sounded like a petulant boy who had had his favorite toy taken from him.

Again that sad smile. "I cannot marry you. I am truly sorry. Please forgive me." And with that, she rose and walked from the solar.

Chapter Three

"You seem upset. Is there something wrong?" Isabeau's voice broke through Beatrice's anxious thoughts. She had tried to pretend that all was well as she sat sewing with Isabeau in the lady's solar but she couldn't stop thinking about Gilbret and his offer of marriage. Never would she subject him to the wrath of the church. Or subject herself to another marriage. At least he would not be here to remind her of his earnest face as he sought to understand why she had refused. A part of her heart broke as she witnessed his confusion. Bastard or no, he deserved someone much better than herself.

"Beatrice?"

Beatrice shook her head and offered her cousin a small smile. "I had a disrupted sleep and feel somewhat tired. Forgive me." The lie slipped from her tongue. What a deceitful woman she had become.

Isabeau gave her a steady look. "It seems to me, cousin, that what ails you is not the lack of sleep."

Beatrice had only confided in Isabeau a few months ago when Isabeau's stepsister, Cicele, arrived at Beauforde. Cicele and Beatrice were cousins but they had not seen each other since they were children. When Cicely had arrived and recognized Beatrice she persuaded Beatrice to confide in Isabeau. Beatrice had told her cousins some of the truth but she needed to protect them so dared not tell them everything.

Isabeau had herself married under false pretenses and was only too happy to swear to keep Beatrice's identity a secret. Thankfully not even Isabeau's husband knew the truth of it.

Beatrice tried to ignore Isabeau's question but it was useless. Where was Godiva or Elizabet when she needed them? They always had a way of deflecting Isabeau from probing too deeply into Beatrice's thoughts.

"And no use hoping Godiva or Elizabet will rescue you." She gave Beatrice a sly smile. "They are with Edward and the twins supervising the new nurse for baby Ralf in the nursery."

Godiva was Isabeau's old nurse and the only woman Beatrice knew who could deflect Isabeau's eagle-eyed observations. Beatrice cast a furtive look around the small solar hoping to find something to divert Isabeau's curiosity but alas there was no hiding from her cousin's question. Even the great lump of a dog was missing. Flea was no doubt with Tillie in the garden or kitchens. The dog and girl were almost inseparable.

There was no hiding from Isabeau's question but did she dare answer her honestly? She trusted Isabeau with her life, but could she trust her with the truth?

Giving a small huff of resignation she decided she could at least tell her some of it. This woman had been her friend for over a year and was like a sister rather than a cousin to her. Albeit a secret cousin.

Beatrice loved her two cousins and missed Cicele terribly. God what a complicated family the three of them had—secret children, duplicitous fathers, and unwanted marriages. At least Isabeau and Cicele had found love with their husbands. Ranulf adored Isabeau and often kissed his wife in full view of the castle retainers. Cicele had been ordered to marry Guyon at Christmas as her father lay dying from a hunting accident. Guyon was named "The Wolf," and he was a terrifying man, but Beatrice had seen something in his expression when he looked at Cicele to suggest there was affection there.

So, her cousins had found good marriages, but it would never be Beatrice's lot in life to find such a happy union. The longing for love and affection in marriage was now a distant memory. Her dead husband had killed that hope long ago.

"Gilbret offered marriage." Beatrice didn't look at Isabeau but began pulling at a loose thread on her kirtle.

When Isabeau didn't respond, Beatrice glanced at her face. What she saw reflected in the green of her cousin's eyes shocked her. Was it sympathy? No, Beatrice recognized it. Pity. She hated that she was pitied and couldn't hold her tongue. "Don't look at me like that, I told him it was impossible."

Isabeau rose from the chair she had been sitting on and came to sit beside Beatrice at the window seat. She was still pale from the trials of childbed, but her color was returning and Isabeau and Ranulf had a fine healthy son.

It was late spring and the sun was beginning to make its presence felt through the glass window. Warmth seeped into Beatrice's bones but it didn't reach her heart. That organ was well and truly frozen.

"I don't know what you see in my expression that you find so offensive, but I was thinking what a shame it will never be."

Beatrice began to say something but Isabeau stopped her with a small gesture of her hand. "Gilbret is a good man, Beatrice, but I worry that you may never be ready to let yourself be loved as you deserve."

Now Beatrice was insulted. "What do you mean I may 'never be ready?'"

Isabeau's brows creased in what Beatrice thought might be

incredulity. "I have watched you for over a year and I have seen you hide behind a wall of meek obedience and reserve, yet I suspect that is not your true nature."

Beatrice couldn't help herself as she huffed a small laugh. "And here I was thinking I had fooled everyone with my demure and reticent demeanor."

"Why won't you let us in?" Isabeau asked in a wistful tone.

Time to restore her defenses. Beatrice couldn't allow anyone in —her heart was too broken, too damaged. And the shame. Never would she invite someone to view her shame. Especially not someone as kind as Isabeau. It was better to keep her away. The only person Beatrice had allowed past her heart's walls was Edward. Her young son deflected the darkness that lurked in her heart and he was all she needed.

"I'm not sure I understand, cousin, but I can assure you I am happy and content here." Beatrice's skin tingled and her chest heaved in suppressed indignation. It was all very well for Isabeau to talk. She had a husband who loved her and a young baby boy who would inherit his father's land and titles. Her cousin knew nothing of the shame that poisoned her and Edward's existence.

Isabeau flinched slightly as though struck by Beatrice's harsh words, but her face remained soft while Beatrice arranged her own expression into something that probably resembled a frozen puddle.

Isabeau's eyes assessed Beatrice for a heartbeat; then she smiled. "I am happy that you are here, and that you have found safety and security behind our walls, but I fear that it will not be enough. Perhaps you would do well to accept Gilbret's offer and then you would be sure to evade your father's schemes."

Isabeau knew nothing of Beatrice's odious father's schemes, but it wasn't Isabeau's fault. Beatrice had lied about what she was truly hiding from and marrying Gilbret would never be an option.

"I haven't been entirely honest with you."

A smile slid across Isabeau's beautiful face. "Now that is a surprise."

Beatrice had the grace to laugh along with her cousin. "I admit I may be slightly closed when it comes to divulging what keeps me here." She had been grateful that her cousin had kept her secret, not even telling her husband that Beatrice was a noblewoman hiding from her father on the pretext of keeping her young son safe. But perhaps it was time to tell her why she couldn't marry. "I was repudiated but my husband then he did the honorable thing and died before he could remarry." To be divorced and cast as the whore by her husband still stung. But it was the shame of having Edward's name forever tarnished and his future stolen that was so painful. Some days Beatrice imagined she might actually bleed from the wounds inflicted by her vengeful husband. She cursed his dead blighted soul.

"My father struck an arrangement with my dead husband's brother. Everlyn would inherit Folkingham and grant my father a manor of his choosing. But first, they had to be rid of me and Edward." She couldn't bring herself to explain anymore.

"Oh, Beatrice, that is despicable," she said as she laid her hands over Beatrice's, giving them a small squeeze. "But I don't understand why you can't marry and have Gilbret protect you from them?"

Beatrice searched her cousin's face and saw only concern and confusion. "Repudiation means that I become dishonored and my son illegitimate. I cannot remarry; the church forbids it."

Isabeau didn't move to hug her. The last thing Beatrice needed or wanted was pity. "In truth, cousin, I suspected something like that."

"You are not shocked? I am deemed a whore and little Edward nothing more than a nobleman's by-blow," she spat as bitterness boiled in her stomach threatening to surge up her throat. To be labeled such because she had refused to return to her violent husband was still a raw wound even after all this time.

"I am sorry, Beatrice," Isabeau whispered as she took Beatrice's hand in hers. They sat like that, neither speaking while the internal rage within Beatrice's chest calmed into the tiny ember she had lived with for almost two long years.

BEATRICE TRIED NOT to look but her eyes strayed to the high table and sought Gilbret. He continued to watch her from his higher vantage point. A small smile played at the corners of his mouth whenever their eyes met, sending hot and cold shivers along her spine.

"You are not hungry?" Godiva's concerned voice whispered in Beatrice's ear.

She turned to look at the older woman who had been Isabeau's nurse and was now her maid. She was as astute as a fox and just as wily. It wouldn't do to reveal too much of her own agitation. If Godiva got wind of it, she would ferret it out, and Beatrice didn't have the stomach to revisit the topic.

"I am well, just women's complaints."

"Humm." The woman eyed her suspiciously but returned to her own meal without further interruption.

Beatrice didn't realize she had been holding her breath and almost coughed as she took a deep gulp of air.

"I suspect that Gilbret is indeed 'women's complaints,' but I would be happy to complain." She shot Beatrice a sly smile and then returned her attention to the person sitting on her other side.

Beatrice's face burned with mortification. If Godiva suspected that there was something between Gilbret and herself it was possible that the whole bloody castle knew. The meager meal sitting in Beatrice's stomach threatened to reappear. Swallowing frantically

Beatrice strove to sit still rather than flee from the hall. The meal was interminable but, finally, they were excused from the table allowing Beatrice to make a hasty retreat albeit at a speed that was deemed polite.

She needed air so she chose to walk to the small garden that nestled into the walls of the castle. It was, strictly speaking, Isabeau's garden but as her maid, Beatrice was permitted entrance whenever she wanted.

She closed the solid oak door into the garden behind her and made for the rose arbor where she could sit and think. Northern spring was always late to make itself known in the garden but now as the end of May approached the flowers and herbs responded to the warmth of the sun and the softening of the earth. Bees buzzed around the lavender while birds cheeped as they gathered food for their growing families. Beatrice loved this time of year when everything was new and full of possibilities.

The sound of feet along the path made Beatrice look up. She expected it to be the gardeners but, no, she couldn't be that fortunate.

She recognized him immediately—her father's oily cleric. When had he arrived? And why, in God's name, had she not seen him in the hall?

"Lady Beatrice, may I sit?" he purred as he nodded his head in a show of respect.

"What are you doing here?" There was no point feigning courtesy, she had learned early in her childhood that the man was a grasping weasel who would sell his own soul for gold.

"That, my child, is no way to greet an old friend," he smiled in a manner that turned her blood cold.

He was dangerous and she had better be on her guard. "I am surprised to see you so far from my father's side." She hoped the barb would find its mark.

"Ah, you think me too attached to your father, but I serve him as

God's agent. Everything I do, I do for God's glory, and your father's soul." He smiled at her but his eyes remained hard.

He folded his habit so it lay in perfect creases across his knees. To the unobservant, the woolen cloth was like any other clerics' plain garb, but on closer inspection, the wool was a fine weave that most likely came from France or Italy. It seemed Father Robin de Wolde had a taste for the finer things in life.

"Imagine my surprise at finding a much-loved daughter among the retainers of the great Baron Beauforde." He turned his cold blue eyes on Beatrice. "Your father will be delighted to learn that I, his humble cleric, have finally located his daughter. He has been worried that something tragic had beset you, and your young son."

A shiver of dread crawled down Beatrice's spine. She would never let this demon, who paraded as a man of God, near her son. Ever.

"I will make arrangements for you to travel with me, as I am sure you are impatient to return to the bosom of your family." His smile made her stomach hitch, but she forced her face into a passive expression.

"I shall not be leaving with you, Father, as my life here is settled."

"You are your father's responsibility," he sneered. "And make no mistake, Lady Beatrice, your father takes his responsibility very seriously. In fact, he has placed a reward of one mark for the person who brings his daughter back to him. I shall eschew the coin of course, but to have your father's thanks will be reward enough."

He rose and bowed to her. "I will make arrangements for our departure at dawn tomorrow." Then he was gone.

It seemed her only option was to run away again, but where to? For almost two years she had evaded her father, but she could not escape him, or his odious cleric, this time. That first year as she hid at St. Leonard's had been the most difficult. But the last year here at Beauforde had been happy. Perhaps if she told Isabeau and Ranulf about de Wolde, they could help her? No. She had already received more than she deserved from Isabeau. She would not ask more.

An image of Gilbret's face danced before her inner eyes. The thought of marriage lingered for a heartbeat before she dismissed it. Impossible. Never would he agree to marry her and risk his soul's eternal damnation. No nobleman, no matter how desperate, would defy the church and accept a divorced woman as his wife.

Dread clawed at her limbs as she sat staring at the lavender at her feet.

Fortuna, it seemed, was spinning her wheel yet again and only a fool would believe that it boded well for the future. And Beatrice was no fool.

Chapter Four

GILBRET HAD WATCHED BEATRICE THROUGHOUT THE MEAL YET SHE avoided him when their eyes met. What would it take to have her agree to his proposal? She couldn't stay here indefinitely. And she couldn't remain unmarried. A widow with the face of an angel was too much temptation for men who longed for a woman's touch. It surprised him that Beatrice had refused the amorous attention of the men who dwelt at Beauforde. She had always been civil but declined their overtures. The men often resorted to fighting over her when they had been drinking but Gilbret liked to think it was his force of will as the seneschal that prevented the men from doing anything more serious than a few punches when it came to the rivalry over who was going to pay court to the beautiful wet nurse. But he was no longer the seneschal, which left Gilbret with the familiar sense of resentment that his future had been dictated by his father.

Turning his attention back to the beautiful widow sitting at the table below the dais, Gilbret had to give her her due. It was Beatrice who had evaded the attention of the men. She had never, in the year she had lived at Beauforde, encouraged any of them. She kept her head down and averted her eyes when any of the men spoke to her.

His own eyes tracked her as she rose and walked out of the hall, but no sooner had she risen than the visiting cleric from Dunstunburgh rose and left. Gilbret had been made aware of the man's presence just as the noon meal began so he had not had time to discover why he was here. Whatever the cleric wanted it was too much of a coincidence for Gilbret as he watched the cleric follow Beatrice. What was the sniveling little cleric up to?

Gilbret walked through the bailey in time to see Beatrice enter the Lady's Garden unaware that she was being followed. The hairs on the back of Gilbret's neck rose as the little cleric stalked Beatrice in the shadows until he slipped in through the garden gate.

Instead of intruding on the pair, Gilbret observed them from just inside the garden's walls. Undetected he saw instantly that Beatrice did not welcome the cleric. Her body became rigid as he approached. Whoever he was, they knew each other, and Beatrice wasn't happy.

Gilbret decided to wait and question the cleric when he left the garden. He didn't have to wait long. The little man with a shifty expression rose and bowed before Beatrice. A cleric bowing before a miller's widow. Who the hell was she? No trifling servant received bows from clerics.

Gilbret walked through the gate and waited. He would intercept the cleric as he exited the garden gate.

The cleric saw Gilbret and quickly turned towards the church. *So that's how it is, is it?*

Gilbret strode after him and caught him before he reached the chapel doors. The man was apt to pray for hours if he didn't get to him now and Gilbret had no intention of waiting all afternoon to get some answers as to who Beatrice was.

"Father, a word if you please." Gilbret purposely kept his voice affable as he drew alongside the man as he tried to hurry his steps.

Being ignored infuriated Gilbret, so he did the unthinkable and grabbed the cleric's arm. The little man jumped with fright.

"Unhand me, sir," he blustered, but to no avail. It would take more than a pretentious cleric to put the fear of God into Gilbret.

"Father, as seneschal I request that you accompany me to my solar so you may inform me as to the reason for your visit."

The little man turned and attempted to stare Gilbret down. "I am Father Robin de Wolde come from Baron Embleton to meet with my friend Father Ascelin." He puffed out his chest. "Now unhand me at once."

Gilbret had to admire the little man's bravado, but he had asked Ascelin if he recognized the cleric who was sitting at the back of the hall when they sat at table and Ascelin had said he had no knowledge of the man.

"Now, Father, that is a lie. I suggest you come with me now, or I shall be forced to have you detained so we can ascertain why you feel, as a man of the cloth, the necessity to lie to me." Gilbret made sure his voice held a threatening tone that he hoped would be enough for the cleric to see reason.

"Very well." He shook his arm loose of Gilbret's hold and waited for Gilbret to lead the way.

Gilbret entered the now empty hall and pulled back the curtain for the priest to enter the chamber and indicated a chair for de Wolde to sit. He poured two goblets of wine and handed one over to his guest before sitting on the opposite side of the table.

"This is an excellent wine," the little man gushed. He took another deep sup of wine, then smacked his lips together in appreciation.

Gilbret was happy to let the silence continue. He had learned long ago that silence was not comfortable for a man who possessed a guilty conscience.

So it was with de Wolde, who began to squirm in his chair as the silence nibbled at his bluster. It wasn't too long before he began babbling. All his arrogance and righteous indignation vanished like mist over the land as the sun rose.

"My master, Baron Embleton, sent me to request an interview with Sir Ranulf concerning rents due." The cleric went to reach for his cup of wine, but his hands shook so much that he placed the cup back on the table.

"So why lie?"

The little man's tongue darted out of his mouth and licked his lips. Gilbret could see the telltale sign of sweat glistening on his upper lip. The man was scared. But why?

"My master has had a bad harvest and is unable to meet his rents and thought it prudent to forewarn his lordship before the rents were due."

"But it is me, the seneschal, who is responsible for collecting rents, so why not seek me out?" Gilbret drummed his fingers on the table as he stared at the man opposite him. Although he was no longer seneschal Gilbret knew everything that went on in Beauforde even though he had been absent for three months. And he knew that Embleton had no such issue with his rents.

Gilbret studied the man sitting opposite him. He looked to be close to three score years which indicated that the little priest had served Embleton for the last twenty years at least. His distinctive cleric's tonsure was almost rendered invisible by his balding head. But the quality of his woolen habit was of note. This man obviously had money. His eyes were a blue that seemed to exude coldness. It took Gilbret all his reserves of strength not to shiver as the man leveled his cold blue gaze on him.

"Then, I apologize if I have been less than diligent. I only arrived as the dinner meal began, and the steward of the hall bade me sit, otherwise I would have come to you directly."

His tone was condescending now that he had regained his earlier haughtiness.

"What were you discussing with Mistress Beatrice in the

garden?" Gilbret enjoyed the momentary shock that passed over the priest's face before it vanished. "And no lies, Father." Gilbret speared him with a cold glare and an even colder tone. "I find it exceedingly tiring when I am confronted with liars."

"Mistress Beatrice?" He said looking puzzled. "Oh, you mean Lady Beatrice." His confusion gave way to a sly smile. "The lady is Baron Embleton's daughter. She fled from her family and has been in hiding these past two years. I was shocked to see her here, and insisted that she accompany me back to her father at first light tomorrow."

Gilbret thought he might topple sideways. Never had he been so shocked at such a revelation, but he managed to maintain his composure. "Did the lady agree to your demands?" God, he hoped not. He managed to keep his tone disinterested as he awaited the priest's reply. Beatrice was a bloody noblewoman. He suspected that she had been lying about her identity, and he had assumed that she was in trouble so he had kept a watch on her to ensure she was safe, but never did he imagine that she was a nobleman's daughter.

"No, the foolish woman maintained that she had no wish to return to her father." The priest had evidently misread Gilbret's expression and thought that Gilbret agreed with him. That was a mistake the cleric would regret.

"Well, since Lady Beatrice is under the protection of Baron Beauforde she will not be leaving against her will." Gilbret enjoyed the man's discomfort at being thwarted. "You will present yourself to Baron Beauforde tomorrow morning and offer Embleton's excuses personally. You may also ask Baron Beauforde if he will allow Lady Beatrice to accompany you. Now I think I have kept you from your prayers long enough, Father. Allow my squire to escort you to the chapel."

"But ..."

"Olivier," Gilbret called.

Immediately Olivier's head popped around the corner of the chamber. "Yes, my lord?"

"Escort Father de Wolde to the chapel and make sure you offer him all the courtesy an honored guest deserves."

Olivier smiled in what could only be described as smug as he nodded to Gilbret. "Of course. Father de Wolde, if you please?"

Gilbret watched as his squire led the priest out of the solar.

Dealing with the priest would be easy; he was a sniveling little bully who needed to be put in his place. Gilbret smiled as he imagined how de Wolde's interview with Ranulf would go. Ranulf despised bullies and would never allow the priest to take Beatrice against her will.

Gilbret released a sigh. He had bigger problems than the cleric. He had to deal with a woman who had too many secrets for Gilbret's liking. Did her being a noblewoman make a difference to Gilbret's hope to save his mother and sister and secure his inheritance? When had he started to think of Wooler as his inheritance? Probably the moment he signed the accursed charter.

Saint's bones, what an unholy mess. He needed to speak with Ascelin and Ranulf and discuss what they should do. It was unthinkable to allow Beatrice to go back to her father. Whatever motivated her to run, it must have been important and Gilbret would give her a chance to explain.

It was clear she had been desperate—no noblewoman would masquerade as a wet nurse unless she was dispossessed of her wits. And everything he had observed of Beatrice in the past year she had resided at Beauforde convinced him that she was not witless.

God help him, a future with a woman as complicated as Beatrice was not what he needed, but if she was in trouble then he would make sure she and her young son were safe. The little fool had refused his offer of marriage but he had seen the flair of hope bloom in her eyes. It had been fleeting but it had been there. Her refusal was based on fear; he was sure of it. How could he persuade her to trust him? He would speak to her again, especially after he had observed her reaction to the little priest. She showed no desire to be taken back to her father.

BEATRICE SAT FOR A LONG TIME. Every fiber of her being rebelled against going back to her father. She had to act and act fast but her legs didn't want to obey her. She had tried to stand but they refused to hold her weight. A small noise alerted her that someone was coming. Hopefully the gardeners, as the only other people likely to be here were Isabeau or Elizabet and she didn't want to talk to either of them. She needed to get her emotions back into some semblance of order and find a solution to her predicament with her father's cleric.

"Ah, there you are." At Elizabet's familiar voice Beatrice groaned. Elizabet was her closest friend and they had shared so much when Beatrice had first come to live at Beauforde castle. It seemed like a lifetime ago that Mother Hild, the abbess of St. Leonard's Abbey, had persuaded Beatrice to go with Isabeau and become wet nurse for Elizabet's twins. Was it only a year ago that Beatrice had been hiding at St. Leonard's when Mother Hild told her she could not stay? At the time it seemed that Beatrice's world would crumble, but God had provided a way, just as Mother Hild had said. Could she be lucky enough for another opportunity to save herself and Edward from her father's schemes?

"What are you doing hiding here?" Elizabet asked as she sat down next to Beatrice on the stone bench. She was a beautiful woman with dark brown eyes and hair the color of a raven's wing. She had found it difficult to be accepted when she arrived due to her foreign ways but being married to Father Ascelin had meant that the people, with all their superstitions and prejudices, had slowly begun to accept her. She was perhaps one of the most serene women Beatrice had ever met. She envied her her calm demeanor. If only she had a portion of the composure Elizabet possessed perhaps Beatrice's life would have been different. But too late now. The past was never to be changed. It was the future that weighed on Beatrice's mind.

"I find I am in need of some quiet so I may think." She tried to soften the testy tone of her voice with a small smile.

Elizabet glanced sideways, then turned her attention to the spring flowers beginning to bloom in the garden opposite where they sat. "My company is unwelcome, but I sense you need a friend, so here I sit."

"I can't talk about it."

"Well, talk about what you can."

There was a logic to Elizabet's comment that appealed to Beatrice. Yes, she could share some things but, God help her, she couldn't trust her secret to anyone.

"Father de Wolde is here."

"Yes, an odious little man," Elizabet said as she shuddered.

Beatrice laughed. "He makes my skin crawl, too." She took a deep breath. "He comes from my father, Baron Embleton, and now that he has seen where I have been hiding, he insists I accompany him tomorrow when he leaves to travel back to Dunstunburgh Castle." Her tone was so flat that Beatrice hardly recognized her own voice.

"You have no wish to return?"

Beatrice had only shared with Isabeau and Cicele because Cicele had discovered her, but could she tell Elizabet?

"My father has threatened to take Edward from me." Panic gripped her chest. Never would she give Edward into the power of her father.

"And?"

Beatrice glanced at her companion. "What do you mean *and*?"

"There is a reason why you have demeaned yourself to pose as a wet nurse for my boys—"

"No, let me finish," she said as Beatrice was about to interrupt. "I suspected that you were no miller's widow but that you were hiding your true identity. No noblewoman would demean herself unless it was a matter of life or death." Elizabet turned and took hold of Beatrice's hands. "Let your friends help."

Beatrice couldn't bear to look at Elizabet's expression. She didn't deserve such love and compassion from those she had been lying to for almost a year.

"I have fallen so far from grace that I can't begin to hope that there is another way out of my father's grasp."

"There is always hope, Beatrice, but it helps to share the burden."

Beatrice wanted to believe there was a way forward and that perhaps it was wise to allow the people she had come to love help her.

"Gilbret has proposed marriage, but I can't marry him."

"Why ever not?"

She didn't want to expose her disgrace but there was no other way. "I am divorced, the church would never allow me to marry again."

"Have you spoken to Ascelin?"

Beatrice huffed a laugh. "What do you think?" She didn't mean to snap but she couldn't seem to keep the scorn from her voice.

Elizabet didn't seem to take offense, in fact, she laughed. "I can assure you Ascelin is not inclined to righteous indignation when confronted with the asinine dictates of the church," she said. "Come, he is at home with the boys, and with some wine in his belly and the boys on his knees he would be willing to solve even the most pressing theological matter."

Elizabet rose and began walking towards the garden gate. Beatrice had little choice but to follow her friend.

And perhaps, just perhaps, Ascelin could offer counsel.

TRUE TO ELIZABET'S word Ascelin was sitting in front of the fire bouncing his sons on his knees. Their laughter greeted Beatrice and Elizabet as they entered the small dwelling.

"Hello, husband, I have brought a supplicant in need of counsel," Elizabet said as she bent and kissed her husband's head. "But first I think these boys might need their clouts changed." She bent further towards one babe and sniffed. "Yes, methinks a change." With that pronouncement, she took both babes in her arms and walked through into the bedchamber.

Ascelin watched his little family until Elizabet closed the door. With a small sigh, he turned to Beatrice. "And what needs bring you to my door, Mistress Beatrice?"

He gestured for her to sit and poured her a cup of wine.

Beatrice settled herself into the chair and supped the wine while trying to organize her harried thoughts. Where to begin?

It all came tumbling out. Her disastrous marriage. Her father's insistence that she retire to a nunnery and surrender Edward to his care, and the disgrace of being repudiated.

Ascelin listened, only asking questions when he needed clarification; otherwise, he sat quietly with his expression never once revealing what he truly thought of Beatrice's tale.

"And now Father de Wolde has said that he will force me back to my father but I can't go back, Ascelin. I just can't." Her last words were almost a sob.

"Come, child, no need to fret. De Wolde has no jurisdiction here. Ranulf will never allow you to leave if you do not want it." He offered her a small smile. "So, his threat to take you back is empty, but it would mean you are almost a prisoner here. For if you venture outside the castle walls your father could seize you at once. No, we must think of a more permanent solution."

Beatrice was relieved to hear that de Wolde couldn't force her to leave, but she often went riding in the woods outside the gates. To lose that freedom would be hard to accept.

"De Wolde said I would forever be my father's responsibility, and as the church would never sanction me marrying another it seems I am to be a prisoner for the rest of my days,"

Ascelin gave Beatrice a small smile. "I understand Sir Gilbret offered marriage."

"The walls have ears."

"Ah, nothing so mysterious. He came and asked me for my advice regarding your refusal. Now I understand why you thought you must decline."

"Of course, I must decline. It is church law."

"Well, that is true when the spouse still lives, but as your husband is dead, strictly speaking, you are free to marry."

"I am?" she squeaked.

"If you think you could make a future with Gilbret then it is my understanding that there are no impediments to such a union." With a self-satisfied smile, he took a large sip of his wine.

Could she marry Gilbret? Her body would not object but what of her heart. It couldn't withstand another rejection and as sure as night followed day Gilbret would never agree to marry her when he found out the truth.

A weight lifted from her chest. She would stay here safe in the knowledge Ranulf would never force her to leave. He might even give her an armed escort if she accompanied Isabeau on their daily rides through the woods.

If not, she would resign herself to life at Beauforde castle as a prisoner, at least until her father died.

Thanking Ascelin and calling out to Elizabet she left their cottage and headed back to her own hovel. Tillie would be there with Edward. The little maid had become something of a nurse to Edward, and both maid and child adored each other's company, but a crawling babbling Edward could exhaust the most ardent admirer; Tillie would welcome leaving Edward with his mother. This time of the day Tillie would appreciate some time to practice her knife throwing and it would give Beatrice a chance to enjoy a quiet solitary supper and to sleep, knowing her father could never hurt her, or Edward, again.

Chapter Five

After almost two long harrowing years her prayers had been answered. She was free. No, her maggot of a father was still a threat, but at least she was certain Isabeau would never allow her to be turned out of Beauforde. Edward was safe. She cast a quick glance at the little body nestled under the covers of her small bed.

She had eaten a small supper and now settled herself into a chair by the fire and began spinning some wool.

A sharp knock on her door interrupted her quietude. Who would be at her door this time of night?

Another sharp knock, followed by a very male voice, "Open the door."

"Gilbret?"

"Yes, Gilbret. May I come in?"

"Keep your voice down, you'll wake Edward," she hissed, as she opened the door. "And draw the men at watch," she mumbled as she unlatched the door. It wouldn't do to have them think she was receiving male callers after dark. She had lived at Beauforde castle for a year and in that time, she had never encouraged male attention.

Now Gilbret was at her door. God knows it would be all over the castle by morning.

He filled the room. Her body reacted to his presence immediately—a small slow pulse of desire began to make an unwelcome appearance. One look at Gilbret's face and all desire fled. Instead fear snagged her in the pit of her stomach. Had he talked to Father de Wolde? Bile scorched her throat as she desperately tried to swallow her growing fear. *Stay calm and breathe*, a small voice counseled somewhere in the back of her mind. With a shaking breath, Beatrice swallowed and willed her body to relax. Forcing herself to concentrate on getting rid of her late-night visitor she straightened her spine and glared at him.

"What in God's name do you think you are doing here?" It took all her resolve not to demand he leave her in peace. Taking a deep breath, she clenched her teeth so tight that her jaw tingled.

He stood before her with an arrogant tilt of his shoulders. An expression every knight seemed to be born with. God, she hated posturing males. His hands rested on his hips while his chin jutted out in an expression of irritated impatience. So, he was still smarting from her refusal to marry him. Instead of an expected sense of relief, she discerned disappointment deep in the pit of her stomach.

His anger was obvious, but she couldn't understand why. Unless de Wolde had told Gilbret who she was. That would explain his visit and the expression he wore. The urge to slap the disdain from his face was overwhelming, but she couldn't afford to offend the man standing before her.

She had to remember she was a servant. She had already rebuffed him once and couldn't afford to insult him further by demanding he leave. If only he knew the favor she did him by refusing his suit. No man would want a woman with such a tarnished reputation. It gnawed at her belly but she fought the impulse to rage at the arrogant oaf standing in her hovel. She had to be careful. One word from him and she could be removed from Beauforde. Ranulf loved Isabeau, but when it came to the castle's safety he would always side with the man who had been his seneschal.

She might keep silent, but she wouldn't be cowed in her own house. So, she returned his stare. Two could play at being belligerent, and by the look of him, his patience wouldn't last that long.

She was right, he heaved a great sigh, and walked to the chair and sat. Which meant she remained standing.

He didn't take his eyes from the flames, but she could tell he was holding on to his anger by a thread. His shoulders were hunched, and his hands gripped his knees turning the knuckles white. He didn't wear gloves. Her only thought, God help her, was how beautiful his hands were—long fingers, and short clean nails. For a fighting man that was a surprise. What would it feel like to have those hands on her?

Sweet saints in heaven, what was she thinking? She shook her head to dislodge the image. Unfortunately, her body was less inclined to obey. A small, warm tingle had taken up residence in her stomach and was making its way down to her core. That wasn't good.

Finally, he looked at her, and she almost ran from the room. His eyes were deep brown, much like cow's eyes—all soft and inviting, but not today. There was no invitation, only a cold glint in their depths that reminded her of her dead husband. She would have been trembling in fear if Walter gave her such a glare, but she wasn't afraid of the man sitting before her. How extraordinary.

Gilbret didn't move but sat in the chair watching her. Blast his eyes. She had little option but to close the door. Although it had been a warm day, it was now cold outside and she didn't want to squander the heat from the fire.

With an exaggerated sigh, she resigned herself to being questioned. She would give him enough truth to keep him satisfied, but no more. "What do you want?"

"For a woman known for her charm you have an acid tongue."

"Forgive me, but I am mistrustful of men who knock on my door under the cover of dark." She wouldn't give him the satisfaction of seeing how his presence unnerved her.

He huffed a laugh. "Imagine my surprise, Lady Beatrice, to have discovered that a woman claiming to be a poor miller's widow turns out to be a noblewoman." He stood up and indicated that she should sit.

Not a chance. His statement made the blood drain from her head and pool somewhere by her toes. She felt stronger standing, so she stayed where she was and raised her eyebrows in the universal gesture of "please explain yourself, and now."

Admitting defeat he sat down, but he faced her. "What are you thinking—a noblewoman pretending to be a miller's wife in need of work?" he asked, enunciating every word.

He was probably confused more than angry. Why indeed would a noblewoman pretend to be a servant? But she refused to feel anything other than self-preservation. She also reminded herself she owed him nothing.

She continued to hold his gaze for several heartbeats. If she told him the truth or at least some of it, he might agree to leave her be. "I fled my marriage. To save Edward I had no other option but to disguise myself, and as Fate would have it, I ended up here under Lady Isabeau's protection."

"Why?"

"Why what?"

"Why did you flee your marriage?"

"Because I feared for my unborn child's safety."

She watched as he stole a glance at the bed. Then with slow, deliberate care, he walked to where her son lay asleep. She forced herself to stay where she was. She couldn't risk getting too close to him. Something about this man unnerved her—called to her at a primal level that she didn't understand. It was much safer to keep her distance.

"Who is the father?"

She snorted. "You jump to the conclusion that I am an unfaithful harlot?" Gritting her teeth to stop from saying more she walked over to the table and poured a cup of wine for her guest. With a sudden pang of resentment, she realized just how tired she was of being cast in the role of whore.

Gilbret accepted the wine when she offered it, but his eyes assessed her with something that she couldn't quite recognize.

"I merely wondered who your husband was rather than accuse you of defiling your vows." He gave her a steady look. "In my experience, Beatrice, only the most contemptible of husbands become violent. They need little provocation to use their fists. I would not blame you for fleeing such a marriage."

The statement was said with such derision that Beatrice could only gape at the man before her. "My husband was cruel. And my father ignored my plight. A curse on men who view women as mere chattels they can dispose of as they deem fit," she spat.

He eyed her with a scrutiny that left her wanting to hide.

"You are a widow in truth?"

"Yes."

Gilbret took a leisurely sip of wine. "Perhaps your husband, like most men, believed that a beautiful face is no reflection of inner beauty." His face softened and transformed him into a man that took her breath away. Standing this close she could smell his scent, and her body reacted with a surge of longing that almost had her leaning towards him.

"They are apt to believe that a woman of beauty is nothing other than duplicitous." Her cheeks burned as though slapped and she was about to reply but he raised his hand to forestall her. "I am not such a man, Beatrice, but it seems many will rise against you. Father de Wolde is such a man and he is dangerous."

She didn't answer. All her life she had been seen only for her face and she was tired of it.

"I am angry, not because you deceived us but because you did not trust us enough to ask us for help." He heaved a sigh. "I also understand your reasons. Given de Wolde's threats I renew my offer of marriage. As a widow, there is no impediment, so I hope you will see me as an alternative to your father's unholy schemes."

Beatrice didn't know what to say. Could she put herself under the power of a man again? God help her, Isabeau's words rung in her ear. She wasn't ready.

"Since the day you arrived, I suspected that you were not whom you claimed to be." He gave her a small smile. "I was prepared to expose your deceit immediately, but as I watched you over those first few months of your arrival, I found you to be a woman of honor and grace, so I left you to find peace and safety among friends."

"Now that you know who I am and how I've ruined myself posing as a wet nurse you cannot seek to marry me. Surely?"

He cocked his head to the side as he watched her. Her upper lip tingled with sweat as she tried to evade his gaze. *Be the demure woman you pretend to be and perhaps he will leave.* A small voice in her head cautioned.

"As I told you this morning, I find myself in need of a wife and you, Lady Beatrice, seem to require a husband."

What in God's good earth could she say to that? She was indeed in need of something. But a husband was not what she had envisaged.

She decided that enough was enough. She straightened her shoulders and offered him her composed expression. "I cannot marry you. And I would never bring my shame upon your family, but I thank you for the honor." She took a small breath. "Now if you will excuse me, Sir Gilbret, I am tired and wish to retire."

She went to move past him but he took hold of her upper arm. Her head snapped up—a demand to release her on the tip of her tongue.

He must have read her expression because he released her but instead of moving away, he took a step towards her. "I am not so easily rebuffed, my lady." His dark brown eyes skimmed over her face before capturing her gaze.

A terrible thought occurred to her. "You would force marriage on me or …"

"I have no wish to force you, Beatrice, but I must marry and I suspect you have a greater need for a husband now that de Wolde has arrived." He inclined his head in the direction of the bed where Edward lay sleeping.

His eyes traveled over her face. "You are a noblewoman and you know how to run a household," he announced. "As the new Baron Wooler, I could offer you the protection and name you require to keep Edward safe."

"I can't." It was all she could say. Now that the discussion was upon her, she didn't have the resolve to contemplate marriage and all it entailed. Not again.

"I'll give you time to reconsider, but so you are clear about what I offer I shall speak plainly. I will give you my name and adopt Edward as my own. You and your son will never have reason to fear me. It is a marriage of convenience and I will never force you to my bed," he said as he held her gaze. "But it is my hope that given time you will learn to trust me and come to my bed of your own free will."

She didn't dare answer.

"In all respects, you will be my wife, Baroness Wooler, and accorded the esteem that title holds. If these terms are agreeable to you then I would insist that we marry on Monday morning. That gives you three days to consider. I need to take up my position at Barmoor castle and can delay no longer."

Her tongue was stuck to the roof of her mouth. Heart pounding in her ears she nodded and swiftly moved past him to open her hovel's door.

As he walked past her, he stopped and ran his finger along her chin. "I am not a cruel man, Beatrice, and you will never have need to fear me. Edward will be my son in every respect. That I promise you."

He gave her a small nod as he walked through the door and out into the night.

GILBRET SEETHED AS he walked through the door. The cool night air, smelling faintly of horse shit and hay as he walked past the stables on his way to his chamber, did little to dampen his heated face. What kind of man becomes so violent that his wife is forced to flee to protect herself and her unborn babe? The fear in Beatrice's eyes told Gilbret all he needed to know about her marriage. He could offer her a safe home where she could live without fear. But would she be able to overcome her past and accept the future he offered?

The prospect of finding another woman didn't appeal. The time and money spent going to London and seeking out a suitable woman was not the only reason he didn't want to consider the option. If he was honest he could so easily fall under Beatrice's spell, for as surely as God sat on his throne in heaven, Beatrice was a beauty.

Gilbret didn't have much experience with women like Beatrice. She reminded him of a mare he once had who had been abused by a knight. The horse was flighty and often overreacted to the slightest provocation. But Gilbret had glimpsed the horse's true nature and so he patiently coaxed her to trust him and eventually was rewarded for his patience.

It was evident to Gilbret that Beatrice needed to be encouraged to trust but he suspected it was shame that held her captive and made her refuse his offer. Gilbret was only too familiar with how difficult it was to throw that unwelcome mantel off one's life. He would be patient and pray that she accepted him before Monday; otherwise he would have to return to Barmoor without a wife.

Images of Beatrice's fearful expression hovered in his mind. Who was her husband? Some maggot-faced knight who had treated her badly. If he wasn't already dead, he'd find the bastard and kill him. Gilbret entered the darkened hall and stalked towards his chamber.

"You look like you have swallowed a snake and it's about to lunge out of your mouth any moment." His squire guffawed as he poured some wine into a cup and handed it to Gilbret.

Gilbret didn't bother responding but he did accept the offered cup of wine. Olivier had been his squire for almost ten years, and if Gilbret ascended to the barony he could grant the lad his spurs when he was old enough. And when he was older, and if he wished to marry, he would grant him a manor when one became available. If he didn't fulfill his father's stipulation and find a wife he would never be in a position to grant Olivier his spurs. He cursed his father's pox-ridden soul.

"What's got you heaving snakes?" Olivier never took any notice of Gilbret's moods, and in truth, Gilbret was thankful for the lad's forthright approach. But not tonight. Something about Beatrice nagged at Gilbret, leaving him unusually irritated. "I have just come from speaking with Mistress Beatrice."

"And why would she give you a dose of the vipers?" Olivier gave Gilbret a sly glance. "She is a beauty, but then you are not one to shy away from a comely face," he goaded as he sat mending Gilbret's torn surcoat.

Gilbret didn't want to admit why he was so angry yet he couldn't deny his reaction to her. Not having her to wife burned his gut much the way cheap wine soured his belly.

"She has lied, and that makes me nervous." *Liar!* His own conscience shot back.

"What has she lied about?"

Gilbret twisted the stem of his wine cup between his thumb and fingers. "She's a noblewoman. Baron Embleton's daughter. She's lived under Beauforde's protection while all this time she pretended to be the widow of a miller." *And she's refused to be my wife.* Although he kept that last bit of information to himself. He sounded petulant and that made him even angrier. He wanted Beatrice and he felt powerless to make her see reason.

Olivier held Gilbret in a long gaze. "Perhaps she was in trouble and a disguise was her only hope." Olivier didn't take his eyes off Gilbret. "And we both know that disguises come in all forms."

If anyone knew about disguises it was Olivier. He was the bastard son of a king. King Stephen's mistresses had been many and varied and some were sadly left to fend for themselves after the king had had his fill. Even though the old king had been dead these past few years there were many who would kill Olivier if his identity was revealed. Gilbret seldom thought about Olivier's mother, but as he looked at the lad sitting before him all he could see was her beautiful, tragic face.

"You look like her."

Olivier had returned to his task but looked up from his mending. "I can scarcely remember what she looked like. Sadness punctuated his quiet statement.

Not wanting to embarrass the boy Gilbret strove for glibness. "Well, you have her eyes, but thank God nothing else about your ugly face resembles her."

The boy's face paled, and then he laughed. "You are just jealous; I think I shall pay the beauteous Lady Beatrice a visit and then we shall see who has the ugly countenance." He wiggled his eyebrows. A boyish grin spread across his face as he returned to his mending.

Although young, Olivier would be handsome, just like his sire and his mother. He was already as tall as Gilbret, but only time would give him the girth to fill in his still skinny body. Gilbret loved him as a brother and would do everything in his power to see him well placed.

With a sigh, he sat at the table and began to study the ledgers that lay there for his inspection. It would be his last opportunity to ensure Beauforde's accounts were all correct. As the night wore on, the column of numbers blurred and the unwelcome face of a beautiful vixen danced across the pages.

Gilbret shook his head to dislodge the image, but it plagued him until he finally gave up his task and readied for bed.

God's bones, he hated being this desperate. His father had maneuvered him into an appalling position and if he couldn't convince Beatrice to be his wife then many lives would be ruined.

Chapter Six

THE FOLLOWING MORNING BEATRICE WAS SITTING ON THE CHAIR facing the furies of hell—Ranulf held an expression that would turn a hardened warrior's bowels to liquid. She couldn't help wriggling in her chair. Evidently, de Wolde had spread his poison and now she must face Ranulf.

She sat before Ranulf and began to explain why she had lied. And why she had run away from her abusive husband and sought shelter, first at St. Leonard's abbey, then as a wet nurse at Beauforde. Unfortunately, as she continued to explain his anger seemed to increase.

Finally, Ranulf put his hand up to silence her. Beatrice glanced at Isabeau, who sat quietly next to her husband. Gilbret stood by the hearth watching her but said nothing. Why he had been invited to watch her fall from grace she had no clue. But somehow his presence assuaged her panic.

Father Ascelin sat at the table recording her confession. They were all gathered in the lady's solar, a place that held so many wonderful memories of her time at Beauforde. It was in this room that she had found true friendship.

This morning, like every morning, Edward was away in the nursery where he played with Elizabet's twin boys while vying for attention from Godiva and Tillie as they cooed over Isabeau's infant son. She had hoped that Edward would grow up together with his cousin and friends. Perhaps they would be fostered together and become squires. Then knights. That hope had blossomed over the past few months but the look on Ranulf's face reminded her that she and her son's futures here at Beauforde might be in danger. She had been a fool to maintain the lie for so long, but she had made her own bed and it seemed she would be lying in it come what may.

"Do you mean to tell me that he had once beaten you to the point of losing your unborn babe?"

Ranulf's anger caused her stomach to clench and she was back cowering under Walter's rage.

Something on her face must have alerted her cousin. "Perhaps you might lower your voice, my love, I think you are frightening my cousin."

Ranulf shot his wife a quick glance, then turned his eyes back to Beatrice. "Please forgive me, Beatrice, I don't mean to frighten you. And of course, you will receive every courtesy now that we have all been informed of your relationship to my wife." His face softened, and he gave Isabeau a small smile. Beatrice couldn't help but notice his sardonic tone when he mentioned her relationship to Isabeau. He turned his eyes back to Beatrice. "I am appalled at Walter's behavior and cannot bring myself to believe he would treat you as such."

She was about to defend herself when he once again held up his hand.

"No, I do not mean to infer that I don't believe you, but that he always presented himself as the most chivalrous of men."

That was the trouble; her husband, Sir Walter de Gant, Baron Folkingham, had the appearance of a good man, but underneath he was all that was putrid and vile. She shuddered just thinking about the way he had treated her. In those first few months of marriage, everything had been well, then he had returned from King Stephen's court and everything had changed.

He drank more and became violent. She had been married for almost a year when she discovered she was with child. Oh, what joy she had, but had kept her joy to herself wanting to be sure before she spoke to Walter and that was when disaster struck. Walter had come to her chamber one night and began yelling that she had not fulfilled her bargain. Where was his heir? She told him that she was with child but he had flown into a rage and had beaten her.

His fists had crashed into her stomach making her fall to her knees. She couldn't remember anything after that. The pain ripping through her body had taken her wits. But she remembered the agony afterwards. And the loss.

After the loss of her unborn babe, she had vowed that if she carried another child, she would never allow her husband to kill it. She could endure his beatings and his occasional visits to her chamber. But never would she sacrifice another child to her husband's fury. It took several more years and she had all but given up hope of another child when finally she discovered she was once again with child. There had never been a moment that she had regretted her decision to flee her marriage once she knew she carried another life within her. And because of that decision, she had been forced to deceive the only people who had shown her love and acceptance. "I'm sorry."

Isabeau was out of her chair and in front of Beatrice in a heartbeat. "No one in this room blames you," Isabeau stated as she gathered Beatrice into her arms.

"But I lied to you," she blubbered into Isabeau's shoulder as she tried to explain.

"That is of no matter." Isabeau took hold of Beatrice's shoulders. "We are here to help. Never doubt that."

Beatrice nodded but couldn't look at the people gathered in front of her.

Gilbret handed her a cup of wine. "All will be well but we need to know so we can help."

Beatrice gathered her shattered pride about her and acknowledged Gilbret then Ranulf. Isabeau had settled herself back in her chair.

"I understand this is difficult, but Gilbret is correct. No one in this room judges you for what you felt you had to do, Beatrice." Ranulf's voice was more gentle now and his eyes sympathetic. "Never would we abandon you but we need to know all the sorry details if we are to assist you."

Beatrice nodded. "When I refused to return and fled Walter repudiated me for abandoning the marriage," Beatrice said as she hung her head in shame.

"I should imagine Walter saw an opportunity when your father's Adulterine castles, which were part of your dowry, had to be returned to their previous owners at King Henry's orders. Convenient to rid himself of his troublesome wife." Ranulf's voice was so quiet Beatrice almost missed his question.

King Henry had ordered that all lands taken from estates during King Stephen's reign be returned to the original owners. That had caused havoc among the barons who coveted land. She, like many other women, found herself a victim of men's political pursuits.

"My father insisted I return to Walter. When I refused and ran away that's when Walter decided that he would be rid of me. I couldn't allow my unborn babe to be put at risk so I escaped to St. Leonard's. Mother Hild sent a cleric to spy on my father and see what was happening." She glanced at Gilbret, but his expression was unreadable so she looked away.

"That is when I discovered that Walter had annulled our marriage."

"Walter didn't know you carried his son?" Father Ascelin asked.

"No, I told no one. Most of my dowry lands were no longer available to Walter. I suspect he found another woman with more land and money. That is, until he died." She couldn't bring herself to mourn Walter. His death had changed nothing. As a repudiated woman she was condemned as a wanton and little Edward, instead of becoming the heir of Folkingham, was labeled illegitimate.

"But since he is dead, and from what I understand the annulment was not finalized, surely you are still wed and Edward is Walter's heir?" Ranulf asked. His face matched the confusion on Isabeau and Gilbret's faces.

"Perhaps I might explain," Ascelin said, "Walter's maternal uncle is Robert de Chesney, Bishop of Lincoln. He is the one who authorized the annulment. In one stroke he removed Edward from the inheritance allowing Walter's brother, Everlyn, to inherit the title and the estates. I'm sure his grateful nephew will endow de Chesney with a sizable estate in thanks." Ascelin's tone betrayed the contempt he had for both Everlyn and de Chesney.

Silence filled the small solar.

Beatrice had expected that her repudiation was due to a powerful ally associated with Walter's family, but she never knew who that was. Now it all made sense.

"I don't understand," Isabeau said as she looked to her husband and then Ascelin.

"Robert de Chesney has huge political and ecclesiastical sway both here in England, but more importantly in Rome."

"But what does Robert gain by disinheriting Edward?"

"As I said I suspect Everlyn has arranged a very generous endowment for his uncle. The land and castles are a prize that many would likely sell their souls for."

"So, on his own authority, he granted Walter an annulment thus leaving Edward illegitimate?"

Ascelin's expression was kind as he looked at her. "I am afraid powerful men have done much worse for half of Walter's estates."

To have attracted such powerful enemies was a terrifying thought. Her father and de Wolde were mere pawns in a much bigger and more dangerous game.

"I have spoken to de Wolde, and he gave me this." Ranulf handed the missive to Ascelin who read it silently.

"Well, what does it say?" Gilbret's impatience was evident in his tone. "I met the man yesterday. He said his visit was about unpaid rents. He strikes me as someone who would happily feather his own nest."

"Nothing to do with rents. He has been sent to all those whom Beatrice's father thinks might offer her succor. The writ is from de Chesney himself stating that if anyone offers her support rather than sending her to her father, they risk excommunication."

"No!" Beatrice couldn't breathe. How could her father do such a thing? Now Isabeau and Ranulf ran the risk of being banished from the sacraments of the church if they didn't hand her over to her father. Little Ralf could not be baptized. How had her life, and the lives of those she loved, become so complicated?

"There is an answer to all this," Gilbret said as he moved to stand beside Ranulf. "Beatrice can marry, and it seems to me that if I marry her, and adopt Edward as my own, then the church can do nothing. And as a married woman Beatrice will be away from her father's grasp."

Beatrice wanted to object, but she couldn't. Gilbret was right. Only marriage would free her from the bishop's vile threats.

"It is true. The church has no rule against a widow remarrying. Thankfully Walter is dead, thus releasing Beatrice to marry regardless of whether she has been repudiated."

Beatrice rose from her chair, terrified her legs wouldn't hold her as she used the table to steady herself. "I agree. I cannot allow Isabeau and Ranulf to be excommunicated, and I cannot allow my father to take Edward." She didn't need to say that her father would most likely find a way to kill Edward. Everyone present understood the threat to her son's life. She turned and looked at Gilbret. "I will marry you." She had no other choice.

Gilbret didn't smile but merely nodded. His expression was inscrutable. Their eyes held for a heartbeat before he turned to speak to Ascelin. "What would it entail to fight against the annulment?"

Beatrice gasped. Was it possible to remove the shame of the repudiation and reinstate Edward's claim? A tiny flicker of hope sprang to life in Beatrice's mind.

Ascelin looked at Gilbret, then Beatrice. "It would require us seeking support from a powerful bishop and persuading him to appeal the annulment. And it will take a great deal of coin."

"It is impossible." Beatrice didn't want to give up, but there was so much against her that she feared she didn't have the will to fight.

"I think I can speak for all in this room when I say that we will support you in any way we can." Ranulf cast a quick glance at Gilbret, who nodded his agreement, before returning his gaze to her. "And I can assure you that our support will ensure that Edward will grow up knowing the protection of his family."

Beatrice didn't want to cry, but that last statement broke through her defenses. Tears slid down her cheeks as she fought for control over her emotions. "I am grateful, truly I am, but I can't let you shoulder that burden. This is a fight that I am not sure can be won and I will do nothing to jeopardize you and Isabeau." She looked over at Gilbret. "Or you, Sir Gilbret."

Gilbret looked to Father Ascelin. "Father, what does the church say about such matters?"

The priest looked up and captured Beatrice's eyes, then he looked at Gilbret. "The church is clear that if a woman is in danger of her life from her husband, then she is under the church's protection and it will grant a legal separation."

Beatrice flopped back against the chair. The church's ruling might work in her favor if she could prove that her life had been in danger.

"What about in the case of abandonment?" Gilbret said as he leaned over the table where Ascelin sat.

"In such cases, every effort must be made to corroborate the allegation. If Lady Beatrice feared for her life, then the church would agree that leaving her husband was legal. Only when the bishop is satisfied that the evidence is beyond doubt does he rule that no crime against her husband has been committed and that the fruit of that union is legitimate. Therefore an annulment on grounds of abandonment is invalidated." Ascelin explained, making sure to look at Beatrice before he continued, "the church must have evidence that grievous harm to your person can be substantiated. If no such evidence can be found, then the annulment will be upheld."

Beatrice couldn't speak. Her short reprieve was just that. Short!

"Surely that was done?" Isabeau's asked, her incredulity evident in her tone.

"That, my lady, is precisely why I shall travel to Folkingham and undertake to ascertain just who was questioned." His smile could only be described as feral as he looked at Beatrice. "I am confident that Sir Walter's nature cannot be hidden and that in Everlyn and de Chesney's haste to have the annulment pushed through they forgot to question you. And those who were privy to your husband's behavior."

"Meaning?" Gilbret asked impatiently.

"Meaning that if de Chesney did not question Beatrice, then he has no case and it can be overruled. Also, from what I hear, Walter was surely incapable of offering his wife and child protection, fidelity, and succor. For those are his marriage vows, and the church, for all its faults, takes the marriage vows very seriously."

"You would do that for me?" Beatrice couldn't quite fathom why this quiet, solemn man would undertake such an arduous task on her behalf.

"My lady, you held my boys to your breast and gave them life, and offered my Elizabet friendship, and dare I say, love. I can do nothing less." He huffed a small laugh. "I assure you Elizabet would hound me out of the house, and out of Beauforde if I didn't offer." He gave her a cheeky smile. "But rest assured, I am honored to do this for you."

Beatrice was speechless as she looked at the people around her. All she had ever wanted was a family to call her own. Now it seemed God had granted her the desire of her heart, for in this room were the people she considered to be her family. And although she had often hoped it would be so she had never really dared believe. Not since she was a girl of ten when her mother had died in childbed, had she been surrounded with such love and loyalty.

"Thank you." It was pitifully inadequate, but she meant it with every fiber of her being.

Isabeau was just about to embrace her when the door of the chamber opened and Joss, Ranulf's squire, entered and whispered to Ranulf.

"It seems Father de Wolde tired of waiting and has taken himself off." He kissed Isabeau on the cheek and left.

"Then we need to act fast. Father when can Gilbret and I marry?" Beatrice asked. For I fear if we delay all hope will be lost."

"Now, my lady, if you wish."

It was strange to hear the honorific. It would take some time for her to get used to being addressed as a noblewoman again.

"Please, Father, call me Beatrice."

He gave her a nod and waited as she turned and spoke to Gilbret. "Well?"

Gilbret's eyes traveled over her face and then settled on her eyes. His gaze was so intense he must surely see into her soul. She would not flinch. She had confessed all, and she would not hide from the shame that sat as a sodden cloak about her shoulders. It seemed an age before he slid his eyes back to Ascelin. "Very well, Father."

It was an inauspicious moment. With one intake of breath, she was as she had been for almost two years. Beatrice l'Aune. A disgraced daughter. Then, she was married—Beatrice de la Haye, Countess Wooler.

Father Ascelin asked them to pledge themselves to each other. Then he blessed them and pronounced them husband and wife. Isabeau stood quietly beside Beatrice holding her hand as Ascelin acknowledged her as their witness.

Ascelin's cleric was scratching his quill across the charter that declared her married and in the power of Sir Gilbret de la Haye.

And so it was that she had sealed her fate. She was married. God help her.

Chapter Seven

Beatrice didn't quite know what to do next. Usually, she would sit with Isabeau and Elizabet in the solar and spin or weave but those activities held little appeal. Her mind was racing as her body buzzed with energy. What had she done? Accepting another marriage was terrifying.

Gilbret stood off to her side and interrupted her thoughts with a slight cough. "I am going for a ride and wondered if you would care to join me?"

She didn't relish the company but she did long for a ride and to feel the wind in her face. She gave him a small nod. "I would welcome it, sir."

"Please, call me Gilbret." He gave her what could only be described as a grimace. "We are married and the formality does not sit well with me."

She didn't know what to say to that so gave him another nod. "I will meet you in the stables when I have changed into something suitable for riding."

Then to her shame, she fled.

The memory of Gilbret's finger tracing the line of her chin the previous evening made her skin tingle. Could she trust him not to be brutal? She would not concede that when she had thought of him her body had become so heated that it hadn't taken her long to learn that thinking about Gilbret was a danger to her health, not to mention her mind.

Gilbret, for his part, had watched her with an intensity that left her discomfited. He had not trusted her, but he had kept his distance and held his tongue.

Now she would have to get used to his attention. Her skin crawled as though covered with hundreds of creeping things at the thought. It would take all her strength to accept his attention in the marriage act, but she could learn to be civil and have a level of companionship.

A stab of envy made her breath catch. Isabeau had what Beatrice had longed for and had never received—a husband who loved and protected her. A loyal partner in the work of marriage and all it entailed.

Sighing, Beatrice made her way to her hovel and took her riding kirtle and surcoat from the chest against the south wall. No sooner had she finished pulling on her boots when there was a knock at her door.

Opening it she came face to face with Gilbret. "I said I would meet you in the stables," she griped. Why was it that men never listened to her? She said what she was going to do, but they seemed intent on forcing her to their own will. She was so tired of trying to mold herself into something malleable that she almost bit her tongue as she clenched her teeth.

Gilbret must have read her expression because he raised his hands in a sign of surrender. "I come to escort you to the hall as Father de Wolde has summoned you."

"I thought he had left."

"Well, it seems he has changed his mind and now insists that you answer his questions. I thought you might appreciate my scowling presence at your side." He gave her a wolfish grin that she responded to immediately.

"Thank you, Gilbret, I would appreciate you putting the fear of hell's fires in him."

They walked back towards the hall in silence. Once inside they were ushered into the small solar behind the raised dais that was Gilbret's temporary chamber. There Ranulf stood while Father de Wolde sat in a chair sipping wine from a silver cup. He seemed completely at his ease.

A tingle of warning crawled over her skin as she entered. De Wolde stood and gave her a courteous bow. "My lady."

She inclined her head but would give him no more.

The cleric raised his eyebrows at Gilbret's presence but didn't comment. Instead, he resumed his seat and continued sipping his wine while Beatrice made herself comfortable as Joss poured her a goblet of wine, too. Ranulf and Gilbret stood beside her. Their presence gave her the courage she needed.

"Well, why do you summon me, Father?"

The priest made a show of placing his cup on the table and wiped his lips on the linen cloth at his elbow. Such a display had Beatrice gritting her teeth. *Who does he think he is, this little nobody with his posturing and his inflated sense of importance?*

"I could not leave, my conscience would not permit it, without once again trying to save you, and your family," he murmured as he gave Ranulf a cursory nod. "From the edict that His Grace the Bishop of Lincoln has issued you, my lady, must return with me to your father's house before you or your friends are condemned even further."

Gilbret made a small movement on her left, but she stilled him by raising her hand.

"Yesterday, Father, you said it was my father who bore the sole responsibility for me. But I understand that as a widow I am free to marry. As such a husband might also bear that responsibility?"

"That is correct, my lady, but with all due respect who is going to marry a woman who is condemned as a fornicator and without her family's support?"

"A fornicator?" she queried as she looked him in the eye refusing to be cowed.

De Wolde made a clucking noise with his tongue. "Now come, my lady, as a repudiated woman you are left with a child that has no name." He leveled unblinking eyes on her. "Thus, an unmarried woman with a child is a 'fornicator.' And no nobleman would marry such a woman."

Despite her concerns about being married, she would take delight in pulling this little man off his perch. "There you are wrong, Father. Baron Wooler, so it seems, is the exception to the rule." She couldn't resist smiling at him as he almost choked on his tongue.

"Baron Wooler?"

"Father de Wolde, may I present Gilbret de la Haye, Baron Wooler, and my husband."

It was almost comical. The little cleric's eyes boggled and he spluttered as he tried to comprehend what she had said.

"But—"

"Father, we will not detain you as I am sure you wish to convey my regards to my father." Beatrice took pleasure in dismissing the man. Joss, Ranulf's squire, took the priest's elbow and escorted him from the chamber.

"Well, I left not an hour ago and already I find that I have acquired another cousin. Albeit through marriage." Ranulf gave Gilbret a large smile and shook his outstretched hand. "God's bones, man, you move fast," he said as he slapped his friend on the back.

Gilbret laughed. "In truth, it was my good wife's decision."

My good wife. Would she ever get used to those words? Probably not.

"Well, I think a toast is in order."

Beatrice didn't feel like celebrating, but it would have been churlish to refuse. Gilbret had saved her from her father's vile schemes and offered to legitimize Edward. But try as she might her heart sank. What awaited her at Barmoor Castle? And would Gilbret keep his word that he would not seek her out until she was ready?

She would have to pay the marriage debt but at the moment that thought was an unpleasant one. Bedding Walter had been enjoyable at the beginning of their marriage but as their marriage progressed he had become cruel in his speech concerning her body and her inability to give him an heir. Sex was unpleasant and for the life of her, she couldn't imagine it being any better with Gilbret.

Thinking about the future made her head spin while her stomach threatened to heave its contents on the rush floor.

Isabeau entered the solar, followed by Elizabet. "I have sent Godiva to the kitchen to inform them we will be celebrating."

"It's Friday." Beatrice was astounded that Isabeau would organize a feast on a fast day.

"Bah, we will eat game and be dammed. If the church can threaten us with excommunication for protecting a friend, then let us celebrate and face their wrath."

"My lady," Elizabet scolded in mock outrage but her smile betrayed her joy.

It seemed everyone was happy for her and Gilbret. Why could she not join in their pleasure? She knew the answer. Her heart would not allow it. Fear and mistrust were high walls and it would take more than a smile and a few words from her new husband to breach their defenses.

"It is too late for a ride, but perhaps you will accompany me to the garden where we may talk?" Gilbret said as he entered the chamber.

Beatrice had returned to the nursery earlier to check on Edward, who immediately upon seeing her had demanded her knee.

"Greedy boy," she cooed in mock scolding as he reached for the food on a table by her elbow.

"He has an appetite, that one." Godiva chuckled as she fussed over baby Ralf who was in his cradle sleeping.

Although Edward was weaned, he still wanted to nestle against her whenever he could. Time was moving so swiftly that Beatrice could scarce believe that he was already two moons past his first birthday. He would be grown before she knew it and would no longer want this closeness. She would hold on to the joy of his closeness for as long as she could.

She was sitting in a chair by the fire, Godiva's voice a pleasant buzz in her ears as the old nurse fussed over Ralf. Elizabet sat at the window seat sewing as her twins crawled about the solar. It was a quiet peaceful place and Beatrice was grateful neither woman spoke.

But now the serenity had been broken with the entrance of her husband and his invitation that they go to the garden.

He seemed amused with the image of her son snuggled into her, sucking his thumb. Surprisingly, there was a softness to his mouth that she had not seen before. And his eyes. God help her, his eyes held a reverence that she had never imagined a male was capable of. Women, yes. But men? Perhaps that was how Ranulf looked at baby Ralf when Isabeau nursed their son. It was an intimate expression that left her somewhat uncomfortable.

"I would be happy, sir, but perhaps you would care to wait until I have changed Edward's clout." She didn't bother trying to hide her pique, but Gilbret didn't seem to notice.

"No, I shall stay here and wait." He shot her a sly smile. "I suspect I will have to get used to seeing such domestic bliss now that I have a son."

"Your son?" Beatrice was incensed. Edward was hers and she would never share him with another.

"If you recall I did say that I would adopt Edward as my son if you consented to the marriage."

So he had. Beatrice glanced over to where Godiva and Elizabet were busy with their work and trying to look inconspicuous. But she was aware they heard every juicy morsel of her conversation and it irritated her no end. Why couldn't he leave and wait for her like any ordinary man? What did he expect she would do? Run away if he didn't keep watch on her? Well, that was a possibility but she wouldn't do that. Not now. She had agreed to the marriage and accepted she was now wed to Gilbret de la bloody Haye for life.

Think, Beatrice. "Perhaps you would be so kind as to find Tillie and ask her to bring some water to my hut so I might refresh myself before I meet you in the garden," she purred, hoping he would take the hint.

"Oh, I will have to escort you to your bedchamber as it is not fitting for a married woman of your standing to be living in the hovel you have called home for the past year."

"How dare …"

"It was Lady Isabeau's idea." His oily smile made her clench her teeth. "You will share my chamber."

She loved her small hovel. It was where she had been comfortable, with no one to dictate her coming or going. Now that small joy had been taken from her. Isabeau, her foot. Her husband was already exerting his control over her and she disliked it immensely. The idea of sharing the same bed had her skin crawling.

Edward's curiosity had got the better of him and turned to see who was speaking. He pulled his little thumb from his mouth with a small *plop.*

Elizabet and Godiva had been silent all this time but now

Godiva interrupted the farce that had been playing out between Beatrice and Gilbret.

"Allow me to change his clout, my lady, then I shall put him to bed for his nap." She gave Beatrice a knowing smile that Beatrice was so thankful for she almost cried.

"Thank you, Godiva."

Beatrice kissed her son's head, straightened her kirtle, and pronounced herself ready to be escorted to her new chamber.

Neither spoke as they walked down the stone stairs that led to an internal walkway that would lead them to another tower. There Gilbret led her to a series of doors.

"I thought—"

"You thought I meant you share my chamber?" He gave her a lopsided grin. "I gave my word, Beatrice, and I am a man of my word. I shall sleep in the solar behind the hall.'"

Why did that sound like a threat?

"These are your chambers until we leave for Barmoor.

"And when might that be?"

"I would like to leave tomorrow but would be happy to travel on Sunday after mass."

They entered a large chamber to find a young girl not much older than twelve or thirteen who greeted them.

"You know Mary, I think. She is to be your new maid," Gilbret said as the girl curtsied.

Beatrice looked at the girl, then at Gilbret. "My maid?" She didn't understand. Mary was a sweet child who always wanted to help. She often brought food for Edward and would stop to play with him before returning to her duties. Her mother had died several years ago and her father had put Mary to work in the kitchens so he could spend his time drinking.

"You have no household staff, and I thought it would be helpful to have someone you knew accompany you to Barmoor."

Mary's round face was full of hope as she waited for Beatrice to accept Gilbret's offer. In one stroke Gilbret had saved a girl from years of thankless drudgery at the hands of her drunken father and given Beatrice a familiar face to keep the loneliness of a new home at bay. Her new husband was kind. And thoughtful. That was a surprise. And one she was not sure she was ready for.

Beatrice looked around her new chamber noticing that Mary had a clean kirtle and gown laid out on the bed. "You have been busy, Mary, but those are not mine," Beatrice said, gesturing towards the unfamiliar clothing.

"If it pleases you, m'lady, Lady Isabeau sent them. She thought they would be suitable for the feast to celebrate your wedding." The girl looked a little unsure. Her green eyes darted between Beatrice and Gilbret until they finally rested on the floor at her feet.

The last thing Beatrice wanted to do was cause the girl discomfort. "It pleases me very well, Mary. Perhaps you would be good enough to help me dress."

The girl's face lit up with such joy that Beatrice couldn't contain her smile. Such a simple gesture, and yet the pleasure reflected on the girl's face was an unexpected gift. In truth, Mary was no child. If she had been born a noblewoman she would have been married by now. Thank God servants tended to marry much later.

"I shall leave you to dress, my lady," Gilbret said as he bowed and left the room.

"But don't you want to talk?" Beatrice called after him.

He turned, his hand poised on the door latch. "It can wait." His eyes slid towards Mary then back to Beatrice. "I would not like to interfere with such important matters as a woman and her new clothing." There was no sting to his comment. In truth, Beatrice detected a humorous note to his tone and offered a small smile in recognition of his teasing. "But I will not tolerate being delayed for my wedding supper, so I shall return to escort you to table." The mock gruffness made her laugh. "Of course, my lord," she replied with equal severity.

. . .

THE REST of the morning was spent with Mary as she helped adjust Beatrice's new gown. Elizabet and Isabeau came later in the morning to add their contribution.

"That color suits you well," Isabeau said as she ran a critical eye over Beatrice. "It brings out the green and yellow in your eyes."

Beatrice didn't want the color in her eyes highlighted. She would much rather have had her usual drab kirtle on rather than this sumptuous gown. Although she couldn't resist running her hand over the fine wool. She had never worn a lavender gown before but as she looked in the polished bronze mirror her eyes seemed greener and more defined. Flecks of yellow only enhanced the green. Who was the woman staring back at her? Terror crushed the breath from her lungs. She couldn't do this. All she wanted was to hide here at Beauforde and raise Edward to be a good man. A strong man and a man who would protect those weaker than himself.

"Fear not, cousin, I will be sitting at your side." Isabeau's smile warmed Beatrice's heart and stilled her fears. Well perhaps not stilled, but at least she didn't think she was about to collapse on the floor with terror.

"You will have to get used to being on the dais as Barmoor is a large castle with many important retainers." Isabeau's words cut like a knife. Beatrice's fragile hold on her composure threatened to give way as she considered how her life would change. Memories of being publicly humiliated by her husband as she sat quietly by his side on the dais made her cringe.

Elizabet must have seen the small shudder. "What bothers you, Beatrice?" Her friend's concern was reflected on Isabeau's face.

She didn't want to tell them. A lifetime of hiding her shame behind a shield of quiet acceptance had left her hulled out and empty. Yet a rage burned in her heart, just under her breastbone. Why was she the one to accept such abuse while others lorded it over her? Fear that Gilbret was hiding a cruel side tormented Beatrice. Walter had been so charming when they had first married. Never would she have believed him capable of the cruel spiteful behavior that was his true character. She couldn't endure another marriage like that.

Elizabet led Beatrice to the bed where Isabeau was seated. "Sit."

Beatrice obeyed. How she hated her meek obedience but she couldn't find the energy or will to do anything else.

"Tell us," Isabeau said as she patted the space next to her.

Beatrice sat and wondered where to begin. "I can't do it," she whispered.

"Can't do what?" Elizabet said as she sat next to Beatrice.

Beatrice looked first at her cousin, then at Elizabet. Oh, how she would miss these two wonderful women. The sisters she had never believed she would have. They were beautiful, strong, and full of compassion as they waited for her to explain.

"I will make him hate me as I did the others." It was a lame statement, but one she believed with all her being.

If it wasn't so serious, she would have laughed at their confused faces.

"I am cursed. My stepmother, my father, and Walter. All of them said so. I am afraid that Gilbret will discover the truth and despise me just as they did." It would only be a matter of time before Edward, too, would turn from her. But she prayed she would have years before that fateful day arrived. She couldn't bear to have her son turn away from her, but in her heart, she knew he would.

"I don't understand?" Isabeau took her hand. "Beatrice, what do you mean? You are one of the gentlest women I have ever known. What lie do you believe?"

Elizabet nodded her agreement, but Beatrice didn't know how to explain. "I can't explain." A despondency settled over her as she withdrew her hand from Isabeau's grasp. "I cannot hope to find happiness with Gilbret. For he too will come to despise me just as

Walter did." *If he doesn't already*. But she kept that sad fact to herself.

A knock at the door stopped any further conversation.

"Come." Beatrice was grateful her voice didn't come out as a squeak.

And there standing before her was her husband. He was so handsome in his surcoat that he almost took her breath away. The thought that he would come to despise her made her cringe from him but she would not let Edward suffer for her fears. Her son would have a name, and if God so pleased, her son would also have his inheritance. But while she had gained security this marriage had nothing to offer her personally except more loneliness and the fear of further rejection. And so, it was with a sinking heart that she rose from the bed, kissed her cousin's and Elizabet's cheeks, and accepted Gilbret's outstretched arm.

Like a lamb led to slaughter she went quietly and with no fuss. What would be the point? Her fate was set and she would accept it with her usual quiet dignity.

Chapter Eight

GILBRET REMINDED HIMSELF TO CLOSE HIS MOUTH AS HE GAPED AT the woman who accepted his arm. She was the most ravishing vision he had ever seen. Since his first glimpse of Beatrice, he understood that she possessed a beauty that threatened to take a man's mind and turn it to custard. But the woman before him now was a goddess. Her gown hugged her figure and settled in a pool of cloth at her feet. But it was her eyes that struck him. They were usually a golden brown, but now shades of green seemed to swallow the brown. It was as though he were looking into a woodland glade with various hues of green and gold. A secret place that some part of him wanted to explore while his rational brain shouted, *Be careful—you can't afford to lose your wits!* There was a darkness in Beatrice that Gilbret had noticed. Times when her eyes shadowed and her expression paled. He would have to be careful and patient if he was to gain her trust.

Well, he might not want to rush her, but he could appreciate her beauty. Although that was a temptation he would likely come to regret. Having her so close and yet beyond reach would test the resolve of a saint. And he was no saint.

"My lord?" A question in her tone.

Shaking his head to dispel the clamor he nodded. "Lady Wife, you look well."

A blush of softest rose colored her cheeks. But she didn't reply; she merely inclined her head. Gilbret wasn't prepared for her response and took a few moments to remember his manners. "Lady Isabeau, Mistress Elizabet." He ushered his wife out of the chamber. The two women walked behind them as they all made their way to the hall and his wedding feast.

His mother and sister were safe and would return to Barmoor when he and Beatrice were settled. And with his marriage, he was now Baron Wooler. A rich and landed title that changed his life. It had been a shock to learn that de Chesney was the force behind Beatrice's annulment. The man was a threat to be sure, but as Beatrice was a widow the bishop had no power over Gilbret's future.

But somehow, he couldn't quite muster the energy to celebrate his good fortune. His uncle, William de Muscamp, could not be trusted. The old snake had coveted the Wooler estates for years. In truth, he suspected his uncle would do all in his power to ensure Gilbret did not succeed in obtaining his father's inheritance. It would not surprise Gilbret if he were to learn that his uncle and Robert de Chesney might conspire against him. Barmoor was an excessively rich barony and the two clerics would benefit from such an endowment. It was imperative Gilbret return to Barmoor as soon as possible to claim his right to the title and estates.

Gilbret glanced at the woman by his side. Had he made a mistake taking this woman to his wife? He would stand by his word and support an appeal to the annulment. But she was a woman who had made powerful enemies. His future might be within his grasp, but it was by no means assured.

They walked on in silence until they reached the hall. There Gilbret stopped and waited for the steward to seat him and his wife. As honored guests, they would be seated on the dais next to Ranulf and Isabeau. Gilbret was used to sitting there, but Beatrice had taken her meals far below the salt. How would the castle retainers react to her elevated position? In their eyes, she was still a miller's widow, not Lady Beatrice l'Aune. How she had kept such a secret for the year she had lived among these people was a mystery to Gilbret.

The woman had been desperate, and he had better be on his guard to ensure he protected her from the men who would see her and her son destroyed. That gave him pause. The woman he had watched and quietly admired for the past year was a stranger to him. What was she really like? He glanced sideways and saw that she was looking at her feet. She was as uncomfortable at her elevation as he would have expected had she truly been a mere miller's widow. But she was a lady and trained to live in the elevated circles of nobles, so why so demure?

A small thread of compassion wove its way around his conscience. "All will be well, Beatrice."

She turned. Her eyes reflected a sadness that surprised him. "Thank you."

He made light of it to hide his discomfort. This woman was a paradox. "For what, my lady?"

"Your kindness with Mary. That was unexpected, but much appreciated. I shall miss living here among friends and a familiar face to accompany me to Barmoor will be welcome." She gave him a small, sad smile.

"You are unhappy to be leaving Beauforde and your lowly position?" He couldn't quite believe she was telling the truth.

She huffed a small laugh. "In truth, Beauforde has been the only home where I have felt safe and valued." She turned her eyes on him. "So, yes, I will miss it very much."

He couldn't respond as the steward of the hall gestured for them to follow him to the dais.

The meal progressed with Father Ascelin pronouncing a

blessing on the wedded couple. And then several courses of fish and game followed.

Jugglers and musicians entertained as they ate.

Gilbret struggled to think. Beatrice confounded him. She was not what he expected. And that made him uncomfortable.

"Do you prefer this type of meal or something more subdued?" he asked as he poured Beatrice some more wine.

He noticed she glanced around the hall before returning her gaze to him. "I find it a challenge. Walter would be in his cups by now and making life difficult for me. I have very little experience of a meal as enjoyable as this."

"Not at your father's house?"

"No. I was eleven summers old when my father remarried. He longed for a male heir." She gave a small shrug indicating that she cared little. "I was a disappointment. An inconvenience at best. My stepmother convinced him to send me to a convent. Then at fifteen, I was brought home to be married to Walter."

Gilbret digested her comment. So, this beauty sitting before him was not the indulged daughter of a wealthy baron he expected her to be. Now, as he watched her from the corner of his eye, he noticed she was reticent about being the center of the celebration. He had thought her reserved nature might hide an arrogant and somewhat superior character. It seemed he had misjudged her.

"When we arrive at Barmoor you will be the lady of the castle. Will that be a problem?" Gilbret tried to swallow as the hand of dread closed around his throat. He had watched his mother wain under the grief of regret and sorrow. Beatrice held the same beaten look. Would she be strong enough to cope with the rigors of being the lady of the castle?

She turned and looked aghast. "But what of your mother? I can't usurp her. It would be too unkind."

Gilbret was pleased that Beatrice truly looked horrified at the prospect of taking control of the household from his mother. "She has long since resided at a nunnery in Kent and has never had the running of Barmoor."

"Your sister has no role?"

"Ah … My sister has also been hidden away in the same nunnery. When my sister had the audacity to disobey my father and fall in love with a mere captain of the guards, he banished her to live out her days in the nunnery. As Baron Wooler, I can bring them back to Barmoor but I had to secure the title first. Thus the haste in our marriage."

"Will they come to live at Barmoor or have they taken their vows?"

"Yes, I hope they will come, but I shall leave that decision to them." Would they come or did they also hate the thought of living in a castle that stood as a reminder of so much pain and humiliation? And what of his sister? Would she forgive him for not being able to help her when she needed him most?

"I look forward to meeting them. Have you decided when we are to leave?"

"If you can be ready, I would like to leave tomorrow."

"So soon?"

"I know it will be a wrench, Beatrice, and I'm sorry, but there is very little time and Whitsun is close. I dare not take any longer." What could he say to ease her pain? "I also want to begin making inquiries about the legality of your annulment." She gave him a quick sideways glance. "As Baron Wooler, I stand a good chance of helping you and Edward. But I must be at Barmoor."

"I thank you, sir." She bowed her head. "As you wish. I will be ready."

Her expression caused something in Gilbret's chest to constrict. They had to leave, as Ascension Day was on Monday and they would be forbidden to travel. He needed to be at Barmoor by then. Looking at his wife and her demeanor, he reminded himself that he had wanted a compliant wife, but at this moment he longed to see some fire behind Beatrice's eyes rather than the docile obedience she presented to him. His disappointment so surprised him that he almost choked on his wine. He chided himself—he didn't want fire and passion in a wife. Then why did it feel as though he had been cheated?

BEATRICE ENDURED THE MEAL. Her skin crawled—all those eyes watching her like insects creeping over her skin. She wanted to retreat to her chamber and eat in peace and hold Edward close. She knew who she was when she held him or fussed over him. But to be a lady who garnered compliments was a source of discomfort. Agitated, she concentrated on eating the small morsels of food placed before her, but in truth, she tasted nothing.

"I know it's a trial, but it will be over soon." Isabeau's quiet voice was a welcome relief.

"I don't wish to be ungrateful …"

"I too endured a meal much like this one," she said, the regret heavy in her voice. "But then I suspect Cicele did not have an easy time of it at Alnwick to begin with, either. It is the way of many marriages."

Beatrice immediately felt chastened. Her cousin, Cicele, had been forced to marry a man she truly loathed. Thank the saints her marriage was as happy as Isabeau's. Cicele's letters were brief, but her happiness shone through. She had married Guyon, a man known by the epithet "The Beast," but fate had favored her. Beatrice would not be so fortunate.

Beatrice noticed a small smile tilt Isabeau's lips as her eyes sparkled with an expression she didn't recognize. Beatrice turned to see that Ranulf was looking at his wife. He bore the same expression. Embarrassed at being privy to such an intimate moment Beatrice lowered her gaze to the trencher in front of her. Isabeau was happily married. Their love and mutual respect were obvious when they were together.

Could Cicele be so blessed? Beatrice prayed every day that her cousin had indeed found the same in her marriage. The Beast was reputed to be a loathsome man, but Beatrice had seen the way he looked at Cicele. She was sure there was more to the man than his vile reputation.

Beatrice sneaked a quick sideways glance at her husband. He was talking to Ranulf, their heads inclined together.

All she could hope for was a modicum of respect and, if she were so blessed, consideration. But love? She had never experienced it, so did not miss it. Edward gave her joy and a sense of purpose. That was enough.

Beatrice turned back to her cousin. "You have found love." She didn't mean to sound bitter but her tone was cold and flat. Beatrice immediately looked at her cousin, ready to apologize for her remark, but judging by her cousin's serene expression no offense was taken.

"I have been truly blessed, and I believe the same is true for Cicele. I will continue to pray that you too will be blessed with a marriage filled with love." Isabeau smiled then. It was radiant. Beatrice wanted to turn her face towards it and never leave. Much like a flower on a spring day basking in the sun's warmth, so, too, Beatrice was filled with warmth in every fiber of her cold and lonely life.

"I shall miss you so much," she said as a sob caught her voice.

"Oh, Beatrice, I shall miss you also." Isabeau took Beatrice's hand and laid it on her lap. "Take courage, Gilbret is a good man."

Tears obscured her view of the tables and people before the dais but she continued to look out over the gathered retainers who had feasted and celebrated her marriage. She didn't dare turn her head and look at her cousin, but she squeezed her hand silently admitting her own sorrow at leaving.

. . .

THE MEAL finally came to an end and Beatrice was escorted from the hall by Gilbret. There were no rowdy or lewd comments from the gathered men as they walked from the hall. That was some small comfort to Beatrice. She remembered the obscene gestures and comments of Walter's men as he led her to their chamber. Thankfully that ordeal was not repeated here. It was late afternoon but there were still hours of daylight left. The men would be off to their various tasks before they returned to the hall for their supper.

"How does Barmoor celebrate Whitsun?" she asked as she turned to Gilbret.

"I expect the same as elsewhere. It is a time of feasting and fêtes and, like Beauforde, will be in the throes of preparation." He smiled down at her. "The cook at Barmoor makes delicious cakes filled with currants and nutmeg." He wiggled his eyebrows at her. "As a boy, I held the record for consuming the most cakes in a single sitting."

Beatrice couldn't help herself, she laughed so hard her sides ached. "So, my lord husband, you were a greedy boy?"

Gilbret executed the perfect expression of an abashed boy. "Yes, it is a sin I must confess to." His smile was light and gave him a boyish quality that Beatrice had no defenses against. His chipped front tooth only added to his charm.

"You, sir, will be a bad influence on my son. He already has a tendency to greediness," she replied in mock severity.

Gilbret leaned closer and whispered into her ear. "I shall teach him all my tricks."

Her body shuddered in response to his breath tickling the sensitive skin below her ear. A warmth began to pool in her most secret of places. God forbid, what was happening to her?

She pulled back as though struck. The look of confusion on Gilbret's face as she jerked away gave her a pang of guilt, but she couldn't let herself be drawn in again. Never would she trust her heart to this man. Not to any man. She needed what little she had left of her heart for Edward alone.

"Forgive me, my lady, if I offended you." His tone was cold and aloof. "I shall leave you to Mary's care." He nodded and turned to walk back towards the stairs.

She was standing outside her chamber door. She had not even noticed that they had arrived, so engrossed with Gilbret that she had failed to keep track of her surroundings. That, more than his nearness, terrified her.

Beatrice didn't want to go to her chambers so she turned and made her way to the nursery on the western side of the castle. It was a lovely, light, airy room where Elizabet and Godiva spent so much of their day. Edward's crying could be heard as soon as she opened the nursery door.

"I was just about to come to get you; his lordship here is in one of his demanding moods," Godiva said as she stroked Edward's head. His little face was flushed pink from his crying.

"Has he had his meal?" Beatrice asked as she took him into her arms. His little body trembled as he snuggled into her.

Godiva nodded. "Yes, but I suspect his back teeth are coming through and he isn't impressed."

Beatrice had no experience with a teething child. Thankfully Godiva did. "What does he need?"

"Give him this so he can chew on it."

Godiva handed Beatrice a small wooden ring.

"I shall go to the kitchen and get some cloves. The oil will help soothe his gums without him having too much."

With that, she was through the door as though the furies of hell were after her.

Beatrice sat by the fire and gave Edward the wooden ring, which he immediately put in his mouth.

A twinge of guilt stabbed at her chest as she thought back to her body's reaction to Gilbret's nearness. She had been so engrossed with him that she had not heard Edward's crying. It was so confusing. Two days ago, she was afraid of him, but now her fear seemed to have turned into something else entirely. And it had robbed her of her diligence towards her son. That would not happen again. That must not happen again.

Marriage to Gilbret, it seemed, was not going to be as easy as she had hoped or imagined. How was she to protect herself from further pain if her body responded to him so easily? She could never allow herself to become vulnerable to her new husband. Walter had taught her that salient lesson. As she stroked Edward's head, she let herself relax into this most pleasurable of tasks. He was content to gnaw on the ring. Saliva ran down his hands and began to drip on her kirtle.

Not wanting to have her new dress spoiled she reached for a linen cloth and wiped Edward's hands.

"You are a grubby boy," she chided. Edward was impervious to the insult as he continued to gnaw on his teething ring.

She would think about Gilbret and his smiles, and the journey to Barmoor, later. For now, she reveled in her son and the assurance that he was safe.

GILBRET DIDN'T UNDERSTAND what had happened. One moment Beatrice was laughing with him, then the next she retreated into that cold distant woman he had known since her arrival at Beauforde.

Something was amiss, but he couldn't quite understand what. He didn't want to think about her rejection and immediate withdrawal. They had been sharing a quiet moment where they were almost friends. So why did it feel like a stab to his chest? It was beyond his comprehension. He didn't care whether she liked him or not. Theirs was a marriage of convenience—they both got what they wanted. Hell's fires he was in trouble.

"Ah, here comes the groom looking fit to spit." Ranulf's comment was met with raucous laughter and several ripe comments.

Gilbret scowled at the men gathered in the pele yard. "Give me a bloody sword," he yelled at Olivier.

The boy sauntered over and handed Gilbret his sword, handle first. "I did suggest she might be too much for you, my lord."

Gilbret wanted to wipe the smirk off his squire's face, but he surrendered to the good-natured jibe.

Gilbret turned to face Ranulf. "I'll wipe that smile off your face, you dung-eating bastard."

Ranulf inclined his head, never taking his eyes off Gilbret. "If you are man enough. I'd wager a wife like Beatrice has sapped your reserves."

Gilbret lunged. But Ranulf was waiting.

It was good to exorcise his frustrations on his opponent. He would have to have held back with any of the other men. But not Ranulf. They fought until exhaustion called a halt to the training.

Ranulf slapped Gilbret on the back. "God's bones, Gil, I'm going to miss you."

Gilbret thought back to the first time he had clapped eyes on Ranulf, who had been sent as a hostage to Matilda's court. He too had been vilified by his father. The boys had formed an alliance that evolved into an unbreakable friendship.

"The castle will be in good hands with Sigeric." Gilbret had apprenticed Sigeric d'Auray years ago and he was now as competent as Gilbret to fulfill the role as seneschal.

"D'Auray is a good man and you have trained him well. But it's not the welfare of the castle I am concerned about, you witless bastard." Ranulf slapped him again. The force was so great that Gilbret almost lost his balance. "You fight like a maid, but you have heart and I will miss my friend."

"God's bones, man, stop hitting me. I'm likely to fall on my face and eat dirt."

"Joss, bring some ale for this frail old man," Ranulf roared at his squire.

"Old?" Gilbret gasped as he tried to regain his breath. Their sparing session had been grueling. And he had savored every moment of it.

"Well, I am younger by at least a week."

Gilbret laughed. As boys, they had always tried to best each other. And Ranulf always brought out the "age" argument when he knew he was beaten.

Gilbret was too exhausted to talk. He took the offered mug of ale and drank it down without stopping.

"Marriage seems to make a man thirsty," Ranulf teased.

Gilbret didn't respond. What could he say? Ranulf knew all the sordid details of Gilbret's father's will. Marriage was only one of many problems Gil faced as he set about being the Lord of Barmoor.

Chapter Nine

BEATRICE'S EYES WERE SORE AND GRITTY AND HER MOOD NOT MUCH
better. She had endured a sleepless night fretting about this very
day. Now after several hours in the wagon being tossed about—the
wooden wheels seemed to attract every rut in the track—she was
just about at her wit's end.

"Enough!"

"M'lady?" Mary's small face was pale and her eyes round. She
was not a good traveler and Beatrice felt a twinge of guilt for not
being more aware of her maid's discomfort. Edward was asleep.
The movement of the wagon seemed to lull him into slumber almost
as soon as they left Beauforde. Beatrice swallowed a cry as she
thought about her beloved friends whose anxious faces could not
hide their concern for her as she set out with her new husband.

Elizabet had hugged her as she walked to the wagon. Ascelin
blessed her, then went to stand next to his wife. Oh, how she would
miss her friend. But it was Isabeau—more a sister than a cousin—
who made Beatrice's heart break. "I shall miss you so much,"
Isabeau murmured as she pulled Beatrice into a fierce hug.

Beatrice's throat refused to open—a lump rendered her incapable of speech. As usual, Isabeau understood. "I am always here," she whispered. A conspiracy between friends. "If ever you need me." Isabeau's green eyes bored into Beatrice.

The intent of the words and gaze left Beatrice in no doubt about what her cousin meant.

Beatrice nodded and swiped the tears from her cheek.

Ranulf stood next to Isabeau. He had said his farewells to Beatrice and was now waiting to bid his friend Godspeed.

Gilbret had helped Beatrice into the wagon and they had been off. Her future was no more certain than it had been three days ago when Father de Wolde had cornered her in the garden. Would Gilbret realize he had made a mistake? Especially if the annulment stood. To be married to a divorced woman was a shame no man could endure.

Dragging her mind back to the discomfort of the wagon, what should have only been a few hours of travel had become several as rain and road conspired to make the journey one of the most uncomfortable in her memory. Fleeing her father and hiding with the pilgrims on the journey to St. Leonard's seemed a trifling matter compared to this tedious and unpleasant journey.

Beatrice smiled at her maid. "It seems neither you nor I are good travelers this morning."

Mary was too busy swallowing to do more than nod at Beatrice.

Yes, it was time to stop. Beatrice had no wish to witness Mary as she vomited over the interior of the wagon.

Beatrice moved to the flap of skin covering the window and poked her head out. Spying a horse and rider just ahead she called, "We must stop."

Without any warning, the wagon lurched to a stop sending Beatrice tumbling backward with her legs and arms flailing about trying to find some purchase.

The side of the wagon was opened and lowered giving Gilbret a perfect view of her legs. The indignity was too much and Beatrice had no qualms about letting Gilbret know exactly how she felt.

"What are you looking at?" she spat as she desperately tried to gain her composure.

The quirk on Gilbret's face did little to soothe her temper. "A pair of rather shapely legs." His smile was playful but Beatrice was not in the mood.

She righted her kirtle and gown and prepared to exit the wagon. "Mary, come and get some fresh air."

The rain had stopped but the ground was muddy from the horse's hooves trampling the ground.

Without a word of apology, Gilbret lifted Beatrice from the wagon and walked to a nearby tree where the ground was not dry but at least it was free of the mud.

A small squeak had escaped her as she had been lifted but even Beatrice had to acknowledge Gilbret's gesture was considerate. "Thank you," she huffed rather ungratefully as he set her on her feet.

Olivier also helped Mary. The little maid's face was crimson. It was a chivalrous gesture, which Beatrice thought rather lovely. Her maid was small and rather pretty, and it seemed Olivier had noticed.

Gilbret turned his head to look in the direction of Beatrice's gaze. "That was thoughtful," Beatrice said as she watched Olivier take Mary to some shelter.

"I could take credit for it, but alas the lad's manners are better than my own." Gilbret's crooked smile made Beatrice's heart flutter. Oh, Lord in heaven, she could get used to that playful smile.

"That, sir, is a lie." She sounded so tart she winced at her tone of voice. "Forgive me, I am not myself this morning." It was a pitiful excuse, but it was the truth.

Gilbret studied her for what seemed an age before he nodded.

"It will be a trying time for you, Beatrice, and I will do all I can to make the transition less onerous." Then he gave her a quick bow and walked back towards Olivier leaving Beatrice standing there watching his retreating back.

Normally Beatrice had an affable temperament but today it had deserted her and she didn't particularly like the woman who was residing in her skin. "Enough, Beatrice, you have made the decision to marry and move to Barmoor, so accept it with grace." The sound of her own voice went some way to soothing her tattered nerves. In truth, she was nervous about arriving at Barmoor.

She would be a stranger among an already organized household. It was one thing to become the lady of the castle, but quite another to be a stranger thrust into a household where she would be neither welcomed nor accepted. Beatrice was under no illusions about her relationship with Gilbret. And the one thing she had learned, even as a small child, was that living in a castle meant that there were very few secrets.

Her nurse used to terrify her with stories of the walls having eyes and ears. She now understood what her nurse meant—servants were everywhere and often went about their duties unnoticed. Yes, the walls did indeed have ears and eyes, and it was as threatening to Beatrice's adult sensibilities as it had been when she was a child.

Gilbret arrived sometime later with a skin of wine and some bread. "I know it's not much but better to have something in your stomach." Did he know she hadn't eaten anything before she left?

"Thank you, but I don't think I can." Her stomach was in her throat and it wasn't only due to the hideous ride in the wagon.

"The wine will offer some comfort," he said as he handed her the wineskin. "It is for your use only," he added as she looked at his outstretched hand.

To her shame, she had expected it to have been offered to others as well.

"You don't know me, Beatrice, but you will come to understand that I am not like your previous husband." His smile was small, but his eyes had a sincerity to them that she recognized.

"I am not used to being cared for. Please forgive my poor manners." She couldn't meet his eye so she kept her gaze on the wineskin as she accepted it from him.

"I wonder if you would care to ride for the remainder of the journey?"

That made her head pop up and look at him. His eyes were assessing her with interest. She would love to ride and couldn't hide the smile that began to spread over her face.

"I take that as a yes."

"Yes," she said as her cheeks lifted and her smile spread across her face. "Oh, but I have no riding cloak." The sense of loss was out of proportion to the situation but she couldn't stop her reaction.

"Lady Isabeau thought you might want to ride at some stage of the journey so she gave me this." He handed her a cloak she recognized immediately. It was the same one Isabeau had lent her when she had discovered who Beatrice was. It was a deep blue woolen garment lined with rabbit skin. It was almost summer but the rain and lack of sun made the day cold. Only Isabeau would have been so thoughtful.

"Thank you." She went to take the cloak but Gilbret playfully pulled it out of her reach. "I shall give you the cloak and a mount if you agree to ride with me."

This new, playful Gilbret was a mystery to Beatrice. She couldn't remember anyone playing with her, even as a child, and, God curse her traitorous heart, she liked it.

"Very well, although I don't take kindly to bribery, sir." She tried to scowl but reluctantly she gave up trying to contain her laughter.

Gilbret bellowed something unintelligible and almost immediately a lovely gray mare with tan markings was led to where she and Gilbret stood.

"I'm afraid I do not have something more fitting your status as Countess Wooler, but Clover is a willing mount who likes to be given her head." Gilbret gave Beatrice a sly glance. "I suspect you like to have the wind rush past your face when the horse is competent."

"So, you think you know me already, husband?" she said as she moved to stroke the horse. "You are a beautiful girl," she whispered into the horse's ear as she ran her hand over Clover's nose and cheek. Clover assessed Beatrice with intelligent brown eyes and tossed her head in protest when Beatrice stopped petting her. "Ah, I see we will get along well, my lovely Clover." Beatrice continued to stroke the mare's neck as she turned to face Gilbret. "Thank you."

Gilbret returned her thanks with a formal bow. "She is only a jennet, but she will do well until you can assess the horses at Barmoor."

"I have never had a horse of my own, and a palfrey seems a little grand for me. I am sure Clover and I will become fast friends." She didn't want Gilbret to think she was ungrateful. In truth, she was delighted. "Why name her Clover?"

"Ah, well I am not usually one to spread gossip, especially when a lovely female is involved, but Clover was a little more rotund in her younger days and had a penchant for clover when she was turned out for the spring."

"So, you are not the only greedy one?" Beatrice couldn't resist teasing him. It was unfamiliar to tease, especially men. Her father and late husband would never have tolerated it, but Gilbret seemed to enjoy the verbal sparring.

"Alas, I have to admit life is much better if I can have companionship in my vices." He wiggled his eyebrows at her which made her laugh.

"You, sir, are a rascal."

"That, wife, I am. Now shall we go or do you need to attend to Edward?"

"Edward!" She had completely forgotten about her son. How had that happened?

"Fear not, he is with Mary. I shall have Olivier take Clover and ride beside the wagon. When you are ready to ride just let him know." Then he was gone, barking orders as he strode past the wagon to his mount.

Beatrice walked back to the wagon, guilt biting at her heels. How, in God's name, had she forgotten about Edward? For the first time since she had known she carried another child, she had never, not for one heartbeat, forgotten about her babe. Until now.

That reality caused a wave of panic to grip her around the neck and strangle every ounce of pleasure out of her time with Gilbret.

It would not happen again. It must not happen again. She couldn't afford to lose her heart to Gilbret. He, like every other male in her life, would discard her as though she were a mere chattel that had served its purpose.

Beatrice returned to the wagon to find that Mary was playing with Edward. A sudden and fierce surge of jealousy reared up as Beatrice watched and heard Edward's gurgled laughter at Mary's antics.

"Thank you, Mary; has he been changed and fed?" Beatrice kept her tone even although everything in her wanted to snatch Edward from the maid. What was wrong with her? She was usually even-tempered and docile. Well perhaps not docile, but she had more control over her temper than she displayed now.

"I am so pleased you are with me, Mary, and it seems Edward shares my view."

Edward clung to Mary as the little maid handed him over to Beatrice. "He likes to play like my younger brothers and sisters did when they were his age." Mary's wistful tone alerted Beatrice to her maid's sadness.

"You miss your family?"

Mary didn't look at Beatrice but continued trying to disengage Edward's fingers from her hair. "I miss my brothers and sisters."

Beatrice didn't bother asking about Mary's father. The man was a drunk who sold his children's labor. If only Beatrice could do something for the other children. She didn't want to think about how Mary's father would turn a profit from his younger daughters. Thankfully Beatrice had mentioned her concerns to Isabeau and she had promised to ask Ranulf to keep a watch on the children. Beatrice also understood the loneliness of being by herself. Mary was without friends and family and that tore at Beatrice's heart.

Edward had tired of pulling Mary's hair and happily went to his mother when she held out her arms to him.

"Did you get something to eat and drink when we stopped, Mary?"

The girl's cheeks flamed red and Beatrice looked away to hide her smile. So, Mary liked Olivier. The poor child, she would soon learn that Olivier's heart was not so easily caught.

"Yes, m'lady, Olivier saw to it." Mary pulled at a loose thread at the hem of her apron rather than look at Beatrice.

"That's good. Perhaps you might like to have a rest while I see to his lordship here."

She nodded as she handed Beatrice a bundle wrapped in waxed linen, then made herself comfortable on the cushions and fell asleep. She looked so young and vulnerable curled there. Beatrice would have to keep a careful watch on Mary. She didn't want anyone taking advantage of her or her innocence. The girl had only ever known Beauforde, and Barmoor Castle was a foreign place for a young impressionable girl.

Beatrice settled to feeding Edward softened bread and soft cheese as the wagon lurched further towards Barmoor and her future.

IT WAS a long and tiring day. They had covered a paltry twenty miles. At this rate, it would take three days to travel to Barmoor. Three days Gilbret didn't have. He had his doubts about his uncle and whether all in Barmoor would be loyal to him. The man would have expected Barmoor to fall to him when his brother died. William would be furious when he discovered that his brother had secretly married Gilbret's mother. It wouldn't surprise him if William had already had spies infiltrate the castle to begin undermining Gilbret's authority. No, he could not afford any more delays.

The wagon was continually getting bogged down in the mud. When there wasn't mud, it was the wheels. The rims separated from the wooden wheels. They had to stop while the smithy fixed the problem. The time it took to remove the wheel and replace it with another was time-consuming and frustratingly slow.

"Do you think we could convince Lady Beatrice and Mary to ride tomorrow?" Gilbret looked at Olivier as he held Maigemor's head so Gilbret could dismount.

"What about Edward?"

"If my good wife is willing, I can carry him with me and we can stop when needs be." It wasn't ideal but Gilbret didn't want to waste another two days traveling. And he was not going to leave Beatrice alone while he rode on to Barmoor.

When Gilbret's feet hit the ground, he walked back towards the wagon. Beatrice had not ridden Clover but had stayed in the wagon all afternoon. Despite the delays, she seemed happy to sit in the relative comfort of the wagon although Gilbret couldn't fathom why anyone would willingly choose to ride in a box as it tossed you about instead of riding on horseback.

He pulled the wagon door open and pushed the hide covering to one side and poked his head inside. "We are at Holystone Priory where we will spend the night."

Beatrice looked relieved as she accepted his hand and descended the wooden steps to the ground. When she turned to take Edward from Mary, Gilbret stepped in to take the child. "He is heavy and you, I am sure, are tired."

She huffed a small sigh. "Thank you, I admit I am tired."

"And a little sore?"

Now she laughed. "They say that traveling in a wagon is to travel in comfort but every part of my body feels as though I've been kicked by a bad-tempered horse."

Gilbret held Edward in his left arm while he offered his right hand to Mary so she could descend the steps. The little maid's cheeks flamed bright red at the courtesy. In truth, Mary looked worse for her ordeal. "Are you unwell, Mary?"

The girl didn't answer but bowed her head and shifted on her feet.

"Alas, it seems we are not good travelers, and the day has been an ordeal for us both." Beatrice gave Mary a gentle smile when her head popped up at her mistress's obvious lie.

So, Beatrice wanted to save her little maid embarrassment. That was a surprise. He had misjudged her again. It seemed his wife was more of a mystery than he had first imagined.

"Let me show you to lodgings for this evening." Gilbret continued to hold Edward who was gurgling his excitement at being held by Gilbret. His little eyes darted hither and thither as he took in his new surroundings. His pudgy little fingers had attached themselves to Gilbret's nose, tweaking it enthusiastically.

Beatrice must have noticed her son's antics. "Please, let me take him before your nose comes loose."

"It will take more than a few tweaks to damage this beak." Gilbret glanced at Beatrice. "If he is to be my son, then he needs to know that he is safe with me." Gilbret didn't bother saying what he thought—that he wanted Beatrice to trust him with her son.

They walked through the courtyard and entered the visitor's chamber where they were met by the prior.

"Ah, Brother Cuthbert, let me introduce you to Lady Beatrice, my wife, and her son Edward." Gilbret waited for Beatrice to exchange a nod to the prior before he continued. "And this is Mary, her ladyship's maid. Olivier will see to her needs if you will be so kind as to escort us to our chambers."

It was unusual to be greeted by the prior, but then the barons of Wooler had endowed the priory with lands. Brother Cuthbert was shrewd enough to recognize an opportunity when it presented itself.

"Of course, my lord, this way."

Cuthbert was also an old friend. He had fought alongside Ranulf and Gilbret back when Empress Matilda was wrestling with her usurper cousin, Stephen of Blois. The monk was loyal to the crown, and a fair, if somewhat unorthodox prior. And although aged, he was still a formidable man.

"Here we are, my lady, I hope you find the chamber to your liking." He gave Beatrice a formal bow and then held the chamber door wide for her to enter. Mary had already arrived and was unpacking Beatrice's chest of clothing.

"I shall leave you to rest and will come back and escort you to the meal." Gilbret handed Edward to Beatrice but the child would have none of it. He screeched in Gilbret's ear.

"God's blood, boy, you are a weapon."

Beatrice wrestled her son from Gilbret's arms. Edward was still crying and clinging to Gilbret and didn't want to let go. "Does he need to nurse?" Gilbret asked as he settled the squirming body into the crook of his arm.

"No, he is weaned. However, he seems to be acquiring a mind of his own."

Gilbret heard the exasperation in Beatrice's tone.

"Fret not, he can come with me."

"Oh, but—"

"He must get used to male company, and you need to rest." Gilbret couldn't resist the jape. "And besides he prefers my company." He had the good sense to leave before he encountered the full force of Beatrice's tongue.

It was going to be fun teasing his wife. That thought surprised and pleased Gilbret in equal measure.

Chapter Ten

BEATRICE WAS SO SHOCKED SHE STOOD GAPING AFTER GILBRET AS
he walked down the stairs that led to the hall. Edward's gibberish
receded as Gilbret's back disappeared.

"Well, I never." Beatrice didn't have words to describe how she
felt about her son's rejection. It stung more than she would have
expected.

"It is good to see him take to his lordship so well."

Beatrice turned to see Mary smiling at her.

"Babes at that age can be a bit clingy, but Master Edward has
taken to Sir Gilbret like a duck to a puddle."

Somehow Mary's words only increased Beatrice's sense of loss.
Edward was all she had, and she didn't want to lose him to another.

"I miss him." The confession was out of her mouth before Beatrice could call the words back.

Mary came over and took Beatrice's hand and led her to a chair.
"Here, m'lady, sit and warm yourself by the fire while I pour you
some wine."

Beatrice let the girl fuss but fear and disappointment curdled her
stomach. She was losing Edward.

Life was so cruel. She had done everything to save her son—endured her father's scorn, risked her life and her soul, by defying the church. She was not ready to relinquish him to another.

"Here, drink this." Mary handed Beatrice a cup of warmed spiced wine. "Don't worry, m'lady, Edward is in good hands. Sir Gilbret often took my brothers with him to the stables or the smithy so they could get used to being around men who were not like my father."

Beatrice almost choked on her sip of wine. She put the cup down and dabbed at her knee where she had spilled some of her drink. Thankfully her kirtle was a deep red and the wine would not stain it.

Mary took the cloth from Beatrice and dabbed at the wine on Beatrice's knee. "I was worried my father would ruin the boys. They were so young and both timid. Sir Gilbret found me one day crying after Da had hit me when I tried to protect them. He went and spoke to my da. After that, he never hit me or the boys again." Mary smiled as she rose from her position beside Beatrice. "There, that won't stain."

Beatrice didn't quite know what to say. Mary's care of her brothers was not altogether unexpected. Beatrice would have endured any amount of beating to save a younger sibling. But Gilbret. He was a man who continually surprised her. He had said he was nothing like Walter or her father, but to her shame, she hadn't really believed him. Perhaps it was time she began to trust him? And reluctantly she also acknowledged that Edward needed male company. He was young, but she didn't want him to cling to her skirts either.

There was a knock on the door. "Come."

Gilbret strode through the door, dangling a laughing Edward by his feet. "It seems his lordship has tired of my company." He righted Edward and handed him to Beatrice. Edward flung his little arms around her neck and tucked his head on her shoulder.

"Ah, I can't compete with a mother's touch." Gilbret ran a finger down Edward's cheek before looking at Beatrice. "He is a winsome child."

Was that regret she detected in Gilbret's tone. Surely not. But he was gone from the chamber before she could ask him.

"Well, you seem to have made an impression." But Edward didn't hear; he was sound asleep on her shoulder. The familiar weight of him soothed something deep inside Beatrice. She recognized it for what it was. A deep soul longing to belong and be of value. Edward had given her purpose and she didn't want to give it up, but seeing him with Gilbret made her realize that if she were to survive her marriage then she must find a way to make herself valuable and useful to Gilbret. But how?

THAT EVENING, as she sat with Gilbret and Brother Cuthbert at table, she listened to their talk of harvests and the constant threat of Scottish brigands raiding their stock.

"We need to have more armed men stationed in the manors between here and the border." The monk spoke with his mouth full. Bits of food were sprayed over the table as he spoke. Beatrice shuddered at the man's uncouth behavior, but Gilbret didn't seem to notice. Although he did tend to lean away from him when he spoke.

She focused on her food and only partially concentrated on her surroundings.

"Beatrice?"

She turned to see Gilbret looking at her with a puzzled expression on his face. The prior had turned to talk to someone on his other side.

"What?"

"Woolgathering?"

"I was, excuse me. What were you saying?" Her cheeks burned

under his scrutiny. She wasn't used to being looked at, especially when Gilbret's gaze was full of genuine interest.

"I was suggesting that perhaps you and Mary might rather ride tomorrow. The wagon's axle needs to be repaired, which I am told will take most of the day."

She stared at him. Her mind couldn't quite make sense of his words. What a dolt she must seem. "I beg your pardon, but I don't understand."

"It will delay our journey another two or three days to travel to Barmoor in the wagon. I thought you might prefer to ride. It would make the journey much more pleasant." He gave her a quick smile "And quicker."

"What of Edward?" The thought of two or three more days in that infernal box was a depressing thought, not to mention another night in the company of the prior, but she couldn't carry Edward for hours. And Mary. What of her?

"I will carry Edward and Mary can ride with Olivier. We should arrive at Barmoor by mid-afternoon tomorrow."

"I must confess to not wanting to travel in that accursed wagon, but I'm not sure I could do without my things for Edward. The wagon offers privacy when necessary." She looked down at her hands, uncomfortable with the topic of soiled clouts when Gilbret was looking at her so intently.

"Your most necessary things would be stowed in panniers with pack horses. And we could ensure privacy when Edward's or your needs demanded it. That would give you enough to go on with when we reach Barmoor. Although as the new lady of Barmoor you would have access to any number of necessities." Gilbret's face remained passive but his eyes shone with unrepressed fervor. To ride beside this man would be a joy.

Beatrice didn't take long to decide. A lightness filled her chest. "Thank you, I think that is a splendid idea. But I cannot force Mary to ride if she does not wish it." Although Mary didn't like the wagon at least it was a safer option than falling from a horse.

"Mary can ride." Gilbret slid her a sly glance. "Olivier taught her and her brothers."

Beatrice could only stare at Gilbret.

A smile split his face. Tiny lines crinkled at the corners of his eyes. Those small telltale lines revealed that Gilbret de la Haye was a man who smiled often. "Mary is an intelligent girl who deserved something more from life than what her sot of a father could provide. I took it upon myself to get Olivier to teach her, and her brothers, how to ride. She took to it with ease. Olivier hates that the girl rides almost as well as him now."

Beatrice knew her mouth hung open but she couldn't quite gather the wit to make it close.

"I like confounding you," Gilbret whispered as he leaned close. He used his finger to push her chin up, closing her mouth. And like a moth to a candle flame, Beatrice was caught in his snare. She could neither move nor resist him. And surprisingly it wasn't as terrifying as she might have thought.

BARMOOR CASTLE WAS something of a surprise to Beatrice. Its stone was washed in soft red hues as the late afternoon sun shone on its walls.

"It's beautiful, is it not?" Gilbret had been riding next to Beatrice for most of the afternoon. He seemed eager to be done with the journey as much as Beatrice had. As he had anticipated it had taken all day to ride the remaining thirty miles to Barmoor.

They stopped and looked at the view. Barmoor sat on an incline that offered unobstructed views of the surrounding plains. A small village sat snugly at the southern base of the castle while a huge mountain range seemed to jut out from the western side of the plain.

It was such a sight that Beatrice had to pause a moment to take it all in.

"My father's great-grandsire was awarded Barmoor by the Conqueror. It was a motte and bailey castle but my father made it what it is today.

"Come, I'm sure you are ready to rest and recover from the ordeal of our journey." He didn't wait for her to agree; he simply led the way expecting her to follow.

The few villagers that were about stopped to tug their forelocks in respect to their new lord. Gilbret waved and smiled as he rode past. He would be a generous and fair lord, not like Walter who had been terse and quick to find fault.

They rode through the entrance of a large barbican, over a bridge and draw, then through the gateway where an enormous portcullis hung above them, and into the lower bailey. Gilbret gave the order for the men at arms to dismount. Grooms milled about waiting to take the horses while shouts of welcome from men on the wall walk filled the air. Gilbret nodded to several men but he continued to walk his mount through to the inner bailey where a woman stood upon the stone steps that led to the large square keep.

Gilbret huffed something that Beatrice didn't catch before he handed Edward to Beatrice, then vaulted from his horse and ran up the stairs to embrace the woman who waited. The woman would have to have been two score years and then some, but she was still beautiful. Her resemblance to Gilbret was evident—her hair was dark, like her son's, but Beatrice could detect streaks of silver among the dark strands. Even from this distance, the woman had a regal presence about her. She was almost as tall as Gilbret and embraced her son with an abandon that caught Beatrice by surprise. She had never witnessed a man so openly affectionate towards his mother. His head was close to his mother's ear as he said something that made his mother laugh and playfully push him away from her. The scene was playful and endearing.

Gilbret returned to help Beatrice down. His smile spoke of his joy to be reunited with his mother.

Beatrice handed Edward down to Gilbret who promptly gave him to his mother who had walked over to where Beatrice sat astride Clover.

"Come, darling, I'm your grand-mère, and we shall become fast friends."

"She has wanted a little someone to dote on for years," Gilbret said as he helped Beatrice from the saddle.

"Yes, well you have finally given me what I have been asking for. Hello, my dear, I'm Sybilla, and very happy to meet you. Welcome to your new home."

Warmth and genuine kindness exuded from the woman standing before her. Beatrice had never met anyone who seemed so open and caring. Yes, Isabeau was kind and gentle, but she was still growing in her confidence. This woman, who was holding Edward in her arms, wore her confidence like a mantle. Beatrice curtsied and resisted the urge to run her hand over her head to check whether her hair and veil were tidy.

"My lady, it is a pleasure to meet you." Beatrice gave the woman a genuine smile before adding, "I see my son has already made a fast friend." Edward had nestled his head on Sybilla's shoulder and was sucking his thumb.

"He, like his mother, will be tired. Come, let me show you to your rooms." She headed towards the stairs but turned almost immediately. "You have no maid?"

"Olivier is seeing to Mary and getting her settled," Gilbret said as he shot his mother an irritated look Beatrice didn't understand.

Of course! Sybilla was supposed to be in Kent with her daughter. Well, that was interesting. The woman was obviously not as biddable as Gilbret had thought. But more astounding was that Gilbret didn't berate his mother for her disobedience. He genuinely seemed pleased to see her even if somewhat irritated now that he had probably thought about it.

Sybilla nodded her approval and then mounted the stairs and led the way into the keep.

A huge, cavernous space, its walls lined with weapons and animal heads, almost took Beatrice's breath away. "Gilbret's father was fond of hunting." Sybilla gave this by way of explanation when she noticed that Beatrice had stopped to stare at the hall.

Two large fireplaces stood at each end of the hall with an even larger one in the middle, presumably where the lord's chair sat. But it was the vaulted ceiling that caught Beatrice's attention.

"I have had the floor rushes renewed. God only knows what was lurking under the old ones." She turned and gave Beatrice a mischievous grin. "Gilbret's father didn't like change and refused to have the rushes completely removed and replaced. I threatened the steward with a day in the gibbet before he plucked up the courage to replace them."

"Even in death he exerts power," Gilbret said in a surly tone.

His mother cast him a disapproving look but said nothing more.

"This way," she said as she began to lead them to the stairs that would take them to the first-floor apartments.

"I shall leave you to get settled, I must see to the men." Gilbret turned on his heel and left Beatrice to his mother's care.

The first-floor apartments were spacious, if a little dim. Wall sconces gave enough light for Beatrice to see a large area with a fireplace against the wall. Its glow gave the room an airy feel.

An enormous bed held pride of place. The furniture was heavy oak and well used but the room had a certain masculine appeal. Sybilla didn't stop until she reached a door concealed between two protruding columns set in the stone wall. She opened the door to reveal a room filled with light from a large window on the outer wall of the keep.

"This is the lady's solar and here is your chamber," she said as she led Beatrice into an adjoining room.

It was a clever design; the solar and chamber were situated behind the lord's chamber and adjacent to a hall that allowed for access from both sides. The difference between the lady's suites and the lord's outer chamber was quite something.

The furniture in the lady's chambers was elegant and painted in soft greens and blues. The walls were painted a soft butter yellow with vine leaf patterns swirling up to the ceiling. A large tapestry depicting hunting scenes hung on the wall opposite the fireplace. The room was warm and restful. The bed sat on a plinth and its four posts were draped in blue woolen curtains.

"It is beautiful." Beatrice heard the wonder in her own voice. Never had she seen anything quite so lovely. A terrible thought occurred to her. "This was your chamber?"

Sybilla smiled as she surveyed the room. "No, I have never lived at Barmoor."

Beatrice wondered at Sybilla's statement until she remembered Gilbret had said that his mother had lived at a nunnery in Kent. "Edward must be getting heavy, let me take him."

"He is asleep and my arms have missed a babe's weight." There was a wistful edge to Sybilla's comments.

"Your daughter is not married?" As soon as she said it Beatrice wanted to bite her tongue. Gilbret had told her that Colette had been sent to St. Ninian's.

Sybilla had sat on a chair facing the fire and held Edward close as she rocked him back and forth.

"Did Gilbret not mention Colette?"

Beatrice's cheeks flamed. "I'm sorry, I can't recall." The lie was only small but it tasted bitter on her tongue. She took the chair next to Sybilla while a young page poured some wine into goblets that sat on the table between the two women.

"Colette will never marry." The bereft tone of Sybilla's voice warned Beatrice not to enquire further, but she couldn't ignore the pain she heard.

"I am sorry for that."

They sat in companionable silence for some time. Both enjoyed the wine and the restful silence. Beatrice liked Sybilla but years of disappointment and abuse at the hands of her father, then her step-mother, and finally her husband had left her wary of strangers. Only time would tell as to the woman's character.

Chapter Eleven

The journey had tired Beatrice more than she would have expected and the thought of going head-to-head with the castle's steward was a step too far. When she had met Sir Ansell Rouille, she almost gasped. He was a terrifying looking man—all wild hair and a scarred face did little to calm her.

"He looks like a bear but he is capable," Gilbret had whispered to her when he had seen her reaction to the steward. As the new lady of Barmoor, she would be instructing him on all manner of things and Beatrice had learned from her time at Folkingham that stewards could be a testy species. Her arrival heralded change and no doubt the rumors and whispers would already be spreading about like flies on a carcass.

Sybilla had managed the castle, and the testy steward, for a few days but she was happy to leave the running of Barmoor to Beatrice. "I have no wish to intrude on your authority, my dear." So, it had been settled.

Stifling a sigh Beatrice would contemplate how best to manage the running of the castle on the morrow. For now, she was content to rest while Edward explored her chamber. Soon he would be walking and wanting to spend time with horses and men—a spike of sorrow stabbed at her chest. Its savagery surprised her. *It won't be long till he is grown and fostered. It was the way of things for boys —they were sent to family or friends where they were trained as pages then squires. Ultimately to become knights. Then I will be left truly alone.*

Pushing away the unwelcome thought of Edward growing more and more independent Beatrice studied the flames in front of her. Were Gilbret and his mother having a discussion? That his mother would defy him yet seemingly receive no punishment spoke of Gilbret's character. Women were always afraid of men who wielded authority with the aid of retribution but Sybilla de la Haye had embraced her son with the ease of a woman who knew she was safe.

Mary reappeared with a wooden bowl in her hands, explaining that Master Roland, the castle's cook, had taken it upon himself to cook fresh greens blended with some mutton stock for Edward.

It seemed that Edward liked the sound of that as he stopped crawling around her chair and hoisted himself up to stand by her knees by pulling at her kirtle. Beatrice scooped him up and placed him on her lap where he squirmed, waiting, but Mary must have taken too long as he reached his hands towards the bowl of food.

"You are a greedy boy," Beatrice scolded. "Where are your manners."

The little boy ignored his mother and continued to babble at Mary.

Feeding Edward was a messy business—as he smacked his lips together in appreciation of Master Roland's offering it dribbled out of his mouth while his hands rubbed the food over his face and onto whoever was unfortunate enough to be holding him.

Beatrice and Mary laughed at Edward's antics as he consumed his dinner.

By the time they had bathed him and settled him to sleep it was almost time for Beatrice to go down to the hall for the evening meal.

"You will also sleep in here with me, Mary," Beatrice said as Edward lay in the middle of the huge bed.

Mary was about to object, but Beatrice placed her hand on her maid's shoulder. "I would prefer it if you were to sleep with me. There is no need for you to use a pallet as the bed is big enough for at least five others as well.

It was true, the bed was enormous and Beatrice would rest easier if she knew Mary was safely tucked up with her rather than down among strangers.

"But his lordship?" Mary's voice betrayed her concern.

"His lordship will be in his chamber, Mary, and I want to make sure you are as safe as we are among strangers."

The girl nodded but her expression spoke of her disquiet about the arrangement.

"You don't snore, do you?" Beatrice teased.

It worked. Mary puffed out her little chest. "No, I do not!"

"That is a relief. Then it is settled. I shall have some viands sent up for you. And there is a chest over there that you may use for your things."

Mary settled herself on a stool by the fire and picked up a chemise to mend from the basket of clothing at her feet.

A knock on the door made Beatrice turn. "Come."

Gilbret entered and looked around the room when he noticed Edward asleep in the bed. "He looks comfortable after his adventures."

"My son has no difficulty with eating or sleeping. In fact, if you get closer you are bound to hear him snoring." Beatrice huffed a small laugh. "Mary and I will have to sleep with our heads under the pillow."

Gilbret gave Beatrice a peculiar look but said nothing about her comment. Instead, he walked around the room admiring the tapestries. "I used to spend my days in here when I was small.

"I thought your mother never lived at Barmoor."

"She didn't. I was sent here to be fostered."

"Your father acknowledged you?"

"Yes, and no. He acknowledged that I was his but never gave me his name. His wife took pity on me and wanted me to excel so she taught me to read and write and taught me numbers." Gilbret gave a deep sigh. "My father objected, of course. 'All a boy needs to know is how to sit a horse and wield a sword.' But Adelle was a Percy and came from a long line of bull-headed people who never took no for an answer. I spent my mornings fighting off my father's sons and most afternoons in here learning my letters."

"It was a happy time?" Beatrice had heard the wistful tone in Gilbret's voice and wondered if she had heard correctly.

"Yes, and again no," he laughed. "I have some fond memories of this room and the woman who showed a young boy kindness in an otherwise cruel and hateful house."

Beatrice had endured her childhood and marriage, so she had no experience of ruing the loss of something cherished.

Gilbret seemed to shake himself out of his musings and turned to face her.

"My lady, it is time to meet the hungry hordes." He gave her a mischievous smile. The one that transformed his face into a playful boy bent on mischief.

Heaving a sigh, Beatrice accepted her husband's arm and walked out of the chamber.

The castle folk would be celebrating their lord's wedding feast and preparing for Whitsun the following week. The mood in the hall would be noisy and full of drunk men. Beatrice shuddered at the prospect.

"Are you cold?" Gilbret asked as he led her out of her suite and down the stairs.

"No, I am just gathering my courage for this evening's meal."

"Fear not, I shall slay the dragons. None shall rip you limb from limb." Again, he bestowed that mischievous smile on her.

She couldn't help herself. Her lips spread of their own accord and by the time they reached the hall she was laughing.

GILBRET WAS aware of the woman beside him. Her posture told him she was not relaxed. Nor was she enjoying herself.

"Is there something amiss?" He had leaned over so he could be heard amid the raucous noise of the castle folk enjoying the celebration. Immediately his senses were on alert. Beatrice smelled of lavender and woman. His gut clenched as his body recognized her feminine scent. He wasn't sure of her. And she had lied with an ease that still concerned Gilbret. But, God help him, he was attracted to her in a way he had never been attracted to another woman before.

Was that such a bad thing? He was married to the temptress. And yes, he had given her his word that he would not force her to pay the marriage debt, but somehow over the past two days, his desire had outstretched his good sense.

"No, I am just out of practice." His eyes fell to her lips as she spoke and it took all his resolve to raise his gaze so he could look at her.

"It will get easier, and as you can see they are happy to have their lord and lady present." He swept his arm out to encompass the crowd before them.

Beatrice heaved a sigh, making her shoulders rise and then slump. Gilbret wanted to ease her discomfort but didn't know how.

Perhaps a change of topic would help. "How did you find my mother?" He cast a quick glance down the table to where his mother sat eating and speaking to the castle priest. She looked happy. And relaxed.

He had been so pleased to see a welcome face when he arrived that he had embraced her before his brain had registered that she had defied him. She did not wish to return to St. Ninian's and Gilbret did not have the heart to banish her from Barmoor.

He turned his eyes back to Beatrice and noticed a slight smile turn up the corners of her mouth. Such a delicious mouth—all curves and plumpness. *Pull yourself together, man!*

"Lady Sybilla is all kindness and care."

"And."

Beatrice turned to face him. "She has taken a keen interest in Edward."

"Is that a problem?" He watched as Beatrice drew her eyebrows together. A scowl never looked so inviting. His eyes ran over her face as she thought about his question. And not for the first time, he cautioned himself about falling under this woman's spell. She would be a competent wife, he was sure of it, and swiving her would be a pleasure. But would he trust his heart to her? No. He would never allow another person to have that much power over him. His mother was an excellent example of someone who had allowed her "love" for his sire to overrule her common sense. And it ruined her life.

"No, I think not." She licked her lips as she continued to scowl. "But I am not used to sharing him." That last statement was so wistful that Gilbret wondered if he had heard correctly.

But he had no time to ask her to explain as he became aware of the crowd descending into silence. That could mean only one thing.

He shot his mother a questioning glance, but she merely gave him a slight shrug, indicating that she knew nothing.

"What's happening?" Beatrice asked as she looked first to the silent men and women before them, then to him.

"I suspect you are about to meet my uncle."

"Your uncle?"

"William de Muscamp, my father's younger brother and the

Prior of Heatherslaw Priory. And the man who assumed he would inherit Barmoor."

Beatrice's expression revealed her confusion.

"My father agreed to marry my mother so that he would have a son inherit the estate. Marrying my mother ensured that I was his legitimate heir." He gave Beatrice a sly smile. "My uncle would have been as surprised as I was to discover that I was no longer the 'bastard son' but the legal heir."

Gilbret turned from Beatrice and rose as his uncle was led by the steward of the hall to stand before the dais. What he wasn't prepared for was the unpardonable insult of his uncle also bringing his father's mistress to be flaunted before his mother. The woman had been forced to leave Barmoor when his father agreed to marry Sybilla. And here she was standing demurely before the dais as though she would be welcome. At least she had the courtesy to look abashed. What was his uncle playing at?

"Uncle, what is the meaning of this?" He tried to keep his tone even but outrage seasoned it. The slight tic at the corner of his uncle's mouth was evidence that he had heard the insult.

"My lord," he demurred but leveled a steely glare at Gilbret. The challenge was plain to see. The enmity between them was palpable as they eyed each other like dogs circling around a bone.

"Imagine my surprise when I learned mere days ago that your father had married your mother," he snarled. "As the new Lord of Barmoor you have the dubious honor of protecting your father's pregnant whore." He inclined his head towards Rosamund as she stood silently beside him.

An audible gasp rippled through the hall.

Speechless, Gilbret glared at his uncle. The insult hung in the air but Gilbret couldn't seem to gather his wits.

"I shall leave the 'lady' with you." His smile was feral as he slid his eyes from Gilbret to Sybilla. "And not wanting to leave the new lady of Barmoor without a token I wish to present her with her own bitch."

"Enough! You go too far," Gilbret snarled.

His uncle ignored the warning and instead nodded towards a small boy who was standing behind him to bring forward a large basket covered with a fine linen cloth.

"This is for you, my lady," he said as he gave Beatrice a very courteous bow.

Beatrice acknowledged him but eyed Gilbret. She, like everyone else in the hall, was waiting for his lead. The atmosphere was so tense beads of sweat gathered on Gilbret's upper lip. His uncle's insult was unforgivable but Gilbret refused to give his uncle the satisfaction of seeing just how much it infuriated Gilbret.

"Lady Beatrice, may I present my uncle, William de Muscamp." As far as introductions went it was barely civil. Withholding his uncle's titles was childish of Gilbret but he didn't care. He gave no acknowledgment to the woman who had caused so much enmity between his father and mother. Gilbret suspected that Rosamund was merely a pawn in a game of his uncle's making.

Gilbret gave Beatrice an infinitesimal nod. She was still looking at him and knew what she had to do. Clever woman.

"You are most kind, Uncle." Beatrice bestowed a radiant smile on his uncle, who almost fell over when he saw it. Beatrice was an extraordinarily beautiful woman and William was not immune to her charms.

"I shall leave this with you and take my leave." His uncle bowed to Gilbret and Beatrice. Then he nodded towards Sybilla, who sat ramrod straight as her eyes focused on the opposite wall.

As the little procession was led from the hall in silence Sybilla indicated for her maid to escort Rosamund from the hall.

Gilbret wanted to roar at his mother to ignore the woman but he remained silent. This was his mother's choice and he would not interfere.

"Come, Lady Rosamund, let me show you to your chamber," his mother's maid said as she led Rosamund from the hall and away from prying eyes.

Only when the steward of the hall had returned to his station to the right of the dais did the clamor of voices fill the space.

Gilbret's hands were shaking as he took his goblet and drank. What was his uncle trying to prove?

"What was that about?" Beatrice asked as she leaned over.

Gilbret turned to look her in the eye. "For some unfathomable reason, my uncle defiled my hall by bringing my father's mistress here to wish us well on our nuptials." Even saying the words had Gilbret seething at the insult.

Beatrice's eyes widened fractionally. "But why would he do such a thing?"

Before Gilbret could answer a plaintive wail came from the basket that had been left on the floor in front of the dais.

"Olivier, take that—" Gilbret spat as he pointed to the basket, "to the stables and have the stable master dispose of it."

"No!"

Gilbret turned to Beatrice. "You wish to defy me?"

Beatrice flinched at his harsh tone, but she didn't cower. "It is a pup and I would value having it."

"I have any number of dogs. You may choose one of those if you so ardently desire a pet," he snarled. God's teeth he couldn't seem to stop himself from spewing his venom.

"You would punish an innocent because of your uncle's insult?" Her tone was incredulous. She didn't take her eyes off his face. "Are you a man who would destroy a life to appease your wounded pride?"

"God's blood, woman, have a care. I am not a man who will allow his wife to kick against my authority." Now he sounded like a fucking adolescent boy who had a fit of the tempers.

"I understand the insult, but the dog in that basket has no quarrel with you. Your uncle's brazen insult is his alone to bear." She spoke with force but she was not angry. That much was clear. "Deal with your uncle, Gilbret, and show some mercy to the pup who has done you no wrong." She leveled her gaze at him. Her eyes were the most extraordinary color—green with flecks of gold but they were shadowed with an emotion he couldn't read. "Please, Gilbret."

He looked down. She had placed her hand on his arm. Never had she voluntarily touched him before. She was making herself vulnerable and although he was furious with his uncle, he would not crush Beatrice to soothe his own wounded pride.

"Olivier, have the dog dealt with, then bring it to Lady Beatrice's chamber."

Olivier did his bidding. All eyes in the hall were on the little drama playing out on the dais.

Her hand was still on his arm. "Thank you."

He lifted her hand to his lips and kissed her knuckles. "I think you mistook my intentions. I was not instructing the stable master to kill the creature, just having him find it a home outside of the castle." The anger was still there but its red-hot glow had dampened. What a fool he'd made of himself. "I am sorry for how I spoke." He kissed her knuckles again. "I do not want a wife who is terrified of me, or what I might say. So please forgive my boorish temper."

She bestowed a beatific smile on him. No trace of fear or disappointment in her serene expression. "No forgiveness necessary. What your uncle did was unforgivable."

She huffed a little sigh and leaned into him. She was shaking ever so slightly. "I must own I am not a defiant woman, Gilbret, but I seem to have forgotten that small point. I am sorry." She offered a tentative smile.

"I would have you speak your mind to me, Beatrice. I am not your father or Walter and as you have witnessed from my mother's actions in defying me, I am not one to punish insubordination." He was still holding her hand. "In truth I want you to challenge me when my pride and temper blur my way."

She slid her hand from his grasp and picked up her goblet. "Shall we drink to it, my lord?"

"You have bewitched me and I may live to regret this, but yes, we will drink to mutual respect."

The meal proceeded without further incident, but Gilbret's attention was already on his uncle. He would pay and pay dearly.

Chapter Twelve

BEATRICE WAS STILL SHAKING AS SHE WAS LED TO HER CHAMBER. What had come over her? To speak to Gilbret the way she had was so out of character that the rest of the meal had passed in a blur.

"I shall leave you, my lady." Gilbret kissed her hand, then turned on his heel and was gone. Her knuckles still tingled from the kiss. She flexed her hand to alleviate the sensation but it was no use. Even through the kidskin of her glove, she imagined his lips on her skin. Stop!

A noise behind her made her turn. Mary was slouched in the high-backed chair by the fire fast asleep.

"Mary, come lie down." Beatrice shook the girl's shoulder.

Mary jerked awake and flung herself from the chair so quickly that Beatrice was taken by surprise. "I'm sorry, m'lady. I should never have been in your—"

"Mary, stop. It is all right. I woke you so you could go to bed." Beatrice lifted the girl's chin so she would look at her. "You have had a very busy few days and I do not begrudge you some comfort when I am not here. Now go to bed. I want to stay up for a while."

"M'lady, it is not proper."

"Ah, Mary, you will learn soon enough that in my own chamber I don't give a fig about what is proper and what is not," she declared as she patted the girl's cheek. "Now off with you." And she gently pushed Mary towards the bedchamber door.

Alone and in front of the fire, Beatrice had time to think. The last two days had been a revelation for her regarding Gilbret. He was like no man she had ever encountered. Yes, he had a temper but, unlike her father and first husband, he kept it in check. Another shuddering wave of disbelief swept over her. She had defied her husband publicly in front of a hall full of retainers.

She wouldn't do that again in a hurry. Her nerves would not withstand it. To cultivate a defiant nature seemed an impossible task. But she could learn to voice her opinions. A little shudder reminded her that that lesson would take some learning.

A soft knock on the door interrupted her brooding.

"Come."

Olivier came through the door carrying the basket. There was no noise or movement under the linen cloth making Beatrice's pulse kick in panic.

"The pup?"

"She is asleep," Olivier said as he laid the basket down beside the hearth. A page had followed Olivier and was carrying a bowl and a large lamb's skin. "This is for her, my lady."

Beatrice nodded her thanks and walked to where the squire had laid the basket. Lifting the linen cloth carefully, Beatrice beheld a tiny bundle. Its glorious chestnut coat shimmered in the candlelight.

"She is a timid thing, but friendly enough when you give her food." Olivier's tone suggested he did not object to the dog although his expression was serious.

"Thank you, Olivier. You may go."

"My lady." Olivier looked a little uncomfortable.

"What is it?" Beatrice asked.

"Do you want me to return and take her to the stables for the night?"

Ah, yes, the pup would need to pee during the night and Beatrice had only just become accustomed to a full night's sleep. Edward had been a wakeful baby and Beatrice was in no mind to have the ordeal repeated by a dog.

"Yes, that would be much appreciated."

Olivier was almost at the door before Beatrice called him back. "Olivier?"

He turned but didn't say anything.

"Is where she will sleep safe?" It was a foolish question but Beatrice didn't want the pup to wake and be all alone and frightened.

Olivier must have read her mind because he smiled. "She will be settled with another litter of pups that have just been weaned. She will be in good company, my lady."

"I know it's silly but I didn't want her to be alone and frightened." Why was she explaining herself to Olivier?

"You and Sir Gilbret both," the lad laughed.

Beatrice didn't understand.

"He told me to make sure the pup was placed with the newly weaned litter so, and I quote, 'she won't be frightened when she wakes in the night.'"

"I see," she said as she smiled at the squire's serious expression. She would wager her favorite gown that the lad was enjoying himself. "Thank you, Olivier, you may come back in an hour and take her."

He nodded and then he was gone.

Beatrice was once again alone in her solar. Her hands itched to hold the small bundle. The pup made small snuffling noises as she picked it up and cradled it close to her neck. The pup smelled familiar—warm fur and healthy puppy. Beatrice loved that smell.

Memories of a long-lost love flooded her mind. Tild had been a dog she had rescued as a girl at the convent. The flea-bitten beast had been her only real friend and she had been heartbroken when Tild had died.

She would not cry, but even as she chided herself warm tears streaked her cheeks. "I shall name you Amica, and we shall be fast friends." The pup, still asleep, nuzzled into Beatrice's neck and began to snore.

Beatrice lowered herself onto the chair and relished the warmth of Amica's little body. "It seems that my husband is truly a man that I can trust to be kind," Beatrice said out loud. "We shall find a happy home here, I think." She closed her eyes and let hope settle over her for the first time in what seemed like a lifetime.

GILBRET PACED while his mother sat in a chair watching him.

"Gilbret, please stop that. It's making me quite ill watching you pace like a caged bear. Sit and talk to me."

Gilbret stopped and leveled an impatient glare at her. "For God's sake, Mother, he brought *her* into my hall. And for some unknown reason you have given her a chamber. What were you thinking?" For the life of him, he couldn't understand why his mother was not breathing fire after the insult William had inflicted. "If I could I would flay the skin from his back for what he has done."

"And that, my son, is what he is counting on." She sounded impatient.

What the hell was she upset with him for? It was William, the pox-ridden bastard, whom she should be angry with.

"He will expect you to retaliate and then you would face a harder time than I suspect you do now."

Gilbret eyed his mother suspiciously. "What do you mean?"

He had a sinking feeling in his gut. He was not going to like what was coming.

"Tell me." He didn't bark at his mother but it was close.

"If you didn't fulfill your father's terms then William stood to gain an even larger portion of the estates, including my dower lands. Not just Barmoor."

Gilbret took a moment to let that information sink in. "Why didn't you say anything?" His mother had sat there silently while his father's cleric had waited for Gilbret to sign the charter. The cut of betrayal from his mother was swift and deep.

"I am sorry, Gilbret, but your father forced me to remain quiet."

Well, his mother may have lied but Gilbret had fulfilled his father's will.

"I am married. He gains nothing by dishonoring me with the presence of that trollop in my own hall."

"Careful, Gilbret, or you may find that the finger you point at Rosamund will also be pointed at me."

Gilbret's mother had defied her father and the church when she became his father's lover for a summer before he married Adelle. God alone knows why but his mother continued to be his mistress and lived at Heaton, a small manor north of Wooler, for several more years before his father sent her south to live out her days at St. Ninian's. Her two bastard children were sent to be fostered at Barmoor. Then when Adelle died, his sire didn't take Sybilla to wife as he had promised but instead threw her over for the beautiful, and young, Lady Rosamund de Grey.

Thankfully Rosamund had no family connections so his father had not married her but instead installed her here at Barmoor, openly flaunting her as his paramour. It was only when his older step-brother, Giles, and his young son happened to both die within a week of each other, leaving his father without heirs, that his mother spied an opportunity and wrote to the king to redress past wrongs.

The king agreed and ordered the marriage making Gilbret his father's legitimate heir.

"Don't you feel aggrieved, Mother?" Gilbret was certainly aggrieved although he did concede her point. But he didn't tell her that.

"No. I don't. Robert married me and Rosamund is now faced with a future as a shunned woman. Without money or connections to buy her a place at a convent where she can live out her days. Her future is very bleak and I am sorry for her. She is to be pitied, Gilbret, not scorned."

His mother was to be applauded for her gracious sentiments but Gilbret was far from convinced. "I suppose you would have her reside at Heaton manor until the babe she carries is born?" he scoffed. The idea was preposterous but one look at his mother's innocent face confirmed she had indeed thought to do just that. "Now just a minute."

His mother smiled and patted the chair next to her. "Come, sit."

When he did, she continued. "If it were not for you, Gilbret, I would find myself in Rosamund's position. I too am a fallen woman, but you saved me from the fate that she finds herself in. So no, I bid her no ill will. And I think your suggestion that she resides at Heaton is very magnanimous." She smiled at Gilbret as she took his hand in hers.

God's bones, he had been well and truly outmaneuvered by his mother. Again.

"Tonight, William was sending you a warning, but why I cannot fathom. Surely, he cannot hope to have the estates now that you are married?"

Gilbret could understand, although he was surprised William had found out so soon. His uncle had numerous contacts and it would not take much for him to inquire about Beatrice. The future he hoped to secure for himself and his mother and sister balanced on a knife's edge. It was probably time he told his mother. "I suspect he knows of Beatrice."

Sybilla frowned. "Tell me."

"She is the repudiated wife of de Chesney's nephew."

"Her husband still lives?" She was about to say something else but Gilbret stilled her by shaking his head.

"No, he is dead, but there seem to be some questions about the legality of the annulment." Gilbret understood that if Beatrice's repudiation was upheld then he would be socially excluded. He may even be excommunicated if he refused to put her aside. It was a future he didn't relish but he refused to be bullied by those whose agendas were not altogether virtuous.

He was a by-blow who had never been accepted. Having his father's titles would make very little difference to those who had despised him all his life. The king, on the other hand, would want his help to keep the Scots at bay.

"I wonder if William has got wind of Beatrice's disgrace and seeks to put you on your guard?" Sybilla said as her brow furrowed in thought.

"You are too smart by far, madam," Gilbret said as he smiled at his mother. She was right of course. William could smell blood and he had wanted to send Gilbret a message—don't get too comfortable at Barmoor. It was quite likely Robert de Chesney and William may have joined forces. They were friends and they both benefited if Gilbret's marriage was deemed illegal.

Gilbret had a gnawing ache in the pit of his stomach despite reassuring himself that his marriage was secure.

He hoped he received word from Father Ascelin soon. Beatrice needed an equally powerful patron and Hugh de Puiset, the Archbishop of Durham, would make a powerful ally.

"Beatrice has the courage to withstand your temper," Sybilla said as she eyed the flames dancing in the fireplace.

It didn't surprise Gilbret. Beatrice was a she-wolf when it came to protecting those she loved. To his shame, everyone would have seen the little scene. Heat singed his cheeks. He had been no better than a surly boy. If he was honest with himself, he had been the very person he had vowed never to become—his father.

"She confuses me."

His mother turned from looking at the fire and stared at him. "What do you mean?"

"She has been trampled on and has never learned to assert herself except for this evening."

"Well, she chose a very public place to question your authority." Sybilla gave Gilbret a shrewd look. "But what I find even more interesting is that you acquiesced. Your father would have sent her from the table just so he could assert his authority."

Gilbret avoided his mother's very perceptive eyes. "I was close to doing just that."

"Then why didn't you?"

Gilbret had been asking himself that question for some time. It was only while sitting and talking to his mother that he found he could answer that question. "I recognized my father in my temper and I refused to be like him."

Sybilla gave him a rare smile. One that spoke of love and something he couldn't name.

"What are you looking at me like that for?" To his horror, he sounded as petulant as a small child.

"I am looking at a man who I am proud to call my son."

A warmth in Gilbret's chest began to radiate through his limbs. His mother loved him. He had never doubted that. But to have her say so openly that she was proud of him for forging his own path made him extraordinarily pleased.

"I loved your father; even when he chose Rosamund, I still could not bring myself to hate him," she confessed. Sybilla was playing with the rim of her goblet. She turned her piercing green eyes on Gilbret. "There is much you don't understand between your father and me, and although he was the only man to ever hold my heart I never felt as proud of him as I do you. He had a temper but never learned to conquer it." She gave him a small smile. "Tonight, you proved you are your own man, and I am so pleased I was there to see it for myself. Now I must away to my bed."

She put the goblet she was holding on the table and stood. "No, stay there." She placed a hand on Gilbret's shoulder as he rose to escort her to her chambers. "I know the way." Then she bent and kissed the top of his head the way she had when he was a boy. "Sleep well, my precious son." Then she was gone.

Gilbret stared into the flames for a long time letting his mind wander where it wanted. Only when the chamber door opened and Olivier walked in did Gilbret rein in his thoughts and concentrate on his squire.

"Did you deliver the dog?"

Olivier nodded as he poured more wine into Gilbret's empty cup. "She will have you eating out of her hand by Lammas."

Olivier was as canny as he was loyal and Gilbret would not curb him. He had been with Gilbret for ten years and knew him better than any living person except, perhaps, Ranulf.

Gilbret missed his friend. What he wouldn't do to be sitting here with him talking about the confusion that he was experiencing over Beatrice. One minute he wanted to throttle her and the next it seemed that she held the thread of his life in her hands.

"I find, my young friend, that that prospect is not as terrible as I might have imagined." Gilbret stood so Olivier could help him with his clothing.

"I like her," Olivier said as he folded the surcoat Gilbret had just discarded.

"God help me, but I like her too," Gilbret sighed as he shed his shirt.

"A beautiful woman with an innocent heart is a rare thing," Olivier said sagely.

Yes, that is what had surprised Gilbret. He had initially believed that she was hiding something when she arrived at Beauforde. He suspected she was duplicitous—out for her own advancement. But not so Beatrice. She had lied to save her son and he commended her for it. Her passion and bravery tonight revealed so much about her character and what she deemed important. Beatrice l'Aune was a protector of those she loved and those who needed her aid.

God help him, Gilbret wanted her to care for him as passionately as she had for the pup. What would it be like to be married to a woman who would be as ferocious as a she-wolf when it came to protecting her family?

Gilbret's mother had failed her two children, but Beatrice had been brave enough to save her son. Could he allow himself to love her?

Chapter Thirteen

A CLOUD OF INCENSE BILLOWED FROM THE THURIBLE AS THE PRIEST intoned the prayers of ascension. His voice was accompanied by the soft tinkling of chains as he swung the censer. The fragrance was so suffocating that Beatrice had to cover her mouth to try and get a fresh breath.

"Are you well?" Gilbret's breath was so close it not only ruffled her veil but caressed her cheek.

Nodding in reply was all she could manage. When would the mass finish? It had begun at dawn and already the sun was slanting through the stained-glass windows over the altar.

Soon they would take Communion and then be free of the cloying scent that made the hairs on her arms and scalp prickle.

Finally, with the priest's blessing, they were released. Gilbret held her elbow as he led her from where they had been standing for several hours, and out of the chapel. "Lean on me."

She had never been so grateful for another's strength. Was it her imagination or could she feel the heat of his skin through her cloak? Something about their proximity thrilled and terrified her in equal measure. Gilbret's closeness fanned the dormant flames of longing into life. Those embers had begun to glow over the past few days. It should have been terrifying but a warmth seeped into the cold recesses of her heart dispelling some of the fear she had carried from the past.

The sunlight made her blink as they emerged from the chapel. "We will break our fast, then it is tradition to climb to Yeavering Bell," Gilbret said as he led her through the lower bailey towards the portcullis that would bring them to the upper bailey and hall.

"Yeavering Bell?"

Gilbret slowed his pace and looked at her. "Come, I'll show you." He took her elbow and led her to the wall walk above the portcullis.

At the top, he pointed west towards the distant Cheviot Hills.

"Where those twin peaks are is where we climb to remember Our Lord taking his disciples up into the mountain before he ascended into Heaven."

"We are to climb those?" Beatrice was a little disconcerted by the prospect of climbing the hills Gilbret had pointed out. They looked small from their vantage point, but experience told her that they would be difficult to climb. And steep.

"It is a tradition that goes back to the Conqueror." He gave her a mischievous smile. "Don't tell me you are afraid of a little climb?"

She recognized his teasing and responded in kind. "A little climb, my lord?" She gave him a demure smile. "That's easy for a man in leggings, but in a gown, it is an entirely different matter."

He leaned in to whisper in her ear, which sent a shiver down her neck and spine. "I can arrange something appropriate for you to wear," he whispered. "If you are as intrepid as I think you are."

It was a challenge and, God help her, Beatrice was never one to shun a challenge. Especially when it was accompanied by a playful grin.

"Very well, I accept." She raised her chin fractionally and

bestowed him with her most imperious glare. "Perhaps a small wager to accompany the challenge?" she teased.

Gilbret's eyes sparkled with mischief. "Very well. I wager a kiss." His eyes held hers in a challenge of a very different kind.

Beatrice couldn't think for the pounding of her heart in her ears. Sweat began to tingle on her skin as a sudden heat engulfed her. She should turn and run. She dared another look at Gilbret's face. There was no arrogance, no threat in his expression. His eyes held hers. Their dark brown irises were almost obscured by the black of his pupils. The desire she felt in her own body was reflected and Gilbret didn't try to hide it. "If you fail to reach the summit, I win a kiss." His eyes bored into hers. "But if you do reach the summit then you win a kiss. Agreed?" The last word was barely audible although his lips were mere inches from hers.

Heat pooled in her lower limbs and her breath came in small gasps. Did she dare give in to this? *Take it. Take what you want.* A small voice commanded in her head. Beatrice decided. "Agreed."

Gilbret smiled as though he had won a great victory. "Shall we?" he asked as he indicated towards the stairs that would lead them to the hall and the viands that awaited them.

Beatrice inclined her head and allowed him to lead her back to the hall.

"How is the pup?" His tone was conversational as he walked towards the oak doors that led to the hall.

"I named her Amica. And she is well." A page had arrived before Beatrice attended the dawn service to bring the dog back to her chamber. She had left Mary and Edward to entertain the pup.

"A good name for a companion dog."

"A companion dog?"

"My uncle breeds dogs designed for nothing other than keeping a lady's feet warm."

Beatrice detected Gilbret's scoffing tone. "You disapprove?"

She was not going to repeat her behavior from the previous evening, but she did want to clarify what was expected of the dog and her.

"Dogs have a task if they are to live at Barmoor. And like the rest of us, they must earn their keep."

"Keeping me company and warm is not task enough?"

Gilbret turned to look at her. For two heartbeats he just stared at her, then his mouth curved into a smile. "If it is all you require from her, then that is enough for me also, my lady."

Beatrice was unsure if he was teasing her or not.

"That frown tells me that you misunderstand me," Gilbret said as he pulled out the chair for her enabling her to sit at the table on the dais. "The dog was a gift to you, Beatrice. I have no claim over it. If you are content to have it merely as a companion then that is your choice."

Beatrice sat while thinking over what Gilbret had just said. It was the first time in her life she had been given governance over her own property. "I suspect that any dog has a talent; Amica may yet surprise you."

Gilbret seated himself next to her. "Then I look forward to the surprise." He gave her a lopsided grin as he poured her some wine.

It was late morning when they arrived at the base of Yeavering Bell. It looked steep. Beatrice huffed a small sigh. Why in God's name couldn't she be back in her chamber with Amica and Edward?

"No use wishing for a reprieve," Sybilla cautioned as she strode past. "It is a tradition that the folk of Barmoor and Wooler take seriously."

Well, if Sybilla could do it, so could she. Gritting her teeth in determination, Beatrice took to the track that wound to the left. She had not taken more than two steps when Gilbret strolled up beside her. "I am here to assist." He gave her a roguish smile, baiting her to say something in retaliation.

"I do not need your assistance," she barked. But then thought better of her reply. "But I thank you, my lord," she said, adding a good dollop of sweetness to her tone and expression.

Gilbret huffed a laugh but kept to her side.

Up in front of Sybilla, the village children were scampering ahead. That had surprised her. "Do they always participate?" She inclined her head towards the children.

"It is a holy day and the villeins have the day free to do as they please. It has been generations now that we have climbed to the top to eat and make merry at the old ruin. Come on, you don't want the children to best their new lady, do you?"

Gilbret took her hand and gently pulled her along.

It took almost two hours to climb to the top and Beatrice was out of breath by the time Gilbret led her to the place where she could look back at Barmoor in the distance. A small gasp escaped as she surveyed the view below. "It is truly beautiful."

The priest had accompanied them and was about to pray so Beatrice disengaged her hand from Gilbret's and stood solemnly as the priest recounted the episode of Jesus's ascension from St. Luke's Gospel.

It didn't take a lot of imagination to envisage the disciples' reaction. Perched up high on Yeavering Bell surrounded by clouds and buffeted by wind Beatrice imagined herself at that auspicious event watching as the Lord disappeared into the air above their heads.

"I believe you win," Gilbret whispered into her ear when the priest had finished. Her cheeks burned and the skin on the back of her neck prickled with anticipation.

She turned to face him, their lips almost touching they were so close. They held each other's gaze for several heartbeats. Beatrice was rooted to the spot. She dared not breathe.

Gilbret's gaze traveled over her face, lingering on her lips before he met her gaze again. "I think I shall let you take your prize in a more private setting." And with that, he stepped back and turned to speak with his mother.

Beatrice didn't realize she was holding her breath. She licked her lips to gather some moisture into her mouth but it was useless. Discombobulated, Beatrice looked around, trying to gather her wits and hoping no one noticed what had just happened. Sybilla gave her a wry glance over Gilbret's shoulder. The woman's expression communicated that she had indeed seen what had transpired and was amused.

Sybilla excused herself from Gilbret and sauntered over to Beatrice. "It seems the climb has you a little flushed," she said, smiling at Beatrice. "Come and sit with me and have some wine to refresh yourself before we walk down."

When they were seated, Sybilla didn't bandy words. "My son is a good man and has chosen well, I think."

Beatrice must have heard wrong. "I'm sorry, my lady, I don't understand."

"You will be good for Gilbret." Sybilla was not looking at Beatrice as she spoke but at Gilbret, laughing with some of the villeins who had accompanied them on the walk to Yeavering Bell. It was almost five miles from Barmoor to Yeavering Bell and Beatrice was surprised to see so many happily walking with the lord's retinue. Gilbret had an easy way about him and men and women of all ranks seemed to feel at ease with him. Beatrice had noticed that about Gilbret even when they were back at Beauforde.

A sudden surge of guilt caught Beatrice by surprise. She had not been the best choice for Gilbret and it saddened her that he should be blighted by her shame. It was of little use to hope that her annulment would be overruled.

Sybilla turned her gaze back to Beatrice. "He told me of your divorce."

What could she say to that?

"I too am a woman who has encountered shame." Sybilla took Beatrice's gloved hand and held it in hers. "My son also knows what it is to face shame. He is no stranger to prejudice and cruel words. What he needs is not protection from such things but a woman who can face them and still stand at his side." Sybilla gave her an earnest look. "I think you are such a woman."

God in heaven. If only it were true, but Beatrice doubted whether her character was as stout-hearted as Sybilla believed.

It was mid-afternoon when they arrived back at Barmoor and Beatrice went straight to her chamber to see Edward. As she opened the door, she heard Mary's laughter and Edward's childish giggling.

"What is so funny?"

Mary was sitting on the rush floor with Edward in her lap. She was throwing a small ball of wool at Amica, who was trying to catch it in her mouth but she kept falling over as she lost her balance. It was the pup's antics that had Edward so amused.

Beatrice sat next to them and watched as they continued to play their game. Edward immediately crawled onto her lap but his focus was once again on the dog.

"Did you enjoy the climb, m'lady?"

"Yes, I did, Mary." Beatrice watched Amica as she came and sniffed at Beatrice's hand. "Have you been in the chamber all this time?"

"No, we ventured outside and looked in on Clover and the stable boys." Mary blushed but didn't meet Beatrice's eyes. "Master Edward and Amica had a nap after their noon meal and now she has been entertaining us for the past while. She is playful and very gentle with Edward."

"It is not Amica I am afraid will hurt Edward, but the other way around."

"Oh no, m'lady, Edward is very gentle. Aren't you my little lord?" she said as she tugged at his nose, making him giggle.

Beatrice's heart swelled as she watched Mary and Edward play.

All thoughts of Gilbret and the kiss she would bestow were tucked safely at the back of her mind.

SIR ANSELL'S expression was unreadable but Beatrice would not be dissuaded. She had put this meeting off for as long as possible but it was no use delaying her duty any longer. After spending time with Edward, Beatrice requested that the steward attend to her in his solar. She was determined to deal with the steward now rather than wait for another day. In her experience, stewards who were not used to the lady being present could be a truculent lot.

She was not proven wrong as he stood before her in his small solar as she sat at his desk. "I would also like an accounting of the spice boxes as well as the larder and dairy," she said as she ran a finger down the column of numbers in the ledger before her.

"I can assure you, my lady, that they are accurate," he said with barely concealed pique. "I have served here for many years and my lord has never had any complaints."

Beatrice stopped reading to look at the aging steward. He was a terrifying man but she would not allow herself to be intimidated. It was conceivable that the man disliked her for any number of reasons, but she was not about to reveal that his disapproval perturbed her. If she was to assert authority over the steward, then she must use her charm and wits.

Smiling her most gracious smile, she fixed the steward with an unwavering look. "And I am sure you have done an admirable job, but nevertheless you will consult with me regarding the expenditure of the hall from now on." She held her ground and didn't succumb to the temptation to look away. Her heart pounded and tiny prickles of sweat irritated her upper lip but, still, she held the steward's glare.

"As you wish, my lady, I shall have them delivered to your solar at your convenience."

"Thank you, Sir Ansell. And perhaps you could have Master Roland come and the three of us might discuss the arrangements I wish to make as the new Lady of Barmoor," she said as she gave him another indulgent smile.

When the castle cook entered the solar it became apparent that the two men did not see eye to eye on anything. They were so at odds that Beatrice had difficulty keeping her face composed as they bickered between themselves. Master Roland's thin sharp-boned face was so in contrast to the fierce countenance of the steward that Beatrice wondered if these men were playing some japery on her. It was unheard of that a cook was not ample about his girth. Master Roland looked more like a whippet than a cook. Yet the viands he served were equal to none. Although in truth she did not have vast experience in that regard.

Master Roland's voice was high-pitched and resolute. "I will not be told how to order my kitchen by you, sir, now that my lady is here."

"I have been overseeing the castle's store with no complaints from my lord for years." Sir Ansell's outrage was apparent in his voice.

It was time for Beatrice to exert her authority or these two would come to blows.

"I will be taking over the role of chatelaine and the daily running of the castle, which will leave you, Sir Ansell, to oversee the larger responsibilities of procurement and management of the staff." She smiled as she waited for him to acknowledge her right to organize such matters.

Reluctantly he gave her a surly nod.

"Master Roland, you will meet with me each Monday and we will discuss meals and the necessary stores required for these, but you will work with Sir Ansell regarding the procurement of the necessary stores so that we do not find ourselves running short." She gave the cook a small smile but kept her eyes on him until he, too, nodded his understanding.

She would be lady of this castle and these men would have to accept that.

"That will be all. I shall discuss the next week's meals tomorrow, Master Roland, as I am sure that Ascension Day activities have you both busy and need none of my meddling."

Both men nodded as she rose to leave the steward's solar.

"Oh, Master Roland," she said as she stopped in front of the cook, "I thank you for your care with my son's viands. They are consumed with vigor." She gave him another smile of appreciation before she moved towards the solar door.

The cook puffed out his skinny chest and smiled with apparent pride that he had been so graciously commended.

With that done, Beatrice walked from the solar hoping she had exerted herself with the necessary blend of decorum and authority befitting the lady of Barmoor.

Chapter Fourteen

The noise in the hall from raucous laughter and people yelling at each other as they gloated over their speed at the climb up Yeavering Bell dissuaded Gilbret from trying to engage Beatrice in any meaningful conversation. He had escorted her from the steward's solar and was disinclined to ask anything more than "I trust it went well?" He was sure she would know how to handle the steward and cook. Both men were used to their own way, but now that he, and not his father, was Lord of Barmoor, he wanted Beatrice to order the arrangements as she saw fit.

When they were seated at table they exchanged pleasantries, commented on the goose that was served at the high table, also a tradition on Ascension Day, and smiled at the behavior of the retainers in the hall. Even the dour steward, Ansell, was not seated on the dais, choosing instead to be with the men drinking ale at the back of the hall.

"Did you have any problem with the steward?"

Beatrice looked from her trencher and followed Gilbret's gaze.

A small frown creased the skin between her brows. Gilbret had come to recognize the sign that she was thinking.

After several heartbeats she turned her eyes back on Gilbret. "I suspect he resents my interference but I am sure he will come to accept my role here."

"Good, I would hate to have to lop off his head." He managed to keep a straight face when Beatrice shot him an incredulous look.

"Ah, if only you would."

It was Gilbret's turn to be shocked until she laughed at his stunned expression.

It was pleasant to have a woman who would equal him in wit and humor.

A current of anticipation sparked between them as they sat, a rippling awareness that set his scalp tingling and his balls aching.

It had been years since he had experienced such a frisson of desire for a woman. His encounters had become a physical release only. He couldn't even remember the last time he had lain with a woman who had not only engaged his lust but also his mind. What would it be like to kiss Beatrice? His mind wandered over images of her lips and the swell of her breasts.

Something touched his arm, bringing his mind back to focus on the present.

As though in a dream he looked to his arm, realizing that it was Beatrice's hand that had jolted him out of his lusty woolgathering.

"Forgive me," he said as he gave her a sheepish grin. "I was elsewhere."

Beatrice held his gaze. The tip of her tongue peeked out from between her lips. She was studying him with rapt attention.

A wave of sudden heat engulfed him. He couldn't breathe. Couldn't concentrate. He was held captive by those amber eyes as they bored into his soul and he was powerless to pull away.

"I asked if you would like to visit my chamber and play a game of Alquerque?" She looked at her hand as though shocked that she had touched him. Immediately she pulled away and averted her eyes. A slight pink tinge to her cheeks only added to her allure.

Gilbret was no clodpate. Beatrice was making herself vulnerable and he was not about to reject her overture.

"I am a mere novice at the game," he said trying for a teasing tone. "But I am a fast learner."

Her eyes appraised him for several heartbeats before she answered. "I can well imagine that is true." She looked at her hands as they rested in her lap. "I am no novice." Her cheeks turned a deeper shade of red as she raised her eyes to look at him. "But I am out of practice."

God's holy bones, she wasn't talking about a board game. The lady was flirting.

Gilbret took a shuddering breath and tried to regain some composure. "You have already won today, my lady, so perhaps you would like another wager?"

Her eyes widened for a moment. Then a sly smile spread across her delicious mouth. "But I have yet to claim my prize," she pouted.

She was pouting. All the blood rushed from Gilbret's brain to his cock. *Say something, you idiot.*

"It would be unfair of me to offer another wager when I have not allowed you to take your reward." He leaned very close. Their lips were mere inches away while their eyes were locked together. Gilbret could smell her—lavender and something he didn't recognize—musk with a hint of spice. It was both calming and intoxicating to his senses.

"If I lose you will have two rewards to claim, and I assure you, my lady, I will be happy for you to claim them when we are in a much more private setting."

All this over the promise of a kiss? He had never been so aroused in his life. He had to touch her.

Lifting his hand to her mouth, he caressed her lips with his thumb. She didn't pull away but he did hear the tiny gasp as he touched her skin. It seemed all the noise in the hall ceased to exist.

It was just the two of them enclosed in a wondrous sensual cloud where they and they alone existed.

To his surprise and delight, she didn't pull away but let him run his thumb over her mouth. "I have been dreaming of your mouth all day." He flicked his eyes up to meet her gaze. He could see nothing but her dark lashes and black pupils. She was as aroused as he was.

"But, first, I think we must play out this game in a more private setting." Reluctantly, he pulled away. Her musky fragrance still lingered in his nose as he resettled himself on his chair. It would take several minutes for his raging cock-stand to subside so he sat neither looking left to Beatrice to see how she was reacting, nor to his right where his mother sat, no doubt intent on watching them.

Beatrice had once again surprised him. Behind a thoughtful detached persona, Beatrice had a playful nature. He looked forward to discovering that playful side of her. What would it be like to make love to her?

That brought Gilbret to a shuddering halt, his wine goblet suspended halfway between the table and his mouth. He didn't want to merely swive his wife. He wanted to make love to her. To cherish her body and explore her mind. To laugh and play as they held each other. Watch her as she shuddered in her climax.

He dare not look at her again. Surely his lust would be plain to see on his face. She was not ready and he would not allow himself to be vulnerable. Not yet. Bollocks, it was too late, he was already falling for his wife. God help him.

Her chamber was well lit and after several minutes of enduring Amica's excited welcome, Gilbret and Beatrice settled to play their game while the pup curled up on her bed in front of the fire.

"You have a board?" Gilbret was surprised.

"It is not mine. I saw it when I visited your mother's chamber earlier and asked if I might borrow it."

"Ahhh. I thought I recognized it, but then one board resembles another to my untrained eye."

Beatrice was laying out her twelve pieces on her white squares but she stopped and looked at him.

"I am beginning to think you are much more skilled than you pretend."

Gilbret clasped his chest in feigned innocence. "I can assure you, my lady, that I am many things but a cad I am not." Was he laying it on too thick? Perhaps, but it was fun to play this game.

"Very well, we shall see," she said as she handed him the little velvet bag containing his black pieces.

Mary and Olivier had retreated to the far corner of the chamber. Olivier read from the little book of fables he habitually carried with him. The leather cover was battered and well-worn evidence that the lad had leaved through its pages many times over the years. Gilbret remembered the day he presented the book to his squire. He had been teaching him his letters and had spied the little book at a stall on market day. Olivier had initially refused the gift but Gilbret appealed to the lad's logic and convinced him that it would help him learn to read. Gilbret cut his squire a quick glance. The lad's voice was a soft drone much like bees on a summer afternoon. Mary sat quietly next to him spinning wool, content to listen.

A sense of peace and comfort enveloped Gilbret. His body thrummed with a slow-burning awareness that he would receive a kiss from Beatrice. She looked mysterious and otherworldly as the flames from the fire created dancing shadows across her face.

She pressed her lips together as she anticipated her first move. If he could he would suspend this moment much like Joshua stopped the sun and moon.

"Well, my lord?"

The note of impatience discernible in her tone made Gilbret smile. Was she as nervous and excited as he was? Possibly. That was what was so exciting. Beatrice was perhaps as eager to taste him as he was her.

The game was fierce. Beatrice had a head for strategy but also a competitive spirit that Gilbret matched.

"What are you doing," Beatrice squeaked when Gilbret took one of her pieces off the board.

"We are compelled to take an opponent if the move is there." Gilbret pointed to the offending piece. "If you don't take your piece it is forfeit."

"We didn't agree to those rules," she snarled as she snatched her piece back. "If you want to play by those rules you have to state them at the beginning of the game."

Gilbret would have liked to continue teasing her, but he didn't want it to escalate into an argument. And she was right, he should have declared whether they were going to compel moves before they began.

"Very well," he said as he eyed her. "But from now on we will play the compelling rule. Yes?"

"Does that mean for the rest of this game, or any games that we play in the future?" Once again, her eyes flared as she glared at him.

Gilbret decided he liked this fierce Beatrice. With her blazing eyes and heaving bust. She had more spirit than any woman he had ever known.

"I like you like this, wife."

Her eyes widened in surprise. "Like what?"

"All passion and determination to win." Gilbret took a slow sip of his wine while keeping his eyes on her. "It makes for a thoroughly intriguing game. Which I won," he teased.

Beatrice didn't respond or take her eyes off him.

Had he gone too far? Pushed her too soon?

She gave him a small smile but held his gaze. "I must confess it is not in my character to be so ... so—"

"Impassioned? Spirited? Competitive?" Gilbret asked. What

would she be like in his bed? A lover who participated rather than passively letting him always take the lead was an intoxicating proposition.

"I own that I am not usually like this," Beatrice said as she eyed him. "You seem to arouse my temper. I become impatient and insistent all at the same time." She tilted her head to one side. "Does it offend you, my lord?"

Gilbret put down his goblet and leaned forward so their faces were closer. "No, my lady, I am not offended."

She huffed a little sigh. "I confess it has always been a part of my character, but when my mother died and my father remarried, he changed. I was determined to please him and my stepmother so I became what I thought they wanted." She gave another little huff of laughter. This one had a tinge of bitterness to it. "But the harder I tried to please them the more distant they became.

"So, I closed off this part of me and refashioned myself into someone who would always be acceptable. Walter came to despise me." She leveled her eyes on Gilbret. "My behavior became a weapon against his cruelty." She turned her eyes to the board in between them breaking their contact. "It is the first time in a very long while that I have allowed my true character to be revealed," she murmured.

Gilbret was out of his chair and came to kneel beside her. "Look at me, Beatrice."

When she turned slightly and met his eye he continued, "You must never hide from me. I am neither your father nor Walter. I want you to trust me enough to be who you truly are." He gave her a small smile, hoping she believed his words. "I can assure you I am more than comfortable with you going head-to-head with me." He lifted his hand and ran his finger over her eyebrows and down her cheek and chin. "I might growl. I have even been known to curse like a Scot. But never would I hurt you or try and mold you into someone you are not."

Beatrice's eyes traveled over his face, finally coming to rest back on his eyes.

"I believe you." Then she moved slightly and laid her lips on his.

Warm soft lips caressed his. Gilbret was too scared to move. Too scared he might frighten her off. The desire to take her in his arms and devour her overwhelmed him, but he kept still and allowed her to take charge of their first kiss. And, as kisses went, it was one he would remember until he took his last breath.

NEED TUGGED AT HER CORE. She wanted this—the taste of his lips, his scent as she breathed him in. Opening her mouth slightly her tongue glided over the seam of his lips asking him to open for her. When he did, she let her tongue delve into his heat. He tasted of wine and the promise of things she had long since denied herself.

No!

Gilbret had pulled his head away just as she was beginning to take the kiss deeper.

Humiliation and something she couldn't quite identify caused her cheeks to burn while sweat pebbled on her neck and arms.

She wanted to flee. To run and never be found.

"Don't hide, Beatrice."

Run! She couldn't look at him. Mortification made her body rigid while her heart pounded in her chest. She had wanted to run her fingers through his hair and, God help her, she wanted to press against him and feel his strength. His masculine power.

"Look at me," he whispered as he lifted her chin to meet his eyes.

When she met his gaze she was a little confused. Desire was so apparent in their dark brown shadows that she couldn't quite make sense of what had just happened.

"I stopped because I didn't want to frighten you with my reaction."

"I don't understand."

"We are new at this, you and I, so I want you to take your time."

"It was only a kiss, Gilbret," she mumbled as she tried to avoid him. Anything to escape his eyes. Eyes that saw too much. Places she wanted to keep hidden were exposed under his gaze and she didn't like it.

He lay his forehead against hers. "No, Beatrice, it was not. You gave of yourself but if I continued to kiss you, I would have taken more than you were willing to give."

He kissed her cheek and rose from where he had been crouching beside her chair. "You claimed your prize, but I will only claim mine when you are ready." He bowed his head. "Sleep well, wife." He turned to leave but suddenly turned back. "Dream of me," he said as he gave her one of his wicked smiles. The smile that made her toes curl in her slippers.

Then he bundled a sleeping Amica into his arms and was gone. Olivier quietly left behind his master.

"You may retire, Mary, I wish to stay here a while longer."

Mary nodded then retired to the bedchamber beyond.

Confusion gave way to anger, which gave way to profound discomfort. Gilbret de la Haye was a man Beatrice could love.

"Oh, Mary, Mother of God, what shall I do?"

There was no answer. There never was.

How long she sat in the chair she didn't know, but eventually the fire became a golden glow. It was time to go to bed but sleep would be elusive. Beatrice had opened the door to her heart and it would be impossible to close it. Not after tonight.

Chapter Fifteen

Sleep eluded Gilbret so it was early when he intercepted Olivier as the lad opened the door to Gilbret's chamber.

"What's got you hopping from one foot to another like a flea on a dog's back?" Gilbret toweled off the water from his face and turned to his squire.

"You are not going to like it."

Gilbret waited. His stomach clenched in anticipation of a punch.

"Cheldric is back, along with Lady Colette."

Gilbret took a moment to digest his squire's words. "But …"

His seneschal was supposed to be in Kent making sure Colette was safe. What in God's name was he doing back here so soon?

"Cheldric is outside," the lad said as he indicated towards the other door of Gilbret's chamber. "Your mother took Colette to her own chamber."

"My mother?" It was not even dawn. What was his mother doing up so early?

Olivier seemed to read his thoughts. "It seems she could not sleep and was on the wall walk when Cheldric arrived."

"Bring him in."

Gilbret finished getting dressed while Cheldric stood beside the fire, waiting.

"Well," Gilbret snarled, glaring at the man before him as he finished tying on his sword belt.

Cheldric's eyes darted from Gilbret to the door as though the huge man was about to flee.

Gilbret was fast losing patience.

"I intercepted Lady Colette just outside of Nottingham."

"Nottingham!" Gilbret roared.

To his credit, Cheldric didn't flinch or break eye contact. "She had escaped St. Ninian's with the help of some pilgrims. I happened to spot her as they were taking refuge from the weather at a small priory north of the town."

"Was she unhurt?"

"Yes, and in fighting fettle."

Gilbret nodded. He had first-hand experience with his sister's fiery temper. She was much more like their father than he was. It would take a strong man not to break her spirit; perhaps Cheldric was such a man? Colette had disobeyed their father by refusing to marry a man twice her age. Rather unwisely she had declared she loved another but refused to say who. His father suspected Cheldric was the man but he could not prove it. So he had banished her to St. Ninian's and imprisoned Cheldric in the dungeon, only releasing him when the steward interceded on Cheldric's behalf. That was two years ago now and Colette had still not forgiven Gilbret. What was he supposed to have done? He was no more capable of helping Colette flee their father's fury than she was. But that mattered not to his sister.

Gilbret trusted Cheldric. The man was honorable and had endured imprisonment rather than confess to the affair with Colette.

"Olivier, have her come to my solar when she has rested."

"Yes, my lord."

"You," Gilbret rasped. "Come with me."

Thoughts of Beatrice fled as Gilbret listened to Cheldric's story. It was mid-morning when Colette, accompanied by their mother, arrived at the solar. A defiant tilt of his sister's chin suggested that she would fight Gilbret tooth and nail.

"Colette." Gilbret inclined his head in a polite gesture of welcome.

"Brother," she snapped, not bothering to hide the cold disdain in her eyes as she met his gaze. "I will not go back."

"And I would not send you back."

That seemed to stall her attack. Good.

"Please, Mother, Colette, sit." He indicated two chairs by the fire. A page poured them some wine. "Leave us," Gilbret said as he stood by the hearth. He was too angry to sit.

"What made you do it?"

Colette looked to her hands—the first sign of hesitancy in her since she had stepped into his solar.

"I was to be taken to Heatherslaw Priory, to our uncle." She looked up and met Gilbret's eye. "I refuse to be his pawn."

Gilbret was surprised that his uncle was involved. But then perhaps not, as he thought about it. His uncle would do anything to ensure he had Barmoor. He had made that clear the night he brought Rosamund to the castle. Thankfully she had agreed to his mother's suggestion and withdrew to St. Leonard's where she would live out her days in peace. It was a good outcome and one his mother had insisted upon. She had been more generous to the woman than Gilbret would have been in her place. He turned his thoughts back to his sister.

"So, you ran?"

"Yes." She began to fidget with the hem of her sleeve. "Several pilgrims were leaving to travel north. I persuaded them to help me."

"No doubt you fed them some absurd story."

That got a rise out of her as Gilbret had intended. "I will be no man's chattel," she bellowed as she flung herself from the chair and stood facing her brother.

"Sit, sister, I have no intention of making you return to St Ninian's or sending you to our uncle."

When she had composed herself, he continued. "What has our uncle to do with this?" He addressed the question to his mother.

She was biting her lower lip in a decidedly nervous fashion. "Several years ago William had threatened that he would take Colette if I dared to marry your father. Of course I defied him, thinking Colette was safe behind St. Ninian's walls." She looked at Gilbret. "Obviously I was wrong."

Gilbret had known moments of rage but at this moment they all paled in the force of his reaction to his mother's words.

It took him several minutes to get his temper and breathing back under control. "I am not angry with you, Mother, but I do wish you had told me this earlier." Then he might have been able to ensure Colette had not put herself in such peril by leaving St. Ninian's.

Her expression was more a grimace than a smile.

"But why did he want to abduct me?"

"He wants to use you as leverage against me."

"But why?"

Gilbret had his suspicions. "If William can claim my marriage invalid then he stands a good chance to inherit the estates." He would need a patron with power and influence at Henry's court to ensure his claim was validated. De Chesney fit the role perfectly. Gilbret's blood ran cold.

William must have discovered Beatrice's past. It wouldn't take much convincing on William or de Chesney's part to hatch a scheme to destroy not only Beatrice's life but also the de la Hayes. Was Everlyn de Gant, Beatrice's brother by marriage, also involved? More than likely as he would inherit Folkingham instead of little Edward. What a godawful mess.

"But how can he do that?" Colette asked as she looked between Gilbret and their mother.

"I think it is best if you hear it from Beatrice."

BBEATRICE WAS SITTING on the window seat sewing a hem when Gilbret arrived. Heat flooded her cheeks when she saw him. Memories of their kiss and his rejection the previous evening invaded her mind. There had been no reprieve in sleep but now as he stood before her with a scowl on his face that would put fear into the dead, her body trembled with humiliation.

"Beatrice," he said as he nodded to her. "I trust you slept well?" He didn't smile and his eyes were not the twinkling playful eyes of the man she had kissed last night.

"What's wrong?" She was on her feet immediately. Gilbret glanced at Mary, who was playing with Edward and Amica.

"Mary, Edward might do with a breath of fresh air. You can leave Amica with me," Beatrice suggested. Whatever it was that had Gilbret so surly it would be best if she alone heard it.

When Mary had gone Beatrice turned to Gilbret. "Something is wrong. What is it?" Fear. Gnawing, visceral fear clutched at Beatrice's throat threatening to choke her. It was that easy to provoke the latent terror that always sat just beneath the surface. Her and Edward's lives were in jeopardy. She was sure of it.

He didn't answer but paced the length of the chamber. A prowling bear ready to attack any hapless victim in its path would have been less intimidating than her husband.

"Please, Gilbret, talk to me."

He walked the few paces that separated them and took her hands. "Don't fret; it is not that bad," he said as he traced small circles over her knuckles. "My sister has arrived."

"Your sister?" Beatrice was confused. Colette was in Kent.

"Yes." Gilbret's resigned sigh gave her a hint as to how he felt about Colette's unexpected appearance. "It seems my uncle is as duplicitous as my father." His gaze was steady as he talked to her. "And I suspect your husband's brother and the Bishop of Lincoln are also involved."

"Everlyn? What has he to do with Colette?" Oh, God in heaven. The sudden realization hit her like a slap across the face. "If they work together, they could make our lives unbearable."

"There is nothing I can prove but I have my suspicions. And if Colette's story is to be believed then it is possible they are in league with each other."

"You don't believe Colette?" Beatrice was unsure why that thought upset her as much as it did. Was it merely because Colette and Gilbret, like many siblings, had a different view of their father or was it that Gilbret's nature erred towards doubt rather than trust?

He huffed a sigh and released her hands. "I am not sure what to believe. And my sister resents me for not rescuing her from St. Ninian's." He began to pace around the chamber. "Colette would do, or say, anything to escape the confinement of St. Ninian's, but even she would find it hard to accuse our uncle if there were no foundation to her story."

"Then why do you doubt her?"

He turned and faced her. For the first time since meeting Gilbret she couldn't decipher his expression. And that sent a shiver down her spine. A cold dread crept over her skin and seemed to encase her chest making it difficult to draw breath.

"I fear that if her story is true, then the likelihood that my uncle and Everlyn and de Chesney have united in their quest to rid themselves of us makes for terrifying enemies."

"No!" Beatrice's knees failed her as she crumpled to the floor. Gilbret was there in an instant, catching her before she hit the floor.

"Come, sit here." He led her to a chair and poured her some wine. "Drink this." She obeyed but her mind couldn't quite catch up with her body. All would be lost. How could she fight against such odds? Edward would have his birthright stolen and she would be forever cast as a whore.

And what of Gilbret? Sybilla would have no home and Gilbret would once again be landless.

After taking a sip of wine and collecting her thoughts she turned to face him. "What can be done?"

He was before her, resting on his haunches, his hands resting on her knees. Their warmth penetrated through the cold that seemed to have invaded her. She appreciated the comfort. He was so strong. So assured. Could he secure the future she was hoping to forge for herself and Edward?

When had she changed her mind about him? They had only been married for a few days yet she felt as though she had known him all her life. A safe harbor that she didn't realize she needed.

To lose what she had never possessed was no great sacrifice. But to lose something that she had finally discovered and wanted, that was tragic. Tears began to prickle at the back of her eyes. Gilbret's face became blurry and distorted. *Shore up your defenses or you will lose so much more,* the voice in her head warned. But it was too late. She had let him in and short of cutting out her heart, she would have to live with the agony of loss. It was too much. Too cruel. She gave in to the sorrow and despair that swept through her and wept.

"All is not lost," Gilbret whispered as he picked her up and settled her on his knee.

Unable to hold back the lifetime of shame that held her in its grip, Beatrice continued to weep.

Gilbret held her—not trying to stop her tears—but he did comfort her with small noises that calmed her nerves and soothed her soul. It took several moments before Beatrice understood what he was saying. He was singing a lullaby. One her mother had sung to her as a child and the same one she sang to Edward when he became tired and fractious.

That small loving gesture seemed to still the tears and quieten her broken heart.

"Will I never be free of the shame Walter inflicted upon me?" She didn't really expect an answer. Not really, so it surprised her when Gilbret replied.

"I will do all in my power to keep you and Edward safe, Beatrice, but I fear if my uncle and Walter's brother join forces with de Chesney then much will be lost. The bishop is powerful and not to be trifled with. But you are my wife and they cannot make me repudiate our vows."

Fine words indeed. But if his mother's and sister's lives were at stake would Gilbret be so committed to her protection? History had proved that he too would deny her. Like all men in her life, Gilbret would not prove the exception—it was just a matter of determining the cost.

How long she stayed entwined in his arms Beatrice could not tell. Mary didn't return with Edward. And Amica continued to sleep in her basket by the fire.

"It is time you told your story to my mother and sister. If we are to prepare for a fight then they deserve to know the truth."

"The truth," Beatrice whispered, "is not always so easy to discover."

Gilbret didn't reply. What could he say? The "truth" was what was believed, not what was true.

Gilbret led her through her chamber door and into his suite of rooms. There, beside the fire, sat Sybilla and another woman who had dark hair and a small elfin face. Both women turned when they heard them enter. Sybilla looked benevolent but Colette's gray eyes had a hard edge to them that warned Beatrice this woman was no docile maid.

Once the introductions were made and they were settled around the table, Gilbret invited Beatrice to tell her story.

He placed his hand on the table palm up, offering her the comfort of his touch. It would be easier to ignore that small unspoken gesture but she needed all her strength and Gilbret's touch would give her the courage to open her soul to these two women.

Hands clasped she told them of her past. Not once did anyone interrupt her. They all sat and listened. Sybilla did gasp when Beatrice spoke of losing her unborn babe after one of Walter's beatings, but apart from that, the three de la Hayes listened in silence. She dared not look at their expressions so Beatrice kept her eyes on the goblet of wine in front of her, avoiding any contact save the hand of her husband.

Silence met her when she had concluded her tale of woe. If she could have, she would have beseeched God to open the floor and have her swallowed up. But even God seemed impervious to her plight.

"Your husband is dead, so there is no legal reason why you cannot marry?" Colette was the first to speak.

"I was told by Father Ascelin that there is no impediment to the marriage so no one can force us to part," Gilbret said as he gave Beatrice's hand a small squeeze.

"The annulment is to be appealed," Gilbret said as he released Beatrice's hand and stood. "If it can be overturned then Edward will receive his birthright."

"But if not?" Colette asked.

"I suspect Everlyn will fight for what he wants. As the Bishop of Lincoln, Robert de Chesney may hold sway over the archbishop but Hugh Puiset is a just man and won't be bullied by de Chesney."

"Can Everlyn and de Chesney do that?"

"Everlyn wants Edward's inheritance. De Chesney holds sway with Rome, and the king will not defy Rome if the pontiff rules against us. If they can destroy our marriage, which I would not put past the pox-ridden curs, then yes, they will do it. "

Beatrice remained silent as they spoke. What could she say? How might she retain some semblance of honor? Her life, and that of her son, was no longer hers to control.

Control? What a naive assumption that was. She had never had control over their lives. She glanced at the faces of her new family. Gilbret wore his usual scowl. When he'd lived at Beauforde he seldom scowled. But since marrying her it seemed that was his permanent expression. She had done that to him.

"If he tries to prove that Edward is not Walter's son, then perhaps he could win," Beatrice whispered.

All faces turned to her then. Heat burned her cheeks while all the moisture in her mouth dried and her throat closed. Her honor and virtue were all she had but even they were to be taken from her.

"I never betrayed my marriage vows," she squeaked. But the memory of that fateful night when her husband accused her of adultery could no longer be ignored. Yes, Everlyn could very easily cast doubt on Edward's right to call Walter "Father."

"Here, drink." Once again it was Gilbret who came to her rescue. "I will fight to the death any man that would make such vile accusations."

"Ah, my son, noble words but be careful. Much is at stake including all our lives," Sybilla cautioned.

Beatrice considered carefully before she spoke. "You still have time to find a wife. Perhaps it would be best if I return to Beauforde and you release me from the marriage." Beatrice looked to the three faces now trained on her. "Edward and I will be safe under Ranulf's care and you will be more secure if you wed another without the stain I carry."

Why was it so hard to say those words? She had secretly thought about them since the day she agreed to this marriage. But now that she had spoken the words out loud, they cut so deep it was likely she would bleed to death.

Chapter Sixteen

For a brief moment, the idea gave Gilbret a sudden rush of relief. Then shame came swift on its heels. To repudiate Beatrice would be to consign her to a lifetime of humiliation and Edward's future would be no better than that of the lowest villein. And in truth he didn't want to repudiate her. He wanted her in his life. In his bed. It was more than lust and that surprised him. When had his feelings for her grown deeper? More complex? He would think on that later. Now he had to act.

"No! It is out of the question," he snarled. "I will never repudiate you. Never!"

The years receded as Gilbret was thrust back in time to when he was a boy and first understood what it was to be labeled a bastard. No name to protect him. No family to offer their support. He was alone and despised all because he was born to a woman who was not married. He would never inflict that on Edward.

"Very well, that is settled," Sybilla said. "But we still have Colette to consider. She is not safe either."

Gilbret took a chance. "Well, then she should marry."

"What. No! Never." Colette gave him a steely glare. "I refuse to be forced into a marriage not of my own choosing."

Gilbret eyed his sister for several heartbeats. "Then choose."

If it wasn't so serious Gilbret might have laughed. Colette's expression was akin to a trout gasping for breath after it had been thrown from the water onto the bank—all boggling eyes and gaping mouth.

"Close your mouth, dear," Sybilla said quietly.

"You have often stated that you wish to make your own decisions, so now make them," Gilbret said. "I will not stand in your way."

"I will marry her."

The three women turned to see who had spoken. Gilbret didn't bother to turn as he'd had Cheldric wait behind the curtain precisely for this moment.

"I won't marry you," Colette squeaked.

Cheldric walked into the chamber and strode to where Colette was sitting. "You pledged yourself to me," he said as his eyes raked over her face. "Have you changed your mind? For mine is as it was two summers ago."

Colette took a shuddering breath. "He will never accept you as my husband," she whispered as she nodded towards Gilbret.

"I have given Cheldric my consent and also offered him the role as constable of Heaton Castle."

Gilbret never gloated, well hardly ever gloated, but on this occasion, he couldn't seem to help himself. "I have bested you, sister, so don't make a fuss and just do what your heart has longed to do for years."

Colette loved Cheldric. It had been obvious to Gilbret even when they were children. Colette followed the boy about like a lost pup.

What saddened Gilbret was that Colette truly thought that he would deny her the choice of husband just as their father had. They had not lived under the same roof for many years, but as children, they had been close. Gilbret made a silent vow that he would ensure they would once again learn to trust each other.

Her eyes were still boggled and she couldn't seem to find her wits. It was a sight Gilbret would cherish.

"It seems, my lord, that your sister is lost for words. A miracle, methinks," Cheldric murmured as he held Colette by his side.

Gilbret huffed a laugh in amusement. "Well, sister?"

Colette turned her gaze from Gilbret back to Cheldric. Her eyes were full of unshed tears "Yes. Oh, a thousand times yes." And flung herself into Cheldric's arms.

"You have the knack for strategy, my son, and are to be commended." There was pride in his mother's tone.

Gilbret had bested his father and it felt good. The cur had abused Cheldric most grievously and consigned Colette to a nunnery all because she had fallen in love with a man their father had despised.

Beatrice was still sitting at the table, a rueful smile on her face.

Had he done the right thing by proclaiming his intention to sacrifice his life, and the lives of his mother and sister, for hers? It was in their wedding vows, but would he truly lay down his life to preserve hers? God, he hoped he would never be put to the test.

A knock on the chamber door interrupted his thoughts. "Come."

Olivier entered the chamber. "This just arrived."

All eyes focused on Gilbret as he took the missive and opened the seal. It was from Father Ascelin.

Gilbret read it—all the blood drained from his face. "It seems Father Ascelin has been busy."

Gilbret pulled out a chair; he didn't think his legs would carry him.

"What does it say?" His mother's question barely registered through the fog of disbelief.

"Father Ascelin has confirmed that Hugh de Puiset, Archbishop of Durham, has not only agreed to support the appeal but finds that there was insufficient evidence in the records for the annulment in the first place."

A great whoosh of air filled the room. Gilbret managed to leap from his chair and catch Beatrice before she slumped to the floor.

"Can it be so?" she asked as she lay in his arms.

"It seems our prayers have been heard." He heard his mother say.

He took Beatrice by her shoulders and led her back to her chair and gave her some wine to drink.

"Unfortunately, that is not all the missive says." Gilbret made sure to sit beside Beatrice. The next few minutes would determine so much.

"It seems Robert de Chesney has uncovered some disturbing new evidence and has asked for a hearing to be held in Alnwick after Whitsun."

"What evidence?" Beatrice asked in a small voice. A gray pallor had robbed her face of color. She looked stricken and he was unable to protect her from what he suspected was an all-out assault on her and her son.

A hearing was a terrifying ordeal. His mind went back to Ranulf and Isabeau's hearing. A small involuntary shudder forced him to relinquish his goblet of wine. If de Chesney and his uncle were behind the "new evidence" then he didn't hold out much hope. But hope he would. He owed that to Beatrice and his mother and sister.

"Ascelin doesn't say, but de Puiset has agreed and we are to present ourselves at St. Andrew's Priory the day after Whitsun."

That was only seven days away. And with no notion of what the new evidence was, they had no choice but to travel to Alnwick and stay with Guyon and Cicele. As sheriff, Guyon would be present although his power would be limited.

At least Beatrice would be with family. Gilbret only hoped

Cicele and Guyon's marriage was sound and that they would support them.

God help them if they didn't.

Chapter Seventeen

A SLOW-SEEPING KIND OF PANIC ENVELOPED BEATRICE. EACH DAY she went about her routine of seeing to Edward and spending time with Amica, then riding to hunt with Gilbret or sitting in the great hall as he dealt with the needs of his retainers.

Colette and Cheldric exchanged vows publicly in the hall. Although the wedding was a muted affair, it was a happy one.

Emotions on the day they left Barmoor to live at Heaton Castle were mixed. Gilbret had decided that Sybilla would travel with Colette and Cheldric but she wanted to travel to Alnwick to support Gilbret and Beatrice. "You will be safer with Cheldric at Heaton," Gilbret said, trying to persuade her. "And besides, I will feel less anxious if I know you are safe behind Heaton's defenses."

Finally, she agreed, and Gilbret and Beatrice waved them goodbye. As she watched them leave, Beatrice didn't want to think about the next few days. Whatever evidence de Chesney, probably with the help of Everlyn, had cooked up it was bound to mean the end of her marriage. Gilbret would fight for his mother and sister's security, but only God and the Fates knew the future.

The castle was so much quieter with Sybilla's absence. Gilbret seemed to withdraw into himself but Beatrice didn't know how to help so she kept her observation to herself.

Most days Beatrice walked to the stables to brush Clover or sometimes just sit and watch Amica and Edward play. Clover had an uncanny knack of calming Beatrice when doubts about the upcoming council robbed her of her composure.

It was during those visits that Beatrice became aware that Amica and Clover had struck up an unlikely friendship. The pup would jump up beside Beatrice until she placed her on Clover's broad back. Terrified that the dog might fall Beatrice had held the dog steady on the mare's back but it soon became obvious that horse and dog enjoyed the game.

If Amica was not on Clover's back she was sitting on the stool Beatrice used to reach the mare's back and rump when brushing her. The horse often nuzzled the pup as she wiggled in ecstasy over the horse's attention.

Tomorrow they would leave for Alnwick. Only God knew if it would be the last time Beatrice could spend time here in the quiet of the stable watching Amica and Clover.

"I would like to do that to you," Gilbret whispered from behind her. His breath caressed her neck as he spoke and she closed her eyes for a moment delighting in his nearness.

She dared not move although every fiber in her body longed to lean back into him and revel in his heat and strength.

"I would start at your neck and work my way down. Perhaps a little nip here and a little nip there."

Beatrice shivered as his breath touched her skin. His words evoked images of his lips on her skin and she was lost in the joy of it.

He wasn't touching her, but still the heat from his body made her skin burn and the hair on the back of her neck rise.

"Would you, my lady wife, be as welcoming of my attentions as Amica is towards Clover?"

Yes, she would. Turning to face the man standing behind her Beatrice smiled a slow seductive smile. "If you are as thorough in your attention as you boast then, yes, I think I would." Then she rose on her toes and kissed him. "But do not tease, my lord, as I find I have no patience for it."

Gilbret's eyes widened for a heartbeat, then squinted. "You, wife, are a vixen." Then he gathered her into his arms and kissed her until her senses were muddled and her body shook with burning desire.

"Ah, woman, the stable is not the place to tempt me," he growled and then stepped back.

She wanted to call him back but she didn't. Instead she watched as he walked through the stable door and out into the bailey.

Amica had lost interest in Clover and was jumping at her legs wanting attention. Scooping down to pick up the dog Beatrice looked about to see if Mary had noticed her and Gilbret's exchange. Her maid was over by Maigemor's stall, Edward chattering away at the horse while he ran his little hand down the courser's neck.

Beatrice sat at table trying to push away thoughts of Gilbret and his words in the stable. She had spent the rest of the day concentrating on arrangements for their travel to Alnwick on the morrow. They would leave at first light in the morning. Cicele and Guyon had written to say they would support her, and Ranulf and Isabeau would travel to Alnwick also. She would have her family about her as she awaited her fate. And heard the lies spun to save powerful men from relinquishing their land.

"You should eat something," Gilbret said as he leaned over and whispered in her ear. It was the evening meal and the hall was a subdued place. The normally loud and cheerful banter from the retainers was nowhere to be heard. Even the musicians played plaintive music that seemed to fit the mood.

"I find I have little stomach for food."

"You will need your strength to face the ordeals that lie ahead."

That was true, but Beatrice couldn't seem to hold down her food. She only had to place a morsel of something near her mouth and she would begin retching. She drank little and ate even less.

"All will be well," Gilbret assured her but she was tired of his empty encouragement.

"You don't know that," she snapped.

To his credit he didn't take his hand from hers. When had he taken her hand? And when had she become so used to his touch that she barely noticed the small caress over her knuckles?

"I have to have faith, Beatrice. And it helps to have a thick skull," he said as he gave her a foolish grin.

Laughter bubbled up and out of her mouth before she could stop it. Gilbret had not lost his sense of humor. It would take more than an ecclesiastical council to dampen his spirits. Or was it that he was good at pretending?

"I have promised you that whatever the outcome I am your husband and I will protect you and Edward with my life."

His expression was so fierce she almost flinched under his ferocious gaze.

"I am so sorry to bring this to your door." Beatrice was no fool and it didn't take a diviner to realize that she had brought this to his house. His uncle would have no claim to Barmoor if Gilbret had married a noblewoman beyond reproach. If only she could go back. She would have refused his offer and stayed tucked away at Beauforde. It would have been half a life but this man would have been free of the shame she would bring to his name.

As she gazed upon his face, she realized something else as well. She loved him. Her instinct was to turn away but she held his gaze and looked deep into his eyes—to his soul. Their brown depths reflected loyalty, bravery, and honor. Perhaps she had loved him from the very beginning but refused to acknowledge it. What a clodpate she had been to deny herself and now it was too late. Or was it?

Taking a deep breath, she made a decision. Not taking her eyes from his she laid her heart bare. "I know not what tomorrow will bring but tonight I want to be your wife." She gave him a smile that she hoped spoke of her desire. "I would like to have you do those clever things with your lips that you spoke of today." She forced herself to keep her eyes on his rather than look away.

She had shocked him. His reaction was small but she had seen it. His eyes widened fractionally before darkening into smoldering brown pools. Desire. She recognized it immediately.

"Are you sure?" His voice was almost a growl. "I have wanted you since the day I saw you but I never allowed myself to believe someone who possessed so much beauty would accept me."

With her free hand she reached up and touched his cheek. "I have been something of a dolt and now, as my future hangs in the balance, I see that it is you I want. So, yes, Gilbret de la Haye, I am sure."

His hand released hers where it rested on the table and cupped her chin. His thumb ran over her mouth sending sparks down her spine and causing an ache in her lower stomach.

"Then I shall come to you when you have Edward settled."

"No. I will not put Edward and Mary out of their bed." She huffed a small laugh when she saw his expression. "They both sleep with me," she said by way of explanation.

To his credit, he didn't bluster about having a servant share her bed.

"I tried that once with Olivier when we were billeted in a freezing inn, but he flipped about like a flea all night," he teased. "And his feet are colder than a winter puddle." He shuddered for dramatic effect.

They both laughed at the absurdity of his statement. When they had regained their composure, he nodded. "I shall be waiting for you." His voice was so low and deep that she felt it rather than heard it. That thrill of anticipation that she thought never to experience again flooded her sending a wanton ache to her womb. Yes, she was ready. And it would be wonderful to be held in his arms and feel his hands on her.

A sudden wave of shyness had her looking at her hand as it rested in her lap. Never had she been so forward. Or so in need of a man's attention.

"Please excuse me, I must see to Edward." She had to leave his presence. She couldn't breathe and her stomach was in knots.

Beatrice rose and nodded to Gilbret, then walked as calmly as she could through the hall and up the stairs that would take her to her chambers.

Walk slowly, with your head held high. And breathe. Yes, breathing was good. Taking a small gulp of air, she nodded to the retainers as she walked past their tables. Was it her imagination or could she feel Gilbret's eyes burning into her back as she left the hall?

As she walked past the benches the fruity fragrance of mead and ale was mixed with the peppery smell of old rushes and the tang of hard-working men's sweat filled her nose and seared her brain. The smells were primal and earthy and reflected her need to be with her husband.

All her senses were on alert as she anticipated what it would be like to be joined with Gilbret.

I am alive for the first time in years. It had never occurred to her that she had been living half a life. But as she walked away from Gilbret with the promise of his body covering hers she admitted to herself she had been walking through life as though half dead. A dream state where nothing save Edward had touched her.

Edward was her life, but Gilbret had become her air and she would never be able to go back to that half-life again.

GILBRET WAS impatient for the hall to quieten and make ready for bed. Ansell sat next to him discussing the arrangements for their journey to Alnwick on the morrow.

Gilbret was not listening but when the silence penetrated his brain, he realized Ansell was awaiting an answer. "Forgive me, Ansell, I was woolgathering."

"You have much on your mind, lord." His steward was a good man and would ensure Barmoor was well protected if William tried to take advantage of Gilbret's absence.

It seemed to Gilbret that although Ansell had initially resented Beatrice's authority the two were now working together without either drawing blood.

"Lady Beatrice tells me that she has found your help invaluable," Gilbret said as he cut his steward a shrewd glance. "I am gratified to hear it."

His steward huffed a sigh. "In truth, lord, I am an old dog and disinclined to perform new tricks," he said as he met Gilbret's eye. "But Lady Beatrice has performed a miracle and keeps Master Roland out of my solar. And for that, I am the lady's most willing servant."

Gilbret smiled at Ansell's wry wit. "The man might be a burr in the arse but his viands are worth much discomfort."

Ansell laughed. "Indeed, lord."

Gilbret forced his mind back to the immediate matters that would not wait. "I have decided to take a score of men to Alnwick, but that should leave enough to ensure the castle's defenses are not compromised.

Barmoor sat on a natural incline but it was his great-grandsire who moved a mountain of dirt to create the large motte on which the castle and bailey sat. From such an advantageous position

Barmoor held unobstructed views of the surrounding plain. It would be impossible for an enemy to approach unobserved.

"Its defenses have never been breached, my lord, and it will take more than that sniveling arse-lick to best us."

Gilbret laughed. As did Olivier who stood behind him. His steward possessed a brusque manner that did little to help ease the sight of his scarred face and wild hair. He looked more beast than man but he was competent. And he was loyal. Those were the only attributes Gilbret needed.

"Then let us hope my uncle has his eyes fixed on Alnwick and the council rather than the estates."

"You have good men at Wooler, Etal, and Heaton. The cur will not get his hands on your birthright, my lord."

Let's hope you are right. Gilbret didn't voice his concern but decided it was best to keep his own counsel.

Ansell and Gilbret continued to discuss the management of Barmoor until the retainers in the hall began to prepare for bed. The tables had long since been pushed back against the wall and the men were now gathering their sleeping pallets and arranging where they would sleep.

Gilbret watched as the most senior men commandeered the warmest spots before the fire. They were the hardened fighters whose skill and rank ensured the warmest place to spend the night. Ansell had his own chamber in the south tower.

A sense of profound disquiet enveloped Gilbret as he looked out over the men who had sworn to protect him and his property. He had resented the king for thrusting him into this position. He had never wanted anything from the man who had treated him and his mother and sister with such disdain, but here he was wanting to protect what was now his. He could not fail his men and those who depended on him. No matter the evidence de Chesney brought to the council Gilbret would spare no effort to ensure he kept his lands. These were his people and he would not abandon them.

It was only as he walked towards his chamber that he began to allow his mind to wander to Beatrice. She would be his. And like his retainers in the hall, he would do whatever was necessary to keep her from his uncle's malice.

"You may leave me."

"My lord." Olivier was astute enough not to question Gilbret. The lad usually slept on a pallet in the same chamber as Gilbret but not tonight. "Might I be so bold as to suggest I sleep in Lady Beatrice's solar?"

Gilbret gave him a quelling look. "Why?"

To his credit, the lad kept eye contact. "Because if Lady Beatrice is not there and is needed in the night, Mary will not have to traverse the empty halls looking for her mistress."

Gilbret, never taking his eyes from Olivier's, walked the few steps to where his squire stood folding his discarded clothing. "I love you as a brother, but, Olivier, if you so much as touch that girl I'll cut off your balls and stuff them down your throat."

Olivier continued to keep his eyes on Gilbret but he raised his chin a fraction in defiance. "I would expect nothing less of you, my lord." His tone was as hard as Gilbret's. "And never would I defile an innocent. You know me better than that."

Gilbret grabbed Olivier's shoulder. "I do know you, but that thing you use to poke most of the kitchen maids with has a mind of its own."

Olivier relaxed under Gilbret's grasp but his eyes held steady. "In point of fact, lord, I have yet to stick it in," he confessed as his cheeks turned a brilliant shade of red. Even in the candlelight Gilbret could see clearly that the lad's confession was humiliating.

Gilbret barked a hard, amused laugh. "God's bones, boy, here I was thinking you had the morals of a goat."

Olivier laughed. "Well, I must be honest," he said as he gave Gilbret a mischievous smile. "It has been handled by most of the kitchen maids."

Gilbret roared with laughter as he slapped Olivier on the back. "Then between the maids and you, the thing will be worn to a stub before you get to use it properly."

Olivier looked wounded. "Father Ascelin said it was better to go blind than to have the thing fall off. So as a good Christian I followed his advice."

Gilbret stopped laughing and leveled a skeptical glance at his squire. "And you believe him? The going blind part?" Over the years he had warned Olivier several times about the dangers of lying with whores. Thank God the lad had heeded his advice.

"No, of course not, but who was I to deny a good man some entertainment," Olivier said as he shot Gilbret an arch smile.

"You are a scary bastard," Gilbret said as he handed Olivier his boots. "Put these away and then get out of here."

Olivier took the boots, which he would clean before he went to bed, and walked out of the bedchamber.

"Olivier," Gilbret called after him.

"Yes, lord."

"Your mother would be proud of you."

Again, Olivier's cheeks turned red. "I hope so." Then he was gone.

Gilbret didn't have to wait long for Beatrice to appear. He had been pacing his chamber unable to settle. No sooner had he sat than he was up and pacing the floor again.

He was nervous. It hit him the moment he heard the small knock on his door. Lust was there. And anticipation. But never had he been nervous. Well not since the first time he had become a man.

"Come." The words rasped his constricted throat as he answered.

One look at Beatrice's beautiful face as the candlelight flickered over her told him she was nervous too.

What a pair they made.

"Come, Beatrice, sit and we shall talk and have some wine." He didn't want to rush this night. And he didn't want to frighten her with his raging lust—his body was already rigid with want.

She settled into the chair by the fire and accepted the wine he gave her. "That was kind of you to have Olivier sleep in my solar."

Gilbret wanted her to think well of him but he couldn't lie. "It was Olivier who offered."

She gave a small nod. "He is as fond of Mary as she is of him."

"He won't take advantage," Gilbret said with a little too much force.

Beatrice gave him a steady gaze. "I would never have allowed it if I thought he would." She continued to study him before she continued, "Olivier is like his lord, honorable and kind, and that is why I accepted his offer to protect Mary and Edward."

Gilbret found he had nothing to say. He stood looking at her like a great dolt.

"Come, Gilbret, sit, as I find I am nervous and need your wit to ease my discomfort." She gave him a beauteous smile and he was lost.

Chapter Eighteen

They talked and spoke of insignificant things—all the while her body tingled with anticipation. She wanted this more than she would have believed a few short days ago.

Rising from her chair she stood in front of Gilbret and reached out her hand. "Take me to bed."

The speed with which he jumped from his chair gave her confidence but Gilbret was not a man to be rushed.

"May I?" he asked as his hand hovered over her décolletage.

She was wearing a linen chemise tied at the neck. Not trusting her voice, she nodded.

His fingers were warm as they caressed her skin but, still, she gasped at his touch. He had beautiful hands—long strong fingers and square clean nails. Walter's had been thick-knuckled and not always clean.

Stop comparing. She chided herself. It would only make her more self-conscious. Walter had often found fault with her body or her lackluster responses.

She shivered as Gilbret ran his finger over her skin tracing a line from her collarbone towards her neck. "Your skin is so soft," he whispered as he retraced the line he had drawn on her neck.

Their eyes met holding her in thrall—completely captivated, she waited.

Slowly, without taking his eyes from hers he leaned in and kissed her. Seldom had she received such a gentle and searching kiss. Her body responded immediately as his tongue licked the seam of her lips requesting entry. Prompted by his urging a smoldering heat began to gather in the cradle of her womb.

Moaning as he cupped the back of her head she allowed him to pull her closer. Beatrice was lost in a sea of sensation. Never had she experienced such a kiss.

His mouth devoured hers with an urgency that drove all doubt from her mind. She wanted this. No! She craved this. Like a cat, she rubbed against him, seeking more, her nipples pebbling as they brushed the linen of her chemise before being pressed to his chest.

How long they kissed she didn't know but she finally pulled away to catch her breath while a delicious aching sensation began to gather between her legs, making her want to push her pelvis into Gilbret's groin.

His smell. His heat. She wanted it all. Hungry for more she leaned into him and devoured his mouth. Their tongues sparred as they explored each other.

"God's bones, you taste wonderful," he growled as his lips skimmed her throat. His breath caressed her chin making her breasts ache with desperation. Every fiber of her body was on fire. She would combust, she was sure of it. Wanting more of his lips and tongue on her skin she tilted her neck to the side to give him greater access.

He gave her a playful little nip with his teeth as he licked a trail of pure fire down to her breasts.

Her body responded as he drew her breast into his mouth

teasing the nipple with his tongue until she was sure she would dissolve into a puddle on the rug at their feet.

She was in heaven … until she wasn't. A blast of cold air had replaced his warm breath.

"Please." A desperate moan escaped as she tried to pull his head back to her aching breasts.

He didn't reply but picked her up and carried her through to his bedchamber. The room was awash with soft candlelight casting a golden glow upon the walls. He placed her on the bed and then straightened to look at her.

Immediately she moved to cover her legs and pull the front of her chemise together to hide her bare breasts.

"Don't." His voice was little more than a growl. "I want to look at you."

It wasn't his tone that stilled her hands but the desire in his eyes. No one had ever looked at her like that.

Yes, there was lust, but it wasn't raw and senseless. He held his desire under control. He would not be like some raging beast who only wanted to plow her.

If she fled back to her chamber now he would not pursue her. Not force her to give more than she was willing to give. No man had ever given her that gift before. That gave her the courage to lay her hands beside her on the bed while her breasts remained exposed to his hungry gaze.

Finally, he climbed onto the bed and lay down beside her, his chin resting on his hand. Slowly, while keeping his eyes on hers, he ran his hand over her hip and down her thigh.

She closed her eyes and reveled in his touch as he explored her body with his fingers. Their heat scalded her skin through the thin material as she made inarticulate little noises of encouragement. Her body responded to each delicious touch with an urgency that made her head swim.

Impatient that he had stopped touching her, she opened her eyes to see that he was kneeling beside her. The front of his shirt was tented with the evidence of his desire. Her eyes were glued to the spot. "Shall I take my shirt off?"

She couldn't speak but she nodded. When his shirt lifted to expose his erection, she inhaled.

"Oh," she moaned as she took in the sight of him. "You are … are …"

"Yes," he coaxed as he watched her devour him with her eyes. "Magnificent."

He barked a laugh at the compliment. "I'm glad you approve." He gave her a silky smile. "May I?" he asked as he lifted the hem of her chemise.

Beatrice knelt and raised her arms over her head in silent invitation. A sudden rush of cool air caressed her skin as the fabric slid from her body.

Although she was self-conscious, she remained still as he looked at her.

"You, wife, are exceptional," he said in a reverent whisper.

Gently he pushed her back as he lay over her. His finger traced the arch of her eyebrow, then the bridge of her nose, and finally her lips. "The first day I saw you, you took my breath away. But never in my wildest dreams did I imagine how beautiful you would be bathed in candlelight." He leaned over and kissed her in earnest. Gone were the gentle, playful kisses. Now he demanded and took all she had, leaving her breathless and aching for him to be inside her.

His elbows supported him but the weight of him on her body drove her into a frenzy.

She ran her hands down his shoulders and up over his arms delighting in the feel of him, moaning his encouragement for her to explore more of him.

When she stroked the curve of his buttocks, he groaned into her neck. "God's bones, that feels so good."

She gave him a little buck with her hips and he responded with a nip to the inside of her neck.

Slowly, with a reverence worthy of a pilgrim, he took her breast into his mouth. She groaned in pleasure as the sensation tore through her.

"You like it?" he asked as his breath made her wet skin tingle.

"Yes." It was more of a pleading cry than an answer but he understood as he recaptured her breast. He laved her nipple, sending her into another bout of ecstasy.

By now she was beyond caring whether she was too demanding. She reached under his stomach and stroked his balls while she pressed up with her pelvis.

He chuckled as he rose slightly over her and held her face in his hands. The smile on his face warned her that he was enjoying making her beg. "It seems I have an impatient wife. And perhaps a little greedy, too."

She slapped him on the shoulder with her free hand. "Don't tease me."

"As you wish." And with that, he rose on his elbows and slid into her with one swift, confident thrust.

He held her face in his hands as he moved in slow deliberate thrusts. But as she arched her hips up to meet him his speed increased.

A delicious pressure built in her abdomen as he thrust into her harder and harder. The intensity of his gaze was too much to bear so she closed her eyes in an attempt to hide.

"Look at me, Beatrice. I want to see your face as you reach your peak."

Heat burned her cheeks as she opened her eyes. There was no escape. No hiding from this man as he claimed her body and soul. A small part of her, the terrified untrusting part, panicked but as she swallowed her fear her heart rejoiced. Never had she experienced something so profound or so powerful.

"Better," he said as he watched her with an intensity that burned her fears to ash.

It was so erotic to be watched in such an intimate way that Beatrice soon forgot to be embarrassed. So caught up in the sensation of Gilbret filling and stretching her she circled her legs around his hips and met him thrust for thrust.

He slid a hand under her buttock, lifting her slightly to fill her completely. She held his gaze as her body began to quiver and shake. Beatrice had never reached her peak before and was a little surprised when she cried out in unapologetic ecstasy at the same time as Gilbret. Her body fizzed with energy while a delicious molten heat seeped through her limbs.

Gilbret slumped on top of her as his body quivered from the effect of his own orgasm—their bodies slick with sweat as they lay together.

All too soon he began to move but Beatrice was not ready to lose contact. "No, please. It feels wonderful." She was still tingling from their lovemaking and didn't want him to withdraw just yet. Never had she been so close to another—his body filled a void deep within her very soul.

Gilbret inched up so he could rest on his elbows but he pressed his groin into her to maintain their contact.

"That, wife, was extraordinary," he said as he placed a kiss on the end of her nose. It reminded her of how she often kissed Edward and she began to giggle. Unfortunately, as she laughed, Gilbret slid out of her—their connection lost.

"What's so amusing." Gilbret harrumphed in the universal tone of a man who thought his prowess had been called into question.

His wounded expression only made Beatrice giggle all the more. "I'm sorry, it's just that you kissed me like I kiss Edward and for a brief moment I found it funny," she confessed as she looked up at him, running her finger over his creased forehead. "And a little inappropriate considering what we had just done."

Gilbret caught her face in his hands and kissed her nose again and again as she squealed in laughter.

Breathless, he fell on his back bringing Beatrice with him.

They lay like that for some time, the silence comforting.

All too soon he left the bed, leaving Beatrice to feel a little bereft. She watched as he walked to the table where he rinsed a linen cloth in the basin of water. His muscles rippled under his skin as he moved. Beatrice was mesmerized as she watched. Gilbret was like a god come to earth. The glow from the candles cast golden hues over his body as he walked towards her—linen washcloth in hand.

After they washed, he pulled the covers over the top of them as they lay side by side.

Beatrice raised herself on her elbow and kissed him soundly on the mouth then tucked herself into him, resting her head on his shoulder.

"Sleep well, husband," she whispered but he didn't hear her. To her amusement, he was already asleep and snoring quietly.

She lay awake watching the candles flicker in the growing darkness. Soon she would get up and untie the bed curtains but for now, she was content to lie in her husband's arms while she tried not to think of the future.

Chapter Nineteen

GILBRET WOKE TO AN EMPTY BED. HE HAD HOPED TO FIND Beatrice in his arms but she had fled early—the bedding was cold where she had lain content and languid after their lovemaking.

He smiled as he thought back to the way her shyness had dissolved and a bold passionate Beatrice had appeared under his touch. They were equals in mind and body. And more than their lovemaking had thrilled him.

The cold reality of what lay ahead gripped Gilbret as he lay in the dark cocoon of his bed. They would ride to Alnwick today and face de Chesney's new accusations the day after Whitsun. Whatever happened Gilbret was determined to protect Beatrice at any cost.

A quiet shuffling noise alerted Gilbret to Olivier's presence. Pulling back the bed curtains he heaved himself out of bed. He had slept and that had been a surprise. Their passion had left him feeling a bone-deep relaxation that had eluded him for years.

Bedding Beatrice was something he would not take for granted. She would be reserved and fretful today and he was patient enough to let her hide in on herself rather than force her to turn to him for comfort. His time would come he was sure of it.

Beatrice was nowhere to be seen as he entered the hall. He sat with Ansell and broke his fast while he waited for her to arrive. The men and horses were ready and they would leave as soon as he was sure Beatrice had eaten.

When she didn't appear after he had finished his viands, he decided it was time to seek her out.

He knocked on her chamber door and entered, then stopped dead in his tracks. She was naked waiting for Mary to bring her a shift. Everything in Gilbret tensed. She was the most beautiful woman he had ever seen. Her skin was a soft honey color in the candle and firelight. She had bathed—her hair lay in a wet rope down her back resting on the rise of her buttocks.

She turned as she heard his approach and the smile she bestowed on him stopped his heart. "I am sorry, lord husband, but I wished to bathe before we left."

His tongue was stuck to the roof of his mouth. He had to cough to dislodge it before he could speak. "I am happy to wait on you and will leave you to finish your bath."

He spun on his heel to leave but Beatrice called him back. When he turned, she was facing him without a shred of embarrassment in her expression. Gilbret had to clear his throat again while his cock, always ready to prove its worth, swelled in readiness to become better acquainted with his tempting wife.

She walked towards him with slow seductive steps. She was glorious. The troubadours sang of women and their beauty but none captured the vision that was walking towards him.

She stopped in front of him in all her naked glory but he dared not look past her eyes, which were riveted to his. When she reached him, she stood on her toes and leveled a kiss that seared his mind and body.

"Whatever happens during the next few days I want you to know that I will cherish what we shared between us last night." She gave him a sad smile and turned back to where Mary was waiting.

Gilbret didn't know what to make of her cryptic comment, but his body raged with unreleased lust, rendering his brain to the consistency of pottage. Best to leave before he did something stupid. Picking her up and tossing her on the table and taking her in one quick thrust would be unwelcome but his mind, once it had seized on the image, couldn't be dislodged. Time to go. And now!

He would speak to her tonight when they were in Alnwick and ask what she meant.

Walking was uncomfortable. The ache in his balls and throb of his cock made him stop so he forced himself to think of what lay ahead. By the time he reached the hall, his body was back under control but his temper was red-hot. De Chesney, curse his worm-ridden soul, would pay for what he had done. Gilbret would make sure of it.

He indicated for Olivier to come. "Lady Beatrice will be down soon; make sure she has had some viands sent to her chamber before we leave."

The lad nodded and strode off towards the kitchens.

Gilbret couldn't sit and wait so he walked out into the bailey to inspect the preparations for their departure. All the while his mind raced. Lust was uppermost but uncertainty nibbled at the edges of his mind. He refused to believe that all would be lost.

BEATRICE STEADIED her breathing as she heard Gilbret leaving her chamber. Mary, bless her, avoided her eyes as she handed Beatrice her shift. Best to say something or the awkward silence would only escalate, making Beatrice's already frayed nerves fit to break. "I'm sorry, Mary, I hope that did not offend you."

Mary looked up in surprise. "No, m'lady, I thought it was astoundingly brave. I could never show a man my body as you did." The girl's cheeks were bright red and she avoided Beatrice's gaze.

"I didn't think I would either, but I find myself feeling rather brave this morning."

Having Gilbret worship her body in a way Walter never had had been something of a revelation to Beatrice. Instead of shame and humiliation when Gilbret arrived to see her naked as she toweled herself dry, she had felt alive and beautiful. She wanted to show him just how much she trusted him and revealing herself had seemed the best way to convey the message.

It had been cowardly to leave his bed without saying a word. At the time she had convinced herself that it was unkind to wake him and she needed to go back to her chamber before Edward awoke. But that was a lie. In truth, she had fallen asleep in Gilbret's arms and awoken with a start. She had needed time by herself to think. And cherish what she had experienced. All could be lost and the fear of losing what she had only just discovered had weighed heavy on her mind.

Now dressed and ready to leave, she took Edward, who had been sitting on a sheepskin rug chewing his wooden teething ring, in her arms and walked from the chamber. Amica, full of her usual energy, bounded beside her. Casting a quick glance about the chamber, Beatrice wondered whether she would see this room again.

If de Chesney conspired with Everlyn to accuse her of adultery, which seemed likely, and the council believed him then she would die a disgraced woman convicted of petty treason against her husband.

"No! I will not think of such things."

"M'lady?"

"Forgive me, Mary, I was chiding myself for entertaining unholy thoughts." She would fight to her last breath rather than allow others to dishonor her. "We must go; I have kept Gilbret waiting too long."

Their traveling chests had already been taken so it was time to carry Edward down to the hall. She kissed his head as he burbled about whatever piqued his interest. He was a talkative child and commented on everything that caught his attention.

Mary, carrying the leather carry bags that contained the clean clots and clothing Edward would need during their journey followed Beatrice and Amica from the solar.

With squared shoulders, Beatrice walked into an unknown and terrifying future.

GILBRET, who had been waiting patiently in the hall, bestowed a smile on her that made her toes curl and her heart flutter. She would never tire of seeing his face. To have found love and then have it ripped from her seemed too cruel. Yes, she did love him. That was perhaps the most unexpected fact of her time spent alone thinking this morning as she lay in her own bed listening to Edward's soft snoring and Mary's breathing.

She loved Gilbret. It wasn't just his handsome face or his kind generous heart. It was that he treated her as an equal—someone who could question him and not be punished or humiliated. He considered her worthy of his respect and that, more than anything else, had captured her heart and was the reason she had given herself so completely to him the previous evening.

"I am sorry, my lord, for keeping you waiting," she said as he came and took Edward from her arms. The child was getting too heavy for her to carry although she was loath to admit it. Time was racing by and Edward was no longer the mewling babe whom she alone could console.

Gilbret's gaze was riveted to hers. "You are welcome to take as much time as you need. I would not hurry you towards Alnwick."

And that was why she loved him. For the first time in her life, she had a husband who was considerate and patient.

"No, I will dally no longer. I must face the council and pray I am found to be innocent of their vile lies."

Gilbret gave her his arm while Edward sat snugly in his other arm as they walked through the hall and out into the Bailey.

Clover gave a soft whinny when she recognized Beatrice. "Good morn, Clover, it is good to see you too," she said as she stroked the mare's nose.

It was twenty-two miles to Alnwick and they would reach Guyon's castle before the sun set unless there was trouble on the road.

It was then that Beatrice noticed the mounted guard that would travel with them. There were over twenty men seated on their horses waiting for them when they rode through into the lower bailey.

She cast a glance at Gilbret in silent question.

"I do not want to encounter trouble and be unprepared." His face was set in a scowl and his eyes were as hard as flint. So different from the man who had made her laugh and her body sing as they lay together in his bed.

Edward was sitting in Gilbret's lap nestled against his chest. He held some of Maigemor's mane in his little hands and was shaking his arms as though he was flicking the reins. She could see Gilbret's mouth moving but was not close enough to hear the words.

"It seems we have a budding squire in our midst." Olivier had ridden up beside Beatrice and was watching with fixed interest at the tiny boy riding with Gilbret.

"It will be some years before he challenges you to the role."

Olivier turned his gaze on Beatrice. She had not noticed before but Olivier possessed the clearest blue eyes of anyone she had seen. They were like a mid-summer sky. If you looked long enough you might be tempted to believe you could see forever. She shook her head slightly to clear the mesmerizing hold they had on her.

Olivier was smiling, but not at her. His eyes were once again focused on Gilbret and Edward. "He would let me ride like that." He sounded so young, so wistful. He turned back to look at Beatrice. "I couldn't ride when he found my mother and me. I was small for my age and terrified of horses but he taught me to trust them."

Beatrice had not heard about Olivier's mother. Were she and Gilbret lovers?

Olivier must have anticipated the question because he gave her a sly smile. "My mother was a favorite of King Stephen. For a while at least. When I was born, she was thrown out and had to make her way. Ranulf and Gilbret found me huddled beside a pig trough one morning and they took pity on me. They also took my mother and cared for her until her death."

"I am sorry, Olivier, I didn't know."

He turned those blue eyes back on her. They weren't exactly cold but they were scrutinizing her as though trying to gauge her character.

"Very few people know I am King Stephen's bastard, and I like to keep it that way." He indicated his head towards Gilbret. "If it hadn't been for him my mother would have died in unthinkable circumstances and I would have followed her to an early grave."

Beatrice slid her eyes from Olivier to where Gilbret rode with her young son in his lap. This man was so much more honorable than any she had ever met. Perhaps with the exception of Ranulf, her cousin Isabeau's husband. It was no wonder Ranulf and Gilbret were friends. They possessed the same depth of honor and chivalry.

Beatrice sighed. She had always assumed men of rank were like her father and Walter, but she now understood that men of wealth could also be honorable and kind.

She turned back to look at Olivier. "You are like him," she said as she smiled. "I see how you care for Mary, and I am grateful."

The boy's cheeks flamed pink. He was unused to compliments but she would not withhold them from him. "If anything happens to me, please take care of her." She could hardly get the words through the lump stuck in her throat.

Olivier turned to look at Mary who rode behind the row of guards at Beatrice's back. "I can never offer Mary more than my friendship," he said as he glanced over his shoulder. "And I will protect her to my last breath." Then he nudged his mount and trotted towards where Gilbret rode at the front of their retinue.

Edward and Mary would be safe. And that more than anything else gave Beatrice the courage to keep riding towards Alnwick.

Chapter Twenty

THE URGE TO RIDE FASTER TO GET THE ORDEAL OVER AND THE impulse to turn back and await fate behind the walls of Barmoor waged a relentless battle in Gilbret's mind. He had never run from anything in his life but the desire to protect Beatrice had him considering the unthinkable—run away and hide so Beatrice would be safe. They could flee to Ranulf's estate in Rouen and live out their days there.

It was all bollocks. He would never flee a fight. And he would never abandon his mother and sister. Cheldric would lose Heaton Castle to the new Lord of Wooler making the three of them landless and with nowhere to live. Ranulf would take them in but what would that say about him? Gilbret de la Haye was a coward—that's what. He was not so craven as to desert his own kin. He was honorable and loyal and would not fail his family.

They rode through Wooler and on to Wooperton where they stopped so Beatrice could attend to Edward. The lad was content to sit on Gilbret's horse and eventually fell asleep. It was a matter of moments to readjust him into the crook of his arm and let the lad sleep. Delays were not an option and his guard would ensure that

William or de Chesney or even Everlyn did not do something stupid.

Brigands were also a possibility as the war between Henry and Stephen had created havoc for the people of these lands. Gilbret was doing his best to make sure that their homes were rebuilt and their crops planted. His retainers would never starve or be exposed to the elements.

They rode through Eglingham by mid-afternoon and would reach Alnwick in good time. Beatrice had kept to herself, and Gilbret respected that. He would not intrude upon her thoughts.

The woman was stoic, which had surprised him. So much of Beatrice's character had confounded him. She was nothing like the woman he had conjured in his mind. Although he would never admit it, he was somewhat ashamed of his prejudice. It was her remarkable beauty that had him confused and unsure of himself. From the very first moment he had laid eyes on her he had been unable to keep his eyes off her. Oh, he'd been careful lest someone notice, but he had watched all the while telling himself lies that he was not interested. She was not one to be trusted. God's blood he was a clodpate.

He cast a quick glance behind him. There she sat upon Clover with a straight back and eyes ahead, Amica tucked into her cloak. She was one of the bravest women he knew. Yes, she held her emotions close but who could blame her? That was not because of arrogance, as he had first assumed, but preservation. Now that he understood some of her past and the things she had suffered at her father and Walter's hands he accepted that it would take time for her to grant him access to the tender parts of her heart.

They rode now in companionable silence as they approached Alnwick but he stopped to offer Beatrice her first view of it. And what a view it was.

"It is beautiful." Her voice was little more than a whisper. Gilbret would not have heard it if Edward had been awake and being his garrulous self. But the child still slept. The movement of the horse seemed to lull him into a stupor.

Alnwick sat atop a hill that overlooked the river Aln. The sun was still high enough to cast a golden glow over the whitewashed stone. The castle was surrounded by a circular wall that extended out to enclose the huge outer bailey and town. A small cluster of huts and buildings tucked into the outer wall seemed to shimmer in the late afternoon sun. Alnwick was thriving and Gilbret was pleased for his friend Guyon.

Ranulf and Guyon had both served Henry and his family for twenty years. Thomas, Guyon's squire, was a man who knew everything. He had spies in every corner of the realm. Perhaps he would be able to shed some light on what the "new evidence" was.

Turning his thoughts back to Beatrice, he cast her a leisurely glance. "Shall we make our way down or do you wish to stay here a little longer?" He didn't want to rush her towards a fate that might very well destroy what they were only beginning to share together and that tore at his chest. In the past week she had taken up residence somewhere in his heart and he wanted her to stay there. Nothing the council ordered would force him to abandon her. Yet an uneasy sense of doom had settled upon him as he neared Alnwick.

"I think I am ready to see Cicele, and the council can wait till after Whitsun." She smiled a small sad smile. "My son seems to have taken up residence in your arms, and I thank you for your kindness to him."

What did she mean? It was almost as though she were bidding him farewell. "Beatrice?" It came out more of a croak than her name.

She turned her face and bestowed a beatific smile upon him. "I fear that it will not go well for me," she admitted before taking a small gulp of air. "I tend to withdraw when I fret, so please be patient with me."

His chest ached and his throat closed, making it impossible to breathe, let alone talk. With a small nudge of his knee, Maigemor moved to stand beside Clover enabling Gilbret's thigh to touch Beatrice's leg. He wanted that contact. Wanted to reassure her but also to reassure himself that he had not lost her. "I will stand by you, Beatrice, but do not isolate yourself. Now, more than ever, you will need people about you. You do not have to face the council alone."

She reached out and touched his arm. The contact sent bolts of fire down his arm making his fingers twitch. Maigemor sensed the change in Gilbret and moved sideways, not understanding what Gilbret required of him. Gilbret ignored the horse and concentrated on Beatrice.

Neither spoke but both understood what the other tried to communicate and, at that moment, Gilbret's heart tumbled down to his toes.

He loved her! With every fiber of his being, he loved her. Perhaps he had always loved her but hadn't recognized it. She had bedeviled him ever since the day she arrived at Beauforde castle. He had assumed it was annoyance and mistrust but that had been a lie. He had been drawn to her as surely as a moth was drawn to a flame. There would be no escape. Whatever she faced he would face it with her.

Without thinking, he leaned over and took her mouth in one fierce kiss that told her what he could not say. Her lips responded to his need. She understood. They were one.

A cough behind Gilbret jolted him back to his surroundings and the retinue waiting behind them. Beatrice's lips clung to his as he began to move. A small sound of annoyance escaped her as he pulled away. "Later, wife, I shall resume my attention."

She licked her lips. The vixen. He leaned over close enough to whisper in her ear. "You will pay for that."

Her eyes rounded in mock innocence as she once again licked her lips in a lazy seductive gesture that was meant to torture a man.

Gilbret straightened in his saddle. Edward was still asleep. "The child has an astounding knack for sleeping," Gilbret said as he huffed a laugh.

Beatrice's laughter set his heart pounding. He wanted to hear her laugh every day. "He does nothing by halves. Sleeping. Eating. Talking. He does it all with a determination that belies his age."

Her tone was full of love and pride. Gilbret wanted that tone directed to his own son. He would love Edward as his own, but now he understood that he also wanted a son with de la Haye blood coursing through his veins.

His father had destroyed that desire early in Gilbret's life. But the possibility of having his own son now dangled seriously close. Fate would determine the future but a hard calloused part of Gilbret's heart softened as he sat on his horse atop a hill looking over Alnwick with Beatrice at his side and Edward tucked into his arm.

Whatever lay before them, Gilbret would not allow his enemies to destroy it.

BEATRICE HAD BEEN SO CAUGHT up in Gilbret's kiss that she had forgotten about the people waiting behind them. Her cheeks burned but it was her tingling lips that caused her the most embarrassment. They were sure to be swollen from Gilbret's hungry attention. What had gripped her to lean into him like that? The answer was so obvious it caused another wave of scorching heat to assault her cheeks. Her body was its own master and it wanted more contact with Gilbret. She dared not look behind her to where Olivier and Mary sat waiting. Knowing looks from the men at arms who rode with them would be too much. Instead, she pressed her thighs together to signal to Clover that she wanted her to move. The horse's response was immediate. "Good girl," she cooed as she patted the mare's neck.

Beatrice led the way down the hill and towards the castle. It was late afternoon but with only three weeks before the summer solstice, the sun still hung high in the sky.

The haze from the angle of the sun and the fires from the village as she approached the main gate made Beatrice's eyes water. As there was no breeze the smoke hung in the air. Its pungent charcoal smell caught the back of her throat, making her cough.

She looked to where Gilbret rode beside her. Edward had woken and was sitting once again on Gilbret's saddle—his back to Gilbret's chest. His little head swiveled right and left as he took in the new scene. She couldn't hear him but she could see his mouth moving. It was Gilbret's voice and occasional laughter that drifted towards her.

Through the main gate and the town, they rode until they reached the inner bailey gate.

Beatrice's stomach hitched in excitement. It had been months since she had seen her cousin and Beatrice had missed her. Isabeau would also be waiting. She would be with her cousins again. Their company would be a balm to her anxious thoughts.

Cicele and Isabeau were both loving and pragmatic. And their husbands were powerful enough to help support her during the council's hearing.

Fate had been kind to Cicele and Beatrice would never begrudge her cousin a happy marriage, but a small ember of resentment glowed at the back of her mind as she considered her own fate.

Grooms dashed forward as she came to a stop before the steps where Guyon and Cicele waited to greet them.

When she was helped from her horse Cicele rushed to embrace her. "You are here."

Beatrice laughed. "Yes, it seems I am."

Cicele held Beatrice by the shoulders and examined her face.

Cicele was an astute woman and Beatrice felt a little self-conscious under her cousin's scrutiny.

Amica wriggled in Beatrice's arms. Placing the pup on the ground, Beatrice straightened and allowed herself to be scrutinized by her cousin.

"You look well, cousin." Cicele glanced over at Gilbret who was handing Edward down to Mary before she turned her gaze back to Beatrice—a calculating glint in her eyes warned Beatrice that her cousin saw too much. "Marriage seems to agree with you."

Beatrice forced herself to return her cousin's steady gaze. It was no use denying it, but Beatrice was not about to discuss what had transpired the previous evening. "Yes, cousin, it does."

Cicele's smile was genuine. "I am glad, for you deserve to be happy." Cicele looked to Gilbret who was conversing with Guyon. "I shall put you in a suite of rooms so that you can enjoy your privacy."

Too embarrassed to reply, Beatrice looked about for Mary. Where was she when she needed her? Beatrice saw Mary standing behind Clover. Edward was hitched on her hip and they were stroking Maigemor's nose. "Edward will need his clouts changed and I need to show her where to go," she said without looking at Cicele.

Cicele was not so easily dissuaded. "Maude will show the girl to your chambers, but you will come with me."

There was no point in arguing so Beatrice indicated for Mary to follow Maude, who was standing behind Cicele, while Beatrice followed her cousin.

"You have a face like thunder," Cicele said ignoring Beatrice's displeasure at being ordered about as she ushered Beatrice into a light-filled room. Tapestries adorned the walls and the furniture was delicate and painted in soft greens and blues. A woolen rug in various colors around the edges covered the floor. Beatrice had never seen anything so beautiful.

"You can take a moment to refresh yourself here before going to Edward."

A twinge of pique nibbled at Beatrice's conscience. But only a twinge. She didn't want to be ordered about. Since being married to Gilbret, she had begun to enjoy the freedom of being her own woman and resented Cicele's high-handedness.

Cicele handed her a cup of wine. "You are not the same Beatrice I left in January."

It was true. So much had changed in such a short amount of time. It was due to Gilbret.

Beatrice huffed a resigned sigh. "Saint's bones, cousin, you are relentless."

Neither chastened nor embarrassed, Cicele looked satisfied with herself.

"That was no compliment, cousin." Beatrice strove for a chiding tone but it fell short.

"Come, sit for a moment and tell me." Cicele indicated a chair with a cushion on the seat and a curved back. It was painted in a soft green. Beatrice had never seen anything that looked so comfortable.

"This is truly lovely, Cicele."

"Don't change the subject."

Beatrice laughed. Oh, how she had missed her cousin's forthright manner. "Very well, what do you wish to know?" Beatrice gave up all pretense at chagrin and smiled at her cousin's impatient expression.

"Everything."

That was Cicele. She wanted everything and would settle for nothing less. "It seems that you too, cousin, have found happiness in your marriage." There was a story here, Beatrice was sure of it.

"Very well, I shall share first." Cicele tried to pout but ended up laughing instead.

"Guyon and I had hurt each other in the past, and there was

much enmity between us, but God has been good and we have found true happiness together."

Beatrice was so happy to hear it that she jumped up and embraced her cousin. "Oh, Cicele, that is indeed a balm to my soul. I am so happy for you."

When they had settled back in their chairs a page arrived with a washcloth and basin of warm water. "You might like to wash before Edward arrives. It will be quieter here for you than in your chamber, as the maids will be unpacking."

That was thoughtful and Beatrice appreciated it.

After washing, she settled back in her chair. "I can only tell you that Gilbret is kind and allows me freedom." It sounded so shallow but only she knew what abuse from a spouse can do to your sense of self.

Cicele gave her a steady stare. "I too understand what it is to be shown respect. That is the start of a true marriage."

Yes. Beatrice thought back to her time with Walter. He had never shown her respect, only bullying. Gilbret was confident in his own status as a man. That was the difference between Walter and Gilbret. Walter had to always prove he was stronger. Cleverer. More of everything.

But Gilbret was already sure of who he was and didn't need to prove it. Yes, he wanted to prove he was worthy of the lordship he had been granted, but he would not do that at the expense of others.

"I find that being respected and genuinely cared for kindles a longing in me." Beatrice couldn't look at Cicele as her poor cheeks burned. Where did all this heat come from? Her face had been aflame for hours. Surely the skin would be peeling off.

Once, years ago, she had spent the day at the river and had fallen asleep. When she woke her face was red and within a few days, the skin began to peel. Her face felt as hot as it did then.

"Guyon tells me Gilbret is the best of men, but I thought you were never going to marry?"

It was time to tell Cicele the truth.

When Beatrice finished her story, she watched for Cicele's response. Would she judge her? Probably not.

Mary had brought Edward to the solar while she was in the middle of telling Cicele what had happened to bring her to this point. Now he sat at their feet playing with Amica and Mary. Vite, Cicele's little dog, deigned to let Amica sniff him but refused to join in their play.

Beatrice had decided to stop caring whether Mary heard her story. The girl had become something of a friend and Beatrice trusted her. Besides, the castle gossip would have hatched a story to rival the truth.

"So, now the council will judge whether the annulment was lawful?"

Beatrice just nodded.

"But what new evidence does de Chesney possess?"

"I can't think, but I fear he will seek to destroy me."

"How?"

"I fled my marriage and the annulment was granted on the grounds of my abandoning my husband. I never told Walter I was carrying his child." Beatrice chewed her lips. "I fear his brother, Everlyn, may seek to accuse me of adultery."

Cicele choked on her cup of wine. She put the cup down and leaned forward towards Beatrice. "Why? How?"

"Everlyn wants Edward's inheritance for his own, and as Walter is dead, he is likely to try and persuade his uncle that I am a disgraced woman. If Everlyn succeeds he will have everything."

"But you didn't do it."

Unshed tears pricked at the back of Beatrice's eyes. Cicele's faith in her was touching. But only God knew if it would be enough.

Chapter Twenty-One

Shouts and laughter filled the town square where the Whitsun fête was underway. Beatrice had spent the last two days concentrating on Edward and Amica. A dread had consumed her and she wanted to spend as much time as possible with her son. The nights were reserved for Gilbret. And oh, what nights. Beatrice was sure she wore a constant pink shade on her cheeks. Just thinking about Gilbret and his clever fingers and tongue would result in wave after wave of embarrassment.

Thankfully, Cicele was too polite to say anything. Maude, on the other hand, had made several comments that sent Cicele into fits of laughter. Beatrice didn't quite see the funny side and had to admit to herself at least that she was becoming more and more dour as the day of the council approached.

But today she had sworn to herself that she would put aside all fear for tomorrow and enjoy the Whitsun celebrations.

"They have pax cakes," Gilbret exclaimed as he rushed towards a stall selling small, spiced cakes.

His face was alight with glee as he purchased several of the treats that were only made for this feast day. "Have one," he offered through a mouth full of cake.

"Are you sure you can spare it?"

He looked to the cake he held out to Beatrice and then to the three he held in his other hand. A frown marred his handsome face as he thought about his offer.

"I can spare one, but if you take a liking to them then I shall purchase more."

"Greedy man," Beatrice chided.

"I did warn you. Now take a bite, they are as good as the ones I remember from Barmoor."

Beatrice bit into the cake and immediately her tongue tingled with the taste of spices and the sweetness of currants and honey. She had never tasted anything so delicious.

"Do you require another, my lady?" Gilbret's voice hummed with satisfaction as he watched her consume her little cake.

"Yes, please." It was greedy but, oh, the flavor and texture were too toothsome to resist.

They spent several hours walking around the square watching the jugglers and listening to the troubadours as they recited tales of heroism and the winsome ladies who captured the heros' hearts.

Cicele insisted on taking Edward with her so Beatrice and Gilbret could have some time together enjoying the festivities. Mary was escorted by Olivier. Beatrice watched as Olivier tried to win a honeyed apple for Mary by competing in a skittles game with Guyon. Alas, he was no match for Guyon, who presented Cicele with the tasty trophy.

"What will become of Olivier and Mary?" Beatrice had noticed Mary's reaction towards Olivier but the squire never showed anything other than kind consideration to the little maid.

Gilbret turned to follow Beatrice's gaze. "Olivier cares for her but he has nothing to offer. No land and no security." Gilbret's gaze raked over Beatrice's face, sending hot sparks down her back. "But I fear Mary may have lost her heart to him."

Beatrice did too. Poor Mary. It seemed it was a woman's lot to be hurt by men. No matter if the man was good and honorable. If Beatrice had the future she hoped for then she would ensure that Mary found a man who cherished and loved her as she deserved.

It was a delightful day and Beatrice had managed to keep her vow and only occasionally let her mind wander to the council and the unknown evidence that would be presented.

Thomas, Guyon's sergeant, seemed to have eyes and ears everywhere but even he could not find out what de Chesney would be presenting.

One sadness was that Isabeau couldn't come to Alnwick. Little Ralf had developed a chill and Isabeau did not want to travel. And Ranulf refused to come without his wife.

"I worry about Ralf; it takes so little for a babe to stop thriving." Beatrice was talking to Cicele in the lady's solar before the evening meal. Edward had devoured his gruel and was sleeping. She would wake him later so he could watch the great fire that was to be lit on the common outside the castle walls when darkness fell. It promised to be a festive night and Beatrice wanted Edward to see it.

"Isabeau is unrivaled in her ability with herbs. Ralf will be well soon, I'm sure of it." Cicele's voice was confident but her expression didn't quite match her tone.

Ebeta, a woman Cicele had befriended, was sitting with Maude and Mary as they sewed and spun. There was never a moment when the demand for clothing was not uppermost on any woman's mind, even on a holiday like today.

"Spring colds, what mother doesn't fret about them?" Ebeta said as she sat spinning wool.

"I remember when Edward had a bad chill and I almost lost my mind worrying about him, but Isabeau assured me all would be well. She made thyme and rosemary teas and sometimes applied a salve of thyme and honey to his chest," Beatrice remarked as she remembered how worried she was. So many children died from chills that often turned to putrid throats and fevers.

"It is one thing to care for another's babe, but quite different when it is your own." This was from Maude who had lost her children and husband years before. Ebeta nodded. She too had lost her husband and baby daughter to a fever only two years before.

Beatrice turned to glance at Cicele who had said nothing.

Her cousin looked up and noticed Beatrice watching her. "Do not fret on my account, cousin. I am resolved to not having a child. God knows Guyon and Vite are children enough for any woman." Her tone was light but Beatrice detected the sadness in it all the same.

"Who will be dancing with you this eve, Ebeta," Maude asked as she sat sewing an elaborate piece of clothing.

The change in topic was welcome and drew the conversation in a more playful direction.

Ebeta's cheeks flamed red but she refused to look at anyone as she sat spinning. Her distaff was wedged into the belt around her waist as her hands worked the thread and spindle.

"Thomas likes to dance," Cicele teased.

All the women laughed at Ebeta's discomfort.

"If I was younger, I would be leaping around the great Whitsun fire like a calf in spring," Maude confessed, and with a straight face, no less.

When they had finished laughing at the image Maude's comment conjured, they settled back into silence. It was comfortable and bittersweet.

I might not have the opportunity to sit like this again. Why was she so dispirited? Morose thoughts had been plaguing Beatrice for days and whenever her mind settled to a quiet task the fears would come and steal her peace.

Gilbret and Guyon eventually arrived to escort Beatrice and

Cicele to the table, promising they would feast on the finest of foods.

And to Beatrice's delight, they did. The Whitsun ale she had consumed during the day had increased her appetite. It was the first time since hearing about the council that she was able to eat with relish.

"Your appetite has returned, I see," Gilbret said as he leaned over to whisper in her ear.

"Don't be thinking to take any credit, sir, it was the ale and those little pax cakes."

"And why would I be taking credit for your increased appetite?"

The innocence of his expression made Beatrice hoot with laughter. "Your talent is lost on wielding a sword."

Gilbret gave her a sly smile. "I thought my sword-wielding skill was something you valued." His heated gaze made her skin tingle and burn. If he continued to look at her like that she was likely to combust like a tree hit by lightning—a small pile of ash on the chair would be all that remained of her.

Gilbret caught her mood and offered her a source of amusement throughout the meal. How would she live without him? There was no possibility of him choosing to remain with her if she were accused of adultery. No man in his right mind would stay with a woman convicted of such a crime.

Everlyn's threat the last time she had seen him had been playing on her mind. Would he be so bold as to accuse her and malign himself in the process? "I will see you dead, bitch."

His words stinging just as much now in her memory as they did that dreadful spring day back at Folkingham. Had she done the right thing? Yes. A thousand times, yes.

A light touch to her arm brought her back to the hall and the man sitting next to her.

"Where did you go?"

She shook her head, not understanding Gilbret's question.

"Just now. You were not here enjoying the meal." The concern etched in the corners of his mouth made him look older than his one score and ten years. What had she brought to this honorable man's door?

A desire to tell him about Everlyn's threat wrestled with a deep sense of self-preservation. It seemed that a lifetime of learning to keep herself safe and away from her father or husband's cruelty was too entrenched. Her father had not believed her, and neither had the priest. No, she would bury the ordeal deep inside her and pray Everlyn's empty threats were nothing more than that. Idle.

"I was thinking of a time long ago," she replied as she gave him a small sad smile. At least it was the truth, just not all of it.

Gilbret had taken his gloves off to eat the meal so when he took her hand his skin was warm and comforting. "I will not fail you, Beatrice. This I can promise."

Despite being in a hall full of people Beatrice disengaged her hand from his and cupped his cheek. "I know you believe this, Gilbret, but do not promise what is not within your power."

A puzzled expression marred his handsome face. A face she had come to love. "God, and the council, will determine our fate. And you, my love, will submit to their judgment because that is what you must do to protect Sybilla and Colette."

She had called him "my love." Did he notice? Never had she declared herself to another like she just did to Gilbret. It felt surprisingly freeing to voice her love. If Fate declared that they must part at least she had spoken true.

Gilbret had not taken his eyes from her, but he did take her hand from his cheek and placed her palm on his chest over where his heart beat a steady rhythm. "I am sworn to chivalry and as such, I never make a promise I cannot keep. I will fight and vanquish the demons of hell before I let anything happen to you." His eyes bored into hers. "This I promise."

He held her palm against his chest for several heartbeats, never releasing her from his gaze. Finally, she nodded. Only then did he release her.

They had made a pact at that moment and, God help her, she knew it would be their doom.

SOMETHING WAS WRONG. He could feel it. She was lying. Well, perhaps not lying but she was withholding something. Something that terrified her. He wouldn't force her to tell him. But he suspected he would find out soon enough.

De Chesney was a callous bastard, but Everlyn was a worm from what Thomas had told Gilbret and Guyon that afternoon as they sat in the lord's solar before the evening meal. "He has been spending coin about town inveigling those who might be useful at the council hearing tomorrow." The disdain in Thomas's voice had been a chilling reminder that Everlyn was dangerous.

Gilbret was aware how easy it was to cast a beautiful woman as a temptress. Men never owned their weaknesses. Instead, they laid the blame for their conduct at the feet of women. It was all too easy to cast aspersion on a woman with a beautiful face or a comely body. Men were apt to believe they were victims when it came to cunning and wanton women. The priests had taught for years that Eve, the mother of all women, had tempted Adam, absolving Adam of any responsibility. What horseshit. Men were responsible for their actions.

It was with a sinking heart that he realized Beatrice would not be given the benefit of truth from her accusers. Perhaps that was what was consuming her tonight as she sat next to him, barely able to conceal her growing anxiety.

Hugh de Puiset, the Archbishop of Durham, was a good man but Robert de Chesney was another matter entirely. Beatrice had attracted some powerful enemies and tomorrow would reveal just what those enemies were capable of.

But not tonight. With a resolve honed from years of facing the enemy, Gilbret turned to escort Beatrice from the hall. They followed Guyon and Cicele through the hall and out into the night. They walked in solemn procession towards the Whitsun bonnefyre outside Alnwick's walls.

A great mountain of firewood was set in the middle of a huge area of flat land next to the river. Already many of the townsfolk were there drinking Whitsun ale and sampling the treats from passing hawkers.

Gilbret would dance with Beatrice and they would pretend that tomorrow was just another day. Then later, in the privacy of their chamber, he would take her in his arms and love her till dawn. His groin began to ache as he thought about her body, especially her breasts. By all that was holy, Beatrice's breasts were a revelation. Like the great earth goddess Gaia from whom the Titans sprang, Gilbret imagined he could spend days, weeks, even years exploring Beatrice's body and he would still never come to a knowledge of her.

His body ached in anticipation. He would wait and he would woo his beloved. She had called him "my love" although he pretended he hadn't heard. But he had. And he understood what she had meant.

Did he love her? Yes. But it had crept up on him and it was only as he watched her in the gloaming that he admitted the truth. She was indeed a beauty but it wasn't her face that had captured his heart. No, it was something much deeper, much more profound. As he watched her laughing at something Cicele said he understood what it was. He loved her complexities. Her mind. Her courage. Even when she hid behind her walls and did not allow him in, he knew her to be honest, loving, and true. She would sacrifice herself to save those she loved.

A sudden thought stopped Gilbret mid-stride. Would she sacrifice herself tomorrow to save him? He turned to look at her but she was caught up in the delight of the moment watching Alnwick's people celebrate the Whitsun fire which had just been lit.

A great *whoosh* filled the night as the crowd stood silently to watch the flames engulf the huge pile of wood. Soon the night was like day and people danced around the fire laughing and shouting, but the darkness that descended upon Gilbret was complete.

Understanding dawned as he stood motionless among the crowd.

Turning to Beatrice, he clasped her arm and towed her to the outer edge of the crowd where he could speak to her without yelling over the noise of the revelers.

She stumbled along beside him but didn't resist his rough treatment. An expression of surprise was on her face, but no fear.

Anger had made him more brutish than he intended. "I'm sorry, Beatrice, I didn't mean to be so harsh," he confessed as he released her arm.

"What's wrong?" Her head swiveled around as she tried to discern the threat.

Gilbret took her by the shoulders forcing her to look at him. "Promise me you will say or do nothing tomorrow that would place you in jeopardy."

Her eyes rounded in surprise before narrowing into a squint. "I shall promise no such thing." The set of her jaw told Gilbret all he needed to know.

"What has Everlyn done?"

Her chin tilted fractionally. "I don't know what you are accusing me of, but I don't like it." Her eyes shifted to look at a point past his shoulder.

"Look at me, Beatrice."

She didn't. And Gilbret's heart sank. He had lost her.

Chapter Twenty-Two

The dawn couldn't come soon enough for Beatrice as she lay in her bed listening to Edward's soft snoring. He lay between her and Mary surrounded by pillows to stop either of them from rolling onto him as they slept. Maude had told her the tragic story of a mother who had rolled on her babe during the night and smothered him. Since then, Beatrice had taken particular care to ensure her son was safe in bed. She did not want to give him up to a cot beside the bed. Not yet.

Memories from days long gone scudded across her mind—some happy but most filled with loneliness and fear. "You are not the sum total of your own or others' mistakes." Gilbret's words as she had lain in his arms on their first night together rattled around in her mind.

She had wanted to take comfort from him last night but the burden of today drove her from him and into her own bed. She could not bear the weight of caring for him as well as herself. Shutting him out as he stood at the edge of the crowd last night had been difficult but necessary for her own protection.

She gently gathered a still sleeping Edward into her arms and lay in the darkness. Three things she had cherished in her life—her son, reuniting with her cousins, and her time with Gilbret. What a paltry testimonial to a life of five and twenty. She had regrets but the past two years had been her happiest. She would face today knowing she had finally known what it was to love.

The troubadours sing of what it is to be loved but they were wrong. It is far more life-giving for the soul to give love. It expands the heart's ability to love beyond pain.

Mary stirred and quietly slipped from the bed. Beatrice didn't want to lie abed so she disengaged herself from Edward's little body and kissed his head. Careful to tuck the pillows around him she pulled aside the bed curtains startling Mary who was bending over a clothes chest.

"Oh, m'lady, you startled me," the girl gushed.

"I could not sleep."

Mary nodded but didn't comment.

It was cold in the chamber and the fire was only a small glow so Beatrice took the cloak Mary offered her and walked to the window to watch the dawn.

She both dreaded and welcomed the day. One way or another she would know her fate, and as terrifying as that thought was it also gave her peace. No longer would she be plagued by the fear that her father could hurt Edward.

Isabeau had promised that if anything happened to Beatrice, she would take Edward and raise him. Gilbret had not yet adopted him. Now it was too late. Edward might never have a name of his own. Fate was cruel but men were crueler.

Heaving a sigh, she turned from the window and watched as Mary poured hot water into the basin for Beatrice to wash. Two young girls had arrived with water and were now coaxing the fire into life by adding new wood and coals to the embers. A page deposited Amica and her bed on the hearth next to the fire, where-upon the pup proceeded to scamper about the chamber in excitement. Her exuberance seemed to absorb some of the tension that lay heavy in the chamber's atmosphere.

WASHED, dressed, and having fed Edward, Beatrice kissed his head and handed him to Mary. "I am unsure what to do," she confessed. Unshed tears burned the back of her eyes and her throat seemed to close, making speech difficult.

"All will be well, m'lady," Mary consoled as she took the wriggling little boy from his mother.

Beatrice was bereft when Edward's weight no longer filled her arms so she scooped Amica up off the floor and placed the dog on her knee. The pup squirmed and bit at the rag toy Olivier had given her that first night. "It is good for their teeth." He had looked a little indignant when he had had to explain himself. The little dog tugged at the rag Beatrice held. The tug of war was a little one-sided but the pup didn't seem to notice. Would she be around to discover what Amica's talent was? A ratter seemed the most likely. Such a sense of loss consumed Beatrice that it was difficult to breathe.

Sometime later Beatrice watched as Mary left, taking Edward to the lady's solar where he would play and be doted on by Ebeta and Maude.

Now alone in her chamber with Amica asleep on her knee, Beatrice waited for Gilbret to arrive and accompany her to the abbey and the council. The waiting was interminable but eventually, he arrived.

He took a sleepy Amica from Beatrice's knee and placed her in her small basket. "I will have a page deliver her to the solar."

Beatrice just nodded. Unable to gather any moisture into her mouth, her throat remained closed. She wanted to say so much but her throat conspired against her.

Gilbret took her hand and raised her to her feet. "I understand," he said as he bent forward and brushed a gentle kiss over her lips.

They walked out of the chamber and through the hall in silence until they arrived at the bailey where Cicele waited. Guyon was already mounted and waiting for her.

To her relief no one said anything. What was there to say anyway? Gilbret led her to Clover who was being held by a groom at the mounting block. Without effort, Gilbret clasped her about the waist and lifted her into the saddle. Her skin tingled at his touch and longing began to flow through her limbs. Would she ever feel his arms around her again? She shut that thought down immediately. It would do no good to be distracted. She needed every ounce of concentration to be directed towards her accusers.

Gilbret mounted Maigemor, and Olivier took up his position at the rear. Then the party of four and a small guard rode out of Alnwick's bailey and towards St. Andrew's Priory.

BEATRICE HAD NOT BEEN present at Ranulf and Isabeau's ecclesiastical council hearing but Isabeau had recounted their ordeal in graphic detail so it was with some surprise that the chamber where the council hearing was to take place today was so small. A table sat on a raised dais with only one throne and a smaller chair behind it. It seemed that the Archbishop of Durham and the Bishop of Lincoln were going to be the only judges in the case.

Several clerics were seated behind a table where they would record the details of the hearing. Father Ascelin was already waiting for them as they walked into the chamber.

"My lady, come this way," he said as he gave her a reassuring smile. She looked behind, wondering why Gilbret and Guyon did not follow. "Only you and I are permitted to stand before the council. They will have to stand with the others over there." He indicated to an area behind them and to their left where there were already several people milling about. She spotted her father towards the back of the crowd. Their eyes met but she refused to acknowledge him. He had long ago made it clear that he cared little for her.

Ascelin led her to a table where several parchments lay. At a table to Beatrice's right, Everlyn and his priest stood waiting for the court to begin. Neither acknowledged her; instead they kept their gaze firmly fixed on the dais.

Within a few minutes, a priest whom Beatrice assumed was the prior led a procession of clerics into the chamber. When the archbishop and bishop gained their seats the Prior intoned prayers of blessing and dedicated the court to God's care and justice.

So it began.

Beatrice had seen Hugh de Puiset on several occasions when he had visited Beauforde castle so she turned her eye to Robert de Chesney. The man was tall and thin and wore a sardonic expression that chilled Beatrice to the bone when he cast her a fleeting glance. There was no compassion in his cold blue eyes as he scanned her face. He seemed devoid of any human emotion and yet he was supposed to be an earthly representative of Christ. Beatrice had learned early in life that the God of the scriptures and the men of the church were not always aligned.

She stole a glance to her left. Father Ascelin was, in her mind at least, the epitome of God's representative on earth—his wit, his compassion, and his honor were all characteristics of the God she had come to love. Robert de Chesney's demeanor spoke of a justice that lay in law and not in divine love. A small shudder skittered down her spine. God help her.

Hugh de Puiset's voice echoed off the stone walls of the chamber. For all its size the chamber was ornate with its vaulted ceiling and stained-glass windows. The flagstone floor was swept clean and a large fireplace where a roaring fire burned gave the room a much-needed feeling of warmth.

It was always a surprise to hear such a high voice coming from such a large man. The archbishop's voice might be a surprise but his tone was grave as he immediately came to the point of the court.

"I have read the details of the annulment between Sir Walter de Gant and Lady Beatrice l'Aune and I find that there was insufficient evidence for such an action. The church is very specific when it comes to the husband's responsibility to protect his wife. In this case, it was within Lady Beatrice's right to seek safety for herself and her unborn child. It is my opinion that the church would not sanction such an annulment and that church law would recommend the unlawful annulment overturned. Consequently, Lady Beatrice would be reinstated as Sir Walter de Gant's lawful wife, thus making any fruit from the union legitimate."

Beatrice swayed on her feet. A loud murmur rose from the gathered crowd behind her but the archbishop silenced them with a swift flick of his hand.

"However, His Grace the Bishop of Lincoln informs me that there is new evidence that has come to light so I have asked him to present such evidence before I announce my final judgment."

Beatrice braced herself for the worst.

Robert de Chesney looked directly at her as he spoke. "I invite Sir Everlyn de Gant to produce the new evidence." Was it her imagination or did she see a small smile crease the bishop's lips as he looked at her?

At that moment she understood what a vole must feel like as it hides in the undergrowth summoning the courage to make a dash for safety, only to have the hawk swoop down and snatch it before it reaches its goal.

Beatrice didn't recognize the priest who would act as Everlyn's counsel. Father Ebberard had been Folkingham's priest and the one who had helped her escape Walter's violence. His absence was a harbinger of impending danger.

"Your Graces," the small weasel-faced cleric said as he offered them an obsequious bow. "Sir Everlyn came to me much troubled in conscience and confessed to a grave sin which I am obliged to read to the court." The priest took a moment to unfurl a scroll on the table in front of him and began to read.

"I, Everlyn de Gant confess that on the night of the 9th day of July in the year of Our Lord 1154 I did commit the grievous sin of adultery with my brother's wife—"

The court exploded with noise as shouts of anger and condemnation rang out. Beatrice was so shocked that she could do nothing but stare over at Everlyn. He never took his eyes from his uncle.

The lying maggot. With his confession, he had condemned her to death.

"Silence!" Hugh de Puiset's voice rang out—the shrillness of it cutting through the crowd's enraged shouts.

Hugh de Puiset looked over to where Everlyn stood. The cur had his head bowed in abject humility.

"This is your sworn testimony?" de Puiset asked.

"Yes, Your Grace," Everlyn replied quietly.

It was japery, but the court would interpret Everlyn's penitent act as sincere.

Robert de Chesney smirked as he looked over at Beatrice but it was the archbishop who spoke.

"This is grievous indeed. Father Ascelin, do you wish to question Sir Everlyn?"

Ascelin bowed his head towards the archbishop and then turned his focus on Everlyn. "When did you come to Father Elias and confess this sin?"

Everlyn lifted his head and glanced at Father Ascelin. "When I received word that she had remarried."

"'She' being Lady Beatrice?"

"Yes."

"Why did you not come forward sooner? It has been over two full years since you committed this sin?"

Everlyn glanced at his uncle, who was staring at someone in the crowd. Beatrice turned and spied Gilbret's uncle standing with her father and Father de Wolde. The vultures were circling waiting to pick her life to the bone.

An involuntary shiver snaked down Beatrice's back. She was doomed. Along with Gilbret and his mother and sister. God help them.

Father Ascelin followed her gaze and then turned back to await Everlyn's reply.

Everlyn cleared his throat, the first sign that he was uncomfortable before he replied. "Her whereabouts were unknown. But when I discovered that she had remarried I feared that her new husband may be cuckolded as the lady's beauty is a snare to any man."

"Are you suggesting that Lady Beatrice has committed the sin of adultery with others?"

"It is possible, as she was a temptress where I was concerned."

Beatrice would not stand for this. It was lies all of it, but Ascelin put his hand on her arm to silence her. Begrudgingly she complied but her pulse thundered in her ears as her cheeks burned. She had not only been publicly denounced as an adulteress but accused of other affairs. All her worst nightmares had come to pass. There was to be no justice.

"Lady Beatrice, how would you answer this charge?" Father Ascelin asked in a strong confident tone.

She looked straight at Hugh de Puiset as she answered. "I am innocent of the charges. Never, upon my mortal soul, have I broken my marriage vows." Grateful her voice didn't betray her terror, she held her head high but lowered her gaze lest the archbishop believed her too forward.

"This is your sworn testimony?" Hugh de Puiset asked her.

"Yes, Your Grace."

"Sir Everlyn, given the extraordinary length of time it has taken you to come forward, I can only assume that you must have confessed to your sin earlier. Our beloved Father Ebberard, God rest his soul, would have acted on such evidence if you had truly been concerned for your mortal soul and made your confession. Therefore, I am inclined to believe that some other inducement has made you come forward."

There was an audible gasp from the crowd behind Beatrice as the archbishop made his remark. Was she to be believed over the word of a knight?

Hugh de Puiset raised his hand for silence. "The church is very clear in matters of adultery. Unless you have further evidence to support your claim, I am of a mind to grant my initial ruling and revoke the annulment."

"I can give a sworn testimony, Your Grace," Father de Wolde's voice rang out.

Hugh de Puiset indicated for him to come forward. "Well, Father, what have you to say?" There was a clear note of dislike in the archbishop's tone.

"I heard Sir Everlyn's confession when I traveled to Folkingham for the funeral of Father Ebberard. He was in great pain and turmoil of spirit. I granted absolution; his penance was to make a pilgrimage to Tynemouth Priory where he would toil with the Benedictine monks there for one month."

"No!" Beatrice couldn't stop herself. The words were out of her mouth before she even had time to think. Such was her outrage.

The chamber erupted into chaos. Shouts and calls for her death rang out. If Ascelin hadn't put his arm around her shoulders she would have fallen to the floor.

"I am doomed," she moaned as she leaned into Ascelin's shoulder. All was lost. No one would dare refute a priest's sworn testimony.

Chapter Twenty-Three

Gilbret stood motionless. All the air in the chamber seemed to evaporate. His lungs burned with the need for air but he couldn't seem to make his chest move. The shit-eating cur was lying. By God's splintered cross he had all but consigned Beatrice to death. His pious act was just that. An act.

Everything in Gilbret wanted to rush to her when she fainted but Guyon restrained him.

"Use your wits, man, and think!" Guyon had counseled. "You can't go rushing to her yet."

It was good advice but he didn't want Beatrice to think that he believed the vile lie.

Stupid, stupid fucking dolt. He should have acted on his gut reaction to the priest when he met him at Beauforde. But Gilbret had never considered that the priest could be so dangerous. Now, de Wolde stood there with Beatrice's accusers. Beatrice was lost and his mother and sister would live out their days in poverty and shame. And what of Barmoor and its people? His people. His uncle was not worthy of them.

"He lies." Guyon's voice barely penetrated the mayhem in Gilbret's mind.

"I said, 'He lies.'" This time Guyon's tone was more a growl and it got Gilbret's attention.

"What?" He couldn't think and he certainly couldn't fathom what Guyon was saying.

"Don't tell me you believe the worm?" Guyon inclined his chin in de Wolde's direction. I have had dealings with the man for some time and he would sell his soul for silver. He has been paid, you idiot."

"Of course, I don't fucking believe him," Gilbret spat. "But it doesn't matter what I believe. He's a priest and his word will stand."

"Are you saying that priests don't lie?" Guyon snarled. "Remember last year when Hexham tried to have Ranulf destroyed? De Puiset never doubted Ranulf over Hexham."

Finally, reason dawned and Gilbret was able to think clearly. Guyon was right. The king and the archbishop never doubted Ranulf because they knew him and knew Ranulf's half-brother, the Bishop of Hexham, for the snake he was. But did de Puiset know de Wolde well enough to believe him?

Gilbret glanced over to where de Wolde stood next to another man Gilbret did not recognize.

"That's Beatrice's worm-ridden father with de Wolde. They both sprang from Satan's arsehole.

"De Puiset may not know Beatrice, but those two turds are worthless. I'll make sure he believes that."

Gilbret glanced back at Guyon and Thomas. Both men wore the same expression of deep mistrust as they stared over at the two men on the opposite side of the chamber.

If Guyon and Thomas already knew l'Aune and de Wolde were worthless curs, surely to God de Puiset also knew de Wolde was an arse-wipe.

Gilbret thought about Beatrice's evasion and fear the previous evening. She was hiding something and he needed to know what. If she knew anything that might help expose Everlyn and de Wolde as the liars they were then he had to find out.

"I need to talk with my wife. Now!"

Guyon nodded, then strode forward to where Ascelin and Beatrice stood before the dais.

Hugh de Puiset had waited for the uproar in the chamber to settle, which it did, as Guyon spoke quietly to Ascelin.

Noticing Guyon, de Puiset motioned towards him. "My lord, you wish to address the court?"

Guyon bowed his head in respect. "As the High Sheriff it is my duty to deal with treason and in the case of adultery, it is a treasonable act against the husband. Therefore, I respectfully request that this matter be heard as a civil case."

"What do you suggest?" de Puiset asked.

"I would ask Your Grace to dismiss the charges of adultery from this court so that I might begin proceedings against the charges as befits a civil law court. It is my opinion that Sir Gilbret de la Haye, Baron Wooler, has been grievously injured by the accusation that his wife is an adulterer."

Hugh de Puiset nodded his assent. "You are right to assert your jurisdiction in civil matters. Perhaps we might meet on St. Barnabas day?"

"I am sorry, Your Grace, but I shall be gone from Alnwick within the next two weeks. I would have no objection if we convened a court as we speak."

Guyon took a huge risk but Gilbret prayed it would pay off.

"I, too, have no wish to prolong the proceedings. Might I suggest you join me on the bench and continue the proceedings here?"

Guyon bowed his head in a show of respect but Gilbret understood exactly what was happening. By insisting the charges be heard as a civil case Guyon, with the help of Hugh de Puiset, had outmaneuvered Robert de Chesney. Now Guyon could steer the court away from Beatrice and focus on undermining de Gant and de Wolde. Clever, very clever.

"Thank you, Your Grace. I accept." Guyon walked to the bench and waited for Robert de Chesney to vacate his chair. The bishop's face was the color of granite as he walked from the dais to stand with his nephew.

Guyon leaned over and spoke to de Puiset, who nodded in agreement.

"The court is adjourned for one hour," de Puiset announced before rising from his throne and walking with Guyon towards a side door.

Now Gilbret turned his attention to Beatrice. She was pale but had recovered from the shock sufficiently to stand straight. She needed to know he trusted her absolutely. As he walked towards her she refused to meet his gaze.

"We need to talk." He wanted to comfort her. To reassure her he didn't believe the vile accusation but his tone conveyed anger, not comfort. Her body trembled as he took her by the arm and escorted her from the chamber. Ascelin and Thomas were close behind.

Gilbret found a small alcove not far from the chamber. It offered a minimal amount of privacy but it would have to do. He gently steered Beatrice into it.

Everything in Gilbret wanted to yell at her. Not because he believed she was an adulteress but because she was hiding something and that put her at risk. Forcing himself to remain calm his next words would determine the future so he chose them carefully.

"Will you look at me, Beatrice?" he asked as his hand hovered near her face. He wanted to touch her, to reassure her, but she was too fragile for that so he let his hand fall to his side.

When she continued to look to her hands rather than him he continued.

"I do not believe Everlyn, my love, but his testimony has a ring of truth so you need to trust us," he said as he indicated to Ascelin and Thomas. Olivier stood behind them making sure no one approached.

Beatrice slowly raised her face and looked at him. She didn't say anything for several heartbeats making Gilbret think she might not reply. Finally, she gave him a small nod and wet her lips with the tip of her tongue. That small nervous gesture made his chest ache as his hands reached to take hers.

"I feared this," she said in a small voice. "He said he would see me dead and he has all but succeeded."

"He has done no such thing," Gilbret snarled, "but you must tell us the truth."

Beatrice glanced past Gilbret to look at Ascelin and Thomas before returning her gaze to Gilbret. "On that night. The 9th day of July," she said as she shuddered. "Walter had struck me and I fled to the stables to be alone but Everlyn followed me. He had only just arrived back from business in Normandy and was shocked at his brother's behavior towards me." She huffed a small derisive laugh. "He was kind and offered me words of comfort but I didn't trust him. Walter and Everlyn were not close but they had been laughing and drinking most of the morning after hunting. I didn't want to make matters worse with Walter, so I said that he should return to Walter and asked him to leave me alone." She glanced up then and Gilbret was struck by the beseeching look in her eyes. She was silently pleading with him to believe her. "He was drunk and tried to force himself on me so I hit him with the only object at hand. An oil lamp."

Gilbret was so angry he began to shake with rage. Immediately, Beatrice backed away trying to disengage herself from his hold. His grip on her was fierce and he couldn't release her. Terror-filled eyes brimming with tears looked back at him but he couldn't make his body react. He was hurting her but he couldn't control his own body.

"Gilbret, let her go." It was Ascelin's calm authoritative voice that finally penetrated his rage-induced inertia.

He dropped her hands as though stung. "Forgive me, I ..." he babbled as he took a step back.

"Olivier, see if you can find some wine," Thomas said as he laid a hand on Gilbret's shoulder.

Gilbret couldn't look at Beatrice. Shame scorched his face making his skin tingle as sweat trickled down the side of his face and neck. What had he done?

They remained silent while Olivier fetched some wine. When he returned there was only one cup. "It was all I could find," he apologized as he handed the cup to Beatrice. She took a small sip and then handed it to Gilbret. His hand touched hers as he took the cup and their eyes met. "Beatrice, I ..."

She gave him a small sad smile. "He called me loathsome names, not even Walter had used such vile language, and told me I had tempted him—a succubus who preyed on men." She looked broken as she stood there surrounded by the three men.

Silently he vowed to make it right. Gilbret didn't move as he didn't want to frighten her but he could speak now that his rage had subsided. "I believe you, and I swear on all that is holy he will pay for his."

"How? The priest's testimony is as God's words."

Gilbret didn't know. He racked his brain thinking about legal precedent. All the years of serving Ranulf and dealing with courts meant he had a good understanding of the law. There had to be a way. If only he could think.

"There is a way, but it's dangerous and I'm not sure it is wise," Thomas said as he stood beside Gilbret.

Three pairs of eyes turned as one and stared at Thomas in silent invitation. "Wager by combat," he said as he met Gilbret's eye.

"No!" Beatrice turned on Thomas with a scowl that would turn a knight's bowels to liquid. "No."

Gilbret's mind raced. It might work. Yes, it was a risk, but it might work. He turned to Thomas. "Explain the terms." Gilbret understood the precepts of the trial by combat but he needed to understand all the ramifications if he was to challenge de Gant's word.

"You must challenge his word. Call him a liar. If he refuses to rescind his allegation against Lady Beatrice then make a challenge for God to judge who is in the right.

"It can only be used in a civil case. But once you have extended the challenge, de Gant has only two options. Rescind or accept."

"But if you fail, you condemn not only yourself to death but also Beatrice," Ascelin said as he looked from Thomas to Gilbret.

"I will not fail," Gilbret pronounced with all the conviction of a knight sworn to a holy crusade.

"You cannot do this, Gilbret," Beatrice pleaded. "Please don't risk eternal damnation. I am not worthy of such a sacrifice."

Gilbret had to shake his head to dispel Beatrice's words. "You are my wife. And that turd—forgive me—would have you maimed or burned for adultery based on a lie. Beatrice, I cannot let that happen. I will see him cut down and fed to the crows for daring to touch you and calling you a whore." He implored her to understand it was the only way.

"If Gilbret doesn't try then you are already condemned, my lady, and will likely die at the stake." Thomas's chilling words cut like a knife into Gilbret's heart.

"God is on the side of truth, my love, please trust me." Gilbret took her hands in his. "It is the only way."

Tears ran down her face and he brushed them away with his thumb. "Trust me," he whispered into her ear as his lips caressed her cheek and chin.

Beatrice had no other option but to accept. De Gant had made sure of that, but Gilbret would not force her. She had to decide their fate.

"I cannot let you sacrifice yourself for me. Think of your mother and sister."

"My mother and sister will be homeless if you die, Beatrice. My father's will stipulates I must marry before Lammas. If they are to have any chance to live in freedom and dignity then I must fight for your honor."

"But Lammas is still a month away," she argued. "You still have time."

His hand cupped her cheek. "I don't want another wife. I chose you. I love you, Beatrice."

"This is all very touching, but the court is due to reassemble." Thomas's voice was an unwelcome one, but he spoke true.

"We are out of time, my love. You must decide. You know what I wish."

Her eyes delved deep into his searching for any hint of uncertainty but she would find none. He was unequivocal. He would save her or die trying.

She must have seen his determination for she leaned in and kissed his lips. "If we are to die, we will die together," she whispered against his mouth.

Gilbret took her mouth in a fierce kiss that sealed their fate.

"So be it," he announced.

They walked back into the chamber together. God, and Gilbret's sword arm, would determine their fate.

Chapter Twenty-Four

"Sir Everlyn de Gant is a perjurer and I demand he rescind his vile allegation." Gilbret didn't bother looking at de Gant; instead, he kept his eyes steady on Guyon who sat with the archbishop on the dais. Guyon's eyes widened for a moment, then he nodded.

"Sir Everlyn, Sir Gilbret has accused you of lying. How do you answer this?"

De Gant's smile was smug as he glanced at Gilbret from across the chamber before returning to look at Guyon. "I have given my oath to this court and what I speak, I speak in truth."

Gilbret took two steps forward and in a clear voice delivered his life, and that of his wife and family, into Fate's hands. "Everlyn de Gant is a liar and has maligned my wife. I, therefore, challenge him to a trial by combat. God will decide who speaks the truth." He thought his voice might betray him but to his relief his voice held and his fate was set.

Guyon showed no sign of surprise. He was one of the most astute men Gilbret had ever known. A civil court was the only court that allowed trial by combat. The church might have subjected

Beatrice to trial by ordeal, but she would have died proving her innocence. Guyon had maneuvered the court into accepting this outcome.

"Sir Everlyn de Gant, how do you respond?" Guyon's voice rang out through the now silent chamber. Everyone present waited. The gathered crowd of clerics and knights smelled blood and would relish the entertainment of a duel.

Gilbret had thrown his glove on the floor before the dais. If Everlyn accepted the challenge he would pick it up. If he refused the challenge, then he would be deemed guilty and die alongside Beatrice as an adulterer.

Gilbret had to give de Gant his due; the knight strolled towards the center of the chamber as though he were going for a leisurely amble in the gardens before bending to retrieve the glove. The man was arrogant and, hopefully, his hubris would play into Gilbret's hand.

Gilbret and Everlyn now stood shoulder to shoulder before Guyon and the archbishop. "On the morrow at dawn, you will attend a mass here at the Priory, then proceed to the common where you shall both fight to the death. No quarter is to be given. Whoever is victorious is deemed to speak the truth and judged by God." Guyon then turned his gaze towards Beatrice. "Lady Beatrice you will sit in a chair under which a pyre shall be constructed. There you will wait for God's determination. Do you agree to this?"

Beatrice walked with her head high and her spine straight until she stood beside Gilbret. "I do, my lord. For God will prove me innocent."

"Very well, it is done." Guyon dismissed the court as men rushed about to begin the preparations for a duel to the death. Whitsun's week-long holiday would ensure that every available person would be present to witness the duel. Villeins and nobles alike would stand shoulder to shoulder to witness God's judgment.

The die was cast and Gilbret would not regret his decision. He would win and make sure Everlyn de Gant regretted ever touching Beatrice.

Guyon and Hugh de Puiset left the chamber to murmurs from the crowd. Carpenters and laborers would spend the day and most of the night constructing a stand for Guyon and the archbishop to sit on and watch the duel. The area designated for the duel was not that large so most would stand and watch.

"I will slice you from your cock to your mouth," Everlyn snarled, "And then watch your whore burn."

Gilbret felt Beatrice shudder beside him so he reached out his left hand and placed it at her back. Ignoring Everlyn, he turned towards Beatrice and escorted her to where Thomas and Ascelin stood.

"You will need meat and light training. Ascelin will escort Lady Beatrice back to the castle," Thomas said. "But you will come with me."

Gilbret wanted to talk with Beatrice but she was already being led away by Ascelin.

"She will do better with women's company, my friend, and you need to concentrate. I have found a squire who can give us some insight into Everlyn's tactics."

Gilbret turned from watching Beatrice's retreating back and faced Thomas. "He is willing?"

Thomas gave him a feral grin. "Whores and ale work a treat."

Guyon's man was many things, but his real talent lay in his ability to gather intelligence and then use that information to assist Guyon, or in this case Gilbret.

Gilbret turned to look for Olivier but his squire was nowhere to be seen.

"Olivier is keeping an eye on our squire," Thomas said anticipating Gilbret's unspoken question. "Your young squire shows potential."

"Potential?" Gilbret asked.

Thomas barked a laugh as they strode out of the priory and back towards the stables. "Olivier has the patience and stealth to be everywhere and yet never noticed." Thomas gave Gilbret a direct look. "You would do well to use that skill in what remains of the day."

Gilbret nodded. He had been trained to meet danger head-on. That approach required strength and very little subtlety but there was a new breed of men like Thomas who lingered in the shadows watching and listening. Guyon had told Gilbret that Thomas's network of spies ran the length and breadth of England and Normandy. Such information was worth a fortune and Guyon took advantage of it.

Gilbret thought about what Thomas had said as they rode the short distance back into the town. They reached a tavern with tables out in front where a buxom barmaid poured ale for a lad who sat opposite Olivier. Thomas and Gilbret dismounted in the ally across the street and watched as the lad, the bum-fluff on his chin giving him away, fondled the tits of a very comely whore who sat on his knee.

Olivier sat opposite. Even from where he stood Gilbret could see that Olivier was pretending to be drunk while the lad was too occupied with his prize to notice the presence of danger.

Thomas and Gilbret watched for several minutes before Thomas walked casually towards the lads. Plonking himself down next to the squire, Thomas flicked a coin at the whore, dismissing her. Everlyn's squire was about to usher a challenge until he saw Thomas sitting next to him. The lad paled and shot a look at Olivier, who was sitting straight and alert.

Gilbret joined the table and waited. The boy seemed to understand immediately as his head swiveled first to Thomas and then to Gilbret.

"I suggest you sit quietly and hear what we have to say," Thomas said almost conversationally.

The squire nodded as his eyes darted about frantically.

"Your master is going to die on the morrow and you will be in need of another. Help us and I will see that you have a place in Lord Alnwick's guard.

The lad's eyes widened at his good fortune.

"Drink and I will talk," Thomas said as he pushed a cup of ale towards the lad and let him drink his fill before he continued.

"Your master, Sir Everlyn de Gant, what are his tactics?" Thomas asked. "And don't think to deceive us; this man will know if you speak the truth." Thomas indicated towards Gilbret.

The lad nodded and proceeded to spill his guts.

An hour later Gilbret was satisfied that he knew how to approach tomorrow's duel.

"That was the most productive hour I have ever spent in an alehouse," Gilbret said as they walked towards the pele yard where they would train until the afternoon meal.

"Productive?" Olivier said with a sour note to his tone. "I was hoping Mattie might show me just how productive it could have been."

"Youth. It's wasted on the young," Thomas teased as he slapped Olivier on the back. "Mattie has a burly husband who would gut you alive if your pecker got anywhere near her."

"She's one of yours?" Olivier asked in an astonished tone.

Gilbret was once again reminded of just how young Olivier was. Perhaps he would ask the lad if he wanted to work with Thomas for a time. As Baron Wooler, Gilbret could use someone with Thomas's skill and it would give Olivier a chance to develop his obvious aptitude as a spy.

If all went as planned and if God and Fortuna were on his side, then Gilbret would discuss it with Olivier.

They arrived at the pele yard to see men already training but as they approached, the men stopped and began clearing a square so Gilbret and Thomas could spar.

"I shall be his partner," Guyon's voice called from behind them.

"Go easy on him, lord, he has to have enough strength to fight that maggot tomorrow," Thomas said as he moved aside so Guyon could enter the yard.

It had been years since Guyon and Gilbret had trained together. Once Guyon struck the first blow, Gilbret remembered just how brutal Guyon could be. Shutting out every noise and thought that might distract him, Gilbret fought for his life.

CICELE WAS PACING the solar as Beatrice entered. She ignored her cousin and went immediately to where Edward was playing with Amica. The pup was pulling on the toy rag that Edward was holding. When the pup dropped it, Edward dangled it in front of her again and the pup would pounce on it sending Edward into squeals of laughter. Beatrice watched her son playing as Mary sat next to him on the floor. Content to watch, Beatrice savored the moment.

It was difficult not to give in to despair but she willed herself to keep calm as she observed her son. There was no point in dissolving into hysterics. If Gilbret failed on the morrow Isabeau and Cicele would ensure that Edward was raised with love and given a future. But what of her son's reputation? The bastard son of an adulterer. An involuntary shudder wracked her body. What had she done?

Her actions had condemned Gilbret to an ignoble death and her son to a shameful future. Beatrice had never regretted her decision to leave Walter, or shun Everlyn's advances, until this moment. If she had stayed, she would have averted all this. But then she would have endured Walter's fists and Edward might have suffered the same fate as her first child.

No, it had never been an option to stay once she knew she was with child again. And Gilbret. Never had she imagined the joy that could be found with a man.

Her father, then Walter and Everlyn, had convinced her that all men were like them, but Gilbret had shown her that what she had believed was in fact a lie. Gilbret's words echoed in her mind: "Not all men are those men." She hadn't understood when he first said it but now, she did.

As she watched Edward and Amica play, she realized that she did believe it. Guyon, Ranulf, Thomas, and even Olivier were all men she could trust. Gilbret had given her that and if she were to die tomorrow, she knew that Edward would be raised to be such a man. That was what she had prayed for when she fled Folkingham. And as she watched her son play she knew her prayers had been answered.

"Come, sit by the fire and tell us what has transpired." Cicele looked at Beatrice with such an intensity that it was obvious her cousin knew what had transpired.

"To speak true, I do not think I have the will to tell it."

"Come and sit," Circle urged her. "We will talk of other things."

Beatrice appreciated her cousin's efforts but to sit and speak of trivial things was worse than speaking of the unthinkable.

"Gilbret called Everlyn a liar and challenged him to a duel by combat."

Cicele's gaze pinned Beatrice to the floor but there was no shock on her face. However, there was an audible gasp from the other three women in the solar. Ebeta sat spinning. Maude was sewing a chemise while Mary mended the hem of one of Beatrice's gowns, but they all stopped in their labors to look over at Beatrice who stood next to Cicele in front of the hearth.

Edward must have tired from his game because he crawled over to where Beatrice stood and demanded to be held. She scooped him up in her arms, inhaling his smell. Her heart threatened to break but she forced the emotion down. She would not mar this last day with tears. "You are my beautiful boy," she crooned as she kissed his cheek.

Amica was not to be outdone and scampered about the room, seeking attention. Vite sprang at her and the two dogs wrestled as the women watched. Edward liked the look of the new game and demanded to be put down.

Vite, Cicele's little black dog, darted about the room teasing Amica and stopped to lick Edward's face as he whizzed past Edward who was sitting on his rump watching the game. Laughter filled the solar and Beatrice let it soothe her shattered emotions. Whether it was tomorrow or when she was a frail old woman, she would cherish this memory for the rest of her life.

Chapter Twenty-Five

It was agreed that Beatrice would take her evening meal in the lady's solar. The hall would be abuzz with gossip about the duel and it was the last thing Beatrice wanted to endure.

Edward was settled and in bed with Mary, which gave Beatrice time to herself as she sat in front of the fire. Her mind couldn't settle on anything—wool, staff, and spindle lay at her feet in a basket. Amica was curled on her knee snuffling in her sleep. The little dog's weight was a comfort to Beatrice.

Quietly the solar door opened. Beatrice didn't need to turn to know who entered.

Her body tensed and her toes curled in her slippers as Gilbret walked into the chamber and sat beside her.

She was grateful he didn't spout mindless words of comfort. She had had her fill of well-meant but inane comments. "All will be well." "The truth will prevail." Yes, they were all charitable and kind but they filled Beatrice with dread.

There were no guarantees. No assurance that Gilbret would be victorious. Everlyn was a knight with a fearsome reputation who would give no quarter to Gilbret.

And Gilbret. Her beautiful, loving, funny Gilbret didn't possess the vicious streak that Everlyn had and would undoubtedly wield to great effect.

Without speaking, they both sat and watched the fire.

Finally, Gilbret broke the silence. "I do not regret one moment or the decisions that have brought us to this place."

Beatrice turned to look at him. Conviction and determination were reflected in his deep brown eyes. Never had she seen him wear such an intense expression. "I have come to love you, Beatrice, and my life is bound to yours."

She couldn't reply. A great lump was lodged in her throat but she reached out her hand and took his in a fierce hold. Her scalp tingled and her skin was on fire. She wanted him.

Without speaking, she rose pulling him with her.

When he faced her, she let go of his hand and pulled him towards her taking his mouth in a kiss that singed her skin.

He responded immediately, taking the kiss deeper. Her breasts were pressed into his chest as he pulled her closer. Their need, their passion, whipped them into a frenzy of kisses. The pressure was almost impossible to endure.

"God's bones, woman, you drive me witless," Gilbret gasped as he broke their kiss.

Gilbret strode to the door and bolted it, then returned to take Beatrice in a possessive embrace. "I want you," he moaned into her ear as he peppered kisses over her chin and neck. A trail of fire was left on her skin as he licked and nipped the swell of her breasts.

Moaning, she responded. Hitching her kirtle up, she leaned against the table, giving herself to him in a way that would have made her blush a week ago.

Gilbret's eyes blazed with desire as he drank in the view she presented to him. Grabbing at his clothing, it was a matter of heartbeats before he was inside her, taking them both to a place where Everlyn de Gant did not exist and death was banished. They moved as one and both screamed their release as they reached their climax together.

Beatrice leaned into Gilbret trying to regain her breath. "That was …" There were no words for what they had both experienced.

One heart.

One mind.

One body. Death itself would not separate them. That was the commitment their bodies had made to each other and Beatrice was thankful. Whatever happened on the morrow she would take Gilbret with her.

Gilbret broke their bond and Beatrice felt empty and forlorn as he slid out of her. He walked over to where a pitcher of water and a stack of linen cloths were kept. He rinsed one and brought it back to her.

"No!"

He looked at her somewhat startled by her brusque tone.

"I want you with me as I sit and await our fate."

He nodded his understanding and put the cloth on the table, unused.

When they had their clothing rearranged into some semblance of order, he unbolted the solar door, then he poured them some wine. Beatrice nestled into his lap. Her head rested on his shoulder. "I love you so much it hurts," she confessed as she sat curled in his embrace. They shared the same cup, sipping wine and settling into a comfortable silence.

Her heart was breaking but if Gilbret was to face his enemy with such stoic determination, then she too would show no weakness. No weeping. No regret.

Finally, Gilbret lifted her off his knee. "You, my love, must sleep," he said as he kissed the top of her head.

"And you?"

"Oh, I will sleep and dream of you," he growled as he gave her a smile that made her skin tingle and her toes curl.

"We will not be able to meet in the morning but know this … I will fight for you until my last breath." His eyes burned into hers, searing her very soul.

She reached up and touched the scar on his chin. "You are the best man I have ever known and your skill and heart will be enough."

He led her out of the chamber, Amica's basket over her arm, and into her own suite on the upper floor of the tower.

"Sleep well, my love," he said as he kissed her. Then he turned and walked away.

She wanted to call him back. To cling to him but she couldn't be that selfish. His back was straight and his hands clenched at his sides. Any sign of weakness on her part and he would crumble. She would not fail. She owed him that.

GILBRET DIDN'T GO BACK to his room but made his way to Guyon's solar where Guyon and Thomas were waiting for him.

When he entered and had sat in front of the fire, Guyon set out the plan for the following day.

"If you fail …"

"I won't fucking fail."

Guyon ignored him. "I have instructed Thomas to give Beatrice a tonic."

"A tonic?" Gilbret was confused. And angry. He couldn't afford to entertain the prospect of failing. And resented that Guyon had mentioned it.

"A tonic so she will feel no pain," Thomas said in a diffident tone.

Gilbret was a little dull-witted while his body still thrummed with pleasure from his passionate lovemaking. It took him a few moments to realize what Thomas and Guyon were trying to tell him. "The pyre?"

Both men nodded at his question.

Beatrice would burn if he died. Guyon and Thomas were thinking of Beatrice. Giving her a tonic so she didn't experience the pain of such a horrific death was not only compassionate, it was illegal. They were taking a huge risk and he was humbled by it. "I am sorry. Forgive me."

Guyon stood and slapped Gilbret on the back. "Don't. You have done nothing to seek forgiveness. You risk more. And it is the least we can do to assuage your fears."

They drank in silence for several moments. The crackle and hiss of the fire was the only noise in the chamber.

Finally, Guyon moved to stand in front of the hearth to stare into the flames.

"What?" Something was wrong.

Thomas spoke. "I have to escort you to the barracks."

"I am to be imprisoned?" Gilbret was so surprised he barely grasped Thomas's meaning.

"Both you and Everlyn are to be kept under guard. I thought my chamber was a better alternative to the cells where Everlyn will spend the night."

"Poor bastard," Guyon said with a grin that showed not one whit of sympathy.

"Satan's cods, I'm pleased neither of you is my enemy." Guyon and Thomas were formidable and although Everlyn would sleep he would not enjoy the experience. They had given Gilbret one small advantage that could sway tomorrow's outcome and Gilbret was grateful for it.

"I can't vouch that Thomas's bed is any better than what Everlyn will sleep on. It's probably riddled with fleas or lice, but it is the best I can do." Guyon sneered.

"Don't forget the rats." Thomas laughed and gulped the last of his wine. "Now, my friend, it's time for you to retire," he said as he looked at Gilbret.

Gilbret was almost to the door when Guyon called him back. "I will do what I can for Beatrice and I will keep Edward safe. And Ranulf will ensure Sybilla and Colette, along with Cheldric, have a place at Beauforde. I give you my oath." Guyon's dark eyes blazed with silent resolve. It was a relief to know that little Edward would be raised by family. Ranulf would ensure his mother and sister were safe inside Beauforde's walls. There was nothing more to do except sleep and pray that God and Fortuna were in accord.

Chapter Twenty-Six

It was the silence that made her skin crawl. Even the birds didn't make a sound. The crowd had fallen silent as soon as she entered the area where the duel would take place and led to the scaffold where she would sit and watch her husband live or die.

As she mounted the steps, they creaked under her weight. It was a tall platform with a chair in the center of the floor at the top. A high railing enclosed the space. Below were hundreds of faggots that would ignite in a blaze of flame burning her alive in moments.

From such a high vantage point she would witness every detail of the duel. Even the platform where the archbishop and Guyon sat wasn't as high. Her stomach cramped as she sat on the chair. Thomas was to be her guard and for that she was grateful. Whatever happened he would be considerate.

It wasn't only the fear of losing Gilbret but the fear of burning that terrified her. She had seen the castle stables burn when she was a girl. The screams from the terrified grooms and horses as the flames engulfed them had given her nightmares for years.

"All will be well, Lady," Thomas whispered as he bent to tie her arms and legs to the chair. There was now no escape.

Cicele had made her drink some warm spiced wine this morn before she left her chamber. Her cousin had put a large quantity of chamomile in it to help soothe Beatrice's nerves. "You will drink this; do you hear me?" Cicele was tyrannical when she wanted to be and Beatrice had complied without protest. In truth, she appreciated her cousin's consideration. The effects of the herb and wine were calming her stomach if not her mind.

Finally, the archbishop and Guyon, accompanied by a large group of retainers, made their way to the platform constructed for them. Cicele gave Beatrice a small nod as she seated herself next to her husband. From where Beatrice sat, she could see her cousin clearly. Cicele kept glancing over at her and giving her small nods of encouragement. Far to the left sat the Bishop of Lincoln, her father, and Father de Wolde. Even from this distance Beatrice noticed the rigid set of her father's jaw. If Everlyn failed, then they would also be shamed and shunned for supporting a perjurer.

The priests had placed a small altar in the center of the ground where Gilbret and Everlyn would kneel and swear their oaths. Once the oaths were done the altar was removed and the priests scurried away.

Now Guyon's herald and sergeant of arms walked out into the center of the huge area where Gilbret and Everlyn would fight. The crowd roared their approval. Their hunger for blood would be met this day. Beatrice took a moment to eye the crowd gathered on three sides of the ground. They were held back by a wooden rail and men at arms stood at intervals of three paces. No one would be able to rush into the arena and disrupt the duel.

Beatrice estimated that the crowd must have started gathering before dawn as there were well over a hundred men, women, and children keenly peering into the area where the two knights would fight to the death. Nobles dressed in fine clothes and accompanied by their squires mingled with townsfolk, villeins, and clerics. The Whitsun celebrations usually lasted a full week giving the people a much-needed break from their usual toil. Today every available person would be present to see the spectacle.

"My lords, Your Grace, ladies, and people of Alnwick, we are here to witness a duel where the victor will be chosen by God. On pain of death, you are forbidden to offer support by deed or weapon. On pain of death, you are to offer no distraction to the two knights."

There was not a sound as all eyes were trained on the herald.

Suddenly he shouted, "Faites dos devoirs!" "Do your duty!" three times as required by law so that all could hear.

The crowd erupted in a mighty cheer as the herald left and the marshal entered with two squires leading Gilbret and Everlyn, who were mounted on their horses, into the arena. Gilbret wore a blue surcoat while Everlyn wore yellow. Their mail shone in the early morning sun sending shards of light in every direction. Both men held their great helms under their arms.

The knights rode their horses into the center of the arena and bowed before the dais where Guyon and the archbishop sat. The herald read the charges and defense and then made the men join hands to make their vows.

"What are they doing?" Beatrice asked Thomas, who stood to her right.

"They are making oaths that their weapons have no magic attached to them and that they will fight fair."

"I thought they had already made their oaths." Beatrice was a little confused that they would have to make oaths for a second time.

"The first oaths were of a spiritual nature, now the oaths are about their weapons, but make no mistake, Lady, there will be no quarter and no 'fair' fighting. Both men will do whatever it takes to kill the other."

Beatrice shuddered at the thought of Gilbret enduring such a fight. Usually, a duel was conducted according to a code of chivalry and valor, but not today.

Now that the men had concluded their oath-taking, they rode to opposite sides of the arena and dismounted.

"Are they not going to fight on horseback?" Once again Beatrice was confused. Knights always rode into battle.

"Gilbret chose to fight with sword alone."

Thomas's brief statement caused a chill to run down Beatrice's spine. Everlyn was a skilled knight and would be a formidable opponent.

Once dismounted, their squires fastened helms on each man's head and handed them their shields, then led their horses away and the gates were bolted. The sergeant of arms walked to the gate and stood guard. No one would be able to enter or exit.

The crowd looked to the marshal, who held a glove high over his head. Almost immediately he threw it forward. As it sailed through the air he shouted the customary command, "Laissez-les aller!" "Let them go!" Before the glove hit the ground and the marshal had shouted the command for the third time, Gilbret and Everlyn unsheathed their swords and advanced on each other.

Sweat pebbled on Beatrice's upper lip but her hands were tied and she couldn't wipe it away. A wave of nausea almost had her gagging but she swallowed her panic and concentrated on Gilbret who stood poised for Everlyn's advance.

The crowd was silent—all eyes were on the men in the center of the arena.

They circled each other with their swords drawn. Not a sound was heard. Even the birds in the nearby orchard seemed to hold their collective breaths as the two men prowled around each other.

Finally, Everlyn struck with snake-like speed but Gilbret defended with his shield reducing the attack to a glancing blow. The fight began in earnest as they slowly assessed each other's strength and skill. But then, as if by silent accord, they began to fight faster and faster. Swinging, thrusting, and parrying with their swords.

Flashes of sunlight caught the blades as they moved in a deadly dance of death.

After several minutes it was clear they were both tiring. Their armor weighed them down and their bodies sweated in the early morning summer sun. From where Beatrice sat, she could see both men's chests heaving as they gulped for breath.

To watch them was like watching a dance—a lethal dance, but there was a beauty to their actions. Everlyn lunged forward, then jumped back to keep out of Gilbret's way.

Gilbret turned suddenly to parry a hostile blow from Everlyn as he brought his sword down in a large arc.

Thus it went. Beatrice leaned forward, hardly daring to breathe.

Neither man seemed to have the upper hand. Their swords clashed high above their heads, then smashed down on their wooden shields. The usually quiet morning air was rent by the lethal song.

Sparks of sunlight danced above the dueling men, causing Beatrice to look away at one point. "Please, God, don't let the sun blind Gilbret," Beatrice prayed when she was momentarily blinded by a brilliant flash of golden light.

Alas, her prayer was not to be answered. Gilbret stumbled as sunlight flashed from Everlyn's sword, blinding him for a heartbeat. Everlyn saw his chance and struck with a vicious blow to Gilbret's right thigh.

Momentarily blinded, Gilbret was unable to protect himself and fell as Everlyn's sword connected with his leg. The mail would protect the skin but if his leg was damaged, Gilbret would be crippled and at Everlyn's mercy.

"Praise God," Thomas gasped as Gilbret recovered and defended another strike to his head that would have had him on his back.

Although both men wore great helms that protected their heads from cutting blows, it didn't protect them from a smashing blow that could temporarily render them off balance.

Everlyn's sword connected with Gilbret's helm, sending Gilbret back several steps. He didn't lose his balance but he was stunned. Everlyn took a step back. That was a mistake. Even Beatrice understood that. Everlyn should have pushed his advantage instead of withdrawing to regain his breath.

Standing apart, it was easy to see their chests rising and falling in great heaving gasps. They had been fighting for almost an hour and were surely exhausted. They could call a short reprieve and take bread and wine to maintain their strength. Both men were commanded to have brought enough food and drink to last the day but neither seemed inclined to take a reprieve.

After a few harrowing heartbeats, the men began their lethal dance again. This time it was Gilbret who would take advantage of an off-balance Everlyn.

Everlyn had tried to kick sand into Gilbret's face but his desperate action only succeeded in making him lose his balance. His arms wheeled about as he tried to regain his balance but it was already too late.

Gilbret struck with a thrust of his sword to the less protected area under Everlyn's right arm as Everlyn was reaching up. There was a gusset between the body armor and the arm. It would not draw blood but it might make Everlyn drop his sword.

The vicious thrust had the desired effect and although Everlyn didn't drop his sword his arm was briefly immobilized.

Gilbret, unlike Everlyn, pushed his advantage by grabbing Everlyn's helm and taking several steps backward before throwing the knight onto his back. The speed and unexpected move caused Everlyn's hand to release his sword as he was flung onto his back.

Gilbret kicked the sword away and yelled down at his opponent, lying immobilized on the ground.

"Confess your lie," Gilbret yelled for all to hear but Everlyn shook his head while his hand sought his sword.

"Confess your lie," Gilbret repeated.

When Everlyn again refused, Gilbret used the steel hilt of his sword to strike Everlyn's helm. The sound of the blow reverberated throughout the arena making Beatrice flinch.

"Confess!"

"By God, I am innocent. She is an adulterous whore," Everlyn screamed. He began kicking at Gilbret but the weight of his armor prevented him from regaining his feet. Gilbret had the advantage and every time Everlyn tried to sit up Gilbret smashed him in the chest.

Then Gilbret did something so extraordinary the crowd gasped. He threw his sword away and straddled Everlyn.

"Confess, you fucking maggot!" Gilbret raged.

"Never," Everlyn yelled back.

"Then be dammed," Gilbret yelled as he withdrew the dagger from his belt.

Everlyn couldn't get to his own short dagger as Gilbret's knees restricted Everlyn's movements.

With his dagger drawn, Gilbret used his free hand to lift Everlyn's helm, exposing his jaw and the leather strap that secured the helm in place under his chin.

Everlyn, understanding what Gilbret was about, began to struggle, frantically searching for purchase.

Within a few minutes, Everlyn's helm was free and Gilbret tossed it aside.

"Your last chance, admit your crime."

"I am innocent," Everlyn screamed, but his reply lacked the confidence of his previous denials.

"Go to hell, you lying bastard." Gilbret plunged his dagger into Everlyn's open mouth. "May God curse your lying tongue," Gilbret roared as the dagger came to rest in Everlyn's brain. Only the hilt was visible.

Everlyn's body gave one enormous spasm, then lay still. Blood pooled at the side of his head. From where she sat Beatrice could see the dagger's hilt and the blood streaming from Everlyn's face.

Gilbret placed his hand on Everlyn's chest and heaved himself up, then turned and faced the crowd. "Have I done my duty?" he roared.

The crowd erupted with one voice. "Yes! Yes!"

Gilbret staggered towards the platform where Guyon and Hugh de Puiset sat. Still wearing his helm, he knelt before them, head bowed, and asked, "God has proved my case," he announced in a loud clear voice.

Guyon rose. "God has proved your case. Go in peace."

The crowd erupted with cheers and shouts but Beatrice's pulse thundered in her ears, drowning out the crowd's shouts.

Thomas cut away the ties at her hands and feet and escorted her down the scaffold stairs where she waited for Gilbret, who was making his way to her.

He had taken off his gloves and mail gauntlets so he could undo the leather strap of his helm.

They stood face to face—a thousand words tumbling around her head but she couldn't catch one.

Gilbret's face looked exhausted and bruises were already appearing on his cheek and chin but his eyes were clear as he looked at her. "It is done, wife." Then he drew her to him, giving her a scorching kiss. Beatrice vaguely heard the crowd erupt in shouts of agreement.

It was over and she was safe.

Providence had proved the day. She kissed her husband back with unveiled passion. The church and the crowd be damned. She would show everyone that the love Gilbret and she shared was true and full of passion.

"I love you," she gasped as he peppered kisses all over her face.

Gilbret pulled back and searched her face. "You, and you alone, gave me the strength to vanquish our foes. You are my equal, Beatrice, and I will love and cherish you till the day I die."

For the first time in her life, Beatrice happily walked into her future with the man she loved walking at her side.

Her buoyant mood was shattered as her father approached them.

"I would talk with you, daughter."

Gilbret went to move in front of her but she raised her hand to still him.

"Speak," she said as she looked her father in the eye. This man had terrified her for years but now as she looked upon him she felt nothing but distain.

"I would forgive you your rebellion and…"

Gilbret's hand was resting on the small of her back and that slight pressure gave her the confidence to speak her mind.

"How dare you," Beatrice snapped as she interrupted her father. "You have proven your character and I have no desire to ever lay eyes on you again." She took a shuddering breath. "You would have seen me burn as an adulterer. You disgust me." With that final barb she turned from her father and walked away.

"Are you well?" Gilbret asked as they made their way to the horses.

She stopped and looked at the man who held her heart. "I will never again allow that worm to have power over me," she said as she smiled. "You have given me the gift of courage and I will never squander it."

Gilbret leaned in and bussed a kiss on her lips. "Let's go home."

Epilogue

BARMOOR CASTLE, NORTHUMBRIA
  St. John's Eve, three weeks later

IT WAS ALMOST three weeks since Gilbret had faced de Gant and the repercussions of that fateful day were still being felt.

Gilbret's uncle had seemingly disappeared after the duel but Gilbret had tracked him down to Heatherslaw Priory the previous week and given him a warning. "On point of death you will never set foot on my land without my permission. You have forfeited any rights." Gilbret glared at his uncle. "Do I make myself clear?"

His uncle had nodded. He was defeated and he knew it. He had been stripped of his position as Prior and was forced to seek succor with the new Prior of Heatherslaw. His uncle would hide behind the priory walls for the rest of his accursed life. Gilbret felt only contempt for the man and vowed that he would purge him from his memory.

Finally, Gilbret's inheritance and his family's future were secure.

They had returned to Barmoor the day after the duel with promises from Hugh de Puiset that Beatrice's annulment would be revoked and Edward would be reinstated as Walter de Gant's heir.

Gilbret now held a charter in his hands from King Henry stating that Gilbret would be the custodian of Folkingham and all thirty estates until Edward reached the age of one and twenty.

What Gilbret had not expected was that the king had decided that Beatrice would not only retain her dower lands but that on her father's death Dunstunburgh Castle and the Barony of Embleton would become hers. Her father had sided with the wrong man and now bore the shame of being associated with a perjurer. He would be forced to live out his days in obscurity. It was a fitting end. Gilbret smiled at the irony. The old bastard had tried to disinherit Beatrice, his only surviving child when she left Walter, but now she would have it all.

It was justice and neither Beatrice nor Gilbret would give the arsewipe another thought.

"Your father will be spitting like the snake he is," he said casually as he handed the charter to Beatrice who sat on the other side of the table playing with Amica. Edward was at her feet, pulling himself up to a standing position and then plunking himself down on his arse thinking he was a very clever fellow.

Gilbret could watch Edward for hours and never grow tired of the boy's antics. He had a stout heart and a sunny disposition and Gilbret looked forward to when he could begin to teach him swordcraft and how to ride a horse.

"You will be busy with Folkingham, perhaps you might consider Olivier as castellan of Dunstunburgh when he is old enough?" she said as she put the charter on the table before her.

Gilbret recognized a trap when he heard it and was careful to avoid a tongue lashing. Although, when he thought about it, Beatrice was an expert when it came to her very talented tongue. The image of Beatrice's head between his legs made him shift in his chair. "I believe Dunstunburgh is yours to dispose of as you see fit." He groaned as he gave her a lopsided smile. "I would never dream of usurping your authority, my lady."

She barked a most unladylike laugh which frightened Amica. The pup jumped off her knee and scampered over to Gilbret begging to be picked up. "I suspect, husband, that the look on your face and the shifting in your seat means that your mind is not on estates or titles," she teased as she raised her eyebrow in silent question.

"Clever wench."

"Mary, might you take Edward and Amica out to see Olivier. I need to discuss a very important matter with my husband."

Gilbret slid his eyes to where Mary had been sitting sewing by the window seat, too far away to hear their conversation but close enough for Beatrice to summon her. The maid had flushed cheeks and didn't meet his eyes as she came and retrieved Amica.

Edward pulled himself up and stood for several moments unaided waiting for Mary to pick him up.

"Clever boy!" All three of them chimed at the same time. Looking very pleased with himself he lost concentration and fell back on his arse. His bottom lip quivered as he thought about crying.

Gilbret jumped up and walked to where Edward sat on the rug next to his mother. He reached down and flung him upside down over his shoulder, asking Beatrice and Mary if they had seen Edward.

The child's laughter filled the solar. All thought of crying was banished.

"Catastrophe averted, very well done," Beatrice purred as she watched Mary leave the chamber.

"I plan on making someone cry, but in pleasure," he murmured as he nuzzled her ear after pulling her out of the chair and into his embrace.

True to his word he did make her cry.

"We must get up or we shall be late for the celebrations," Beatrice said as she lay next to him. They had spent the afternoon in their chamber. God only knew where Mary was, or Edward. But the little maid was used to her mistress's afternoon disappearances.

He gazed down at his wife. Her lips were a rosy pink from his attentions, and her breasts as well. Tiny purple bruises peppered the snow-white skin where he had nipped her. He ran a finger over the area. "Did I hurt you?"

She looked down at her breast, then back up at him. "I should ask you the same thing," she said as she pointed to similar bite marks on his shoulder.

"I seem to have been too occupied to notice that you were trying to devour me."

"I love you, Sir Gilbret," she said as she kissed the bruises she had inflicted.

"And I you." He bent his head to kiss her but she pushed him away.

"No! We will never leave this chamber if I allow you to touch me again." With that, she jumped from the bed as he tried to grab her.

The night air smelled of smoke and magic as Beatrice inhaled. She loved St. John's Eve—the fires, the dancing, and the anticipation that magic stalked unseen about them.

Edward was sitting on her lap, watching the fires. It was late and he should have been asleep but even though he was a child he seemed to understand this night was not meant to be slept through.

Mary and Olivier were dancing around the bonnefyre which had been lit first. The bleached bones were still visible amid the flames but as the night progressed more bones would be added to keep the fire burning till dawn.

A large group of men were standing by the wakefyre drinking ale. Gilbret was at the center of the huddle laughing with his retainers. Villeins, men at arms, and knights stood shoulder to shoulder telling stories and boasting of their drinking prowess.

The summer solstice was a time to celebrate, and although the church named the day in honor of St. John the Baptist, most of the people who gathered around the fires believed in the ancient magic that accompanied such a night.

"Do you want me to take him, m'lady," Mary asked as she plunked herself down beside Beatrice.

"No, go and enjoy yourself. I am content to sit here and watch."

Mary's eyes glowed in the firelight. "I have never had so much fun on St. John's Eve," she panted.

Beatrice turned to her in silent invitation to explain.

"My da always got drunk and became violent," she admitted with a small shrug of her shoulders. "So, I spent the night trying to keep the little ones safe and out of harm's way."

Oh, Mary. What a childhood she must have endured.

Beatrice patted her maid's knee. "Go find someone to dance with, and don't come back till dawn."

Mary's eyes widened. And Beatrice laughed.

"It is tradition to stay awake all night and dance and sit around the three great fires."

Beatrice leaned sideways towards her maid and gave her shoulder a small nudge. "And you just might find a ghost to entertain you for a time," she said as she wiggled her eyebrows.

"What's this about a ghost?" Gilbret said as he came and sat down on Beatrice's other side.

"I was trying to encourage Mary to enjoy herself and to stay open to the opportunity of encountering the magic that lurks about on this night."

"I don't know about magic, but there is a lad over there who could do with some encouragement." Gilbret inclined his head in the direction of the bonnefyre called St. John's Fire. A handsome youth was arm-wrestling with another man as the crowd cheered them on. Beatrice had seen Mary blush as she talked to the lad during the meal.

Mary stood up and slowly walked towards the lad.

"Who is he?" she asked as she watched Mary approach him.

"His name is Rowan and he is the son of the alderman."

"And what of Olivier?"

Gilbret continued to watch Mary and Rowan. "As I told you before Olivier cannot marry as he has no land. And no name." he said in a resigned tone. "Mary needs security. That is something Olivier can never offer."

Beatrice continued to watch as Mary stood beside Rowan. Her presence must have distracted him as he looked up to see who had approached. His opponent took advantage of his momentary lapse. The shriek of defeat could be heard even from where she and Gilbret sat.

"Those two are like circling dogs. One moment playing, then the next snarling and biting at each other," Gilbret announced as he watched Mary and Rowan.

"There is magic between them, but it needs to mature into something that will endure." It was obvious both Mary and Rowan were drawn to each other. It would be some years before they could marry but she hoped it was a future for her young maid.

. . .

Gilbret didn't want to talk of Mary and Rowan. He wanted his wife's company. So he nudged closer to Beatrice and took a very sleepy Edward into his arms.

"I have sat around the fires of this night all of my life," he said as he pulled her closer. "But never have I felt its magic until tonight." He kissed the top of her head as she nestled into him.

They sat like that for some time just watching the fires burn. "Why do they light three fires, do you think?" Beatrice asked as she watched.

"Legend has it that the fires help boost the sun's heat, ensuring a good harvest. But I suspect the church would like us to believe they signify the blessed Trinity."

"I like the idea of the ancients lighting their bonnefyres to encourage the sun," she sighed as she watched the flames.

"I suspect it also has something to do with fertilizing the earth with the ash."

"Very romantic," she teased as she flicked his hand resting on her shoulder.

"Ah, look. The bard is about to sing."

A tall, skinny man moved into the center of the clearing; the three fires shimmered behind him giving him a strangely ghostly appearance.

His voice was clear and carried through the night. He sang of lovers and ghosts. Fairies and magic.

"I have something to tell you," Beatrice whispered as she moved her head so she faced him.

Gilbret's heart began to race. He didn't dare hope as his heart leaped to his mouth, and he didn't dare draw breath.

"I think we can expect a little de la Haye sometime in early spring." Her eyes held his as she searched his face.

Edward was asleep in his arms, but Gilbret couldn't contain his excitement and immediately kissed his wife in front of the crowd. "I love you, Beatrice de la Haye," he murmured as he kissed her again.

"And I you," she said as she rested her head against his shoulder.

It was not the first time Gilbret had silently thanked Beatrice's father for disowning her. His actions had led her to him.

Indeed, the night was full of magic.

Thank You

Thanks so much for reading **_Tempted by Beauty_**. I hope you enjoyed Beatrice and Gilbret's story.

May I ask a favor? I would really appreciate an honest review. Reviews, and telling your friends, helps other readers find books, so please consider leaving a review at Amazon: https://www.amazon.com/dp/B09NV5NNWC

Want More?

Would you like to read more about Beatrice and Gilbret? Sign up for my newsletter and you will receive a BookFunnel link to the bonus epilogue. It is in an e-reader form and PDF so you can download it on your device.

Here's the link to the bonus epilogue for you! It's a year later and life is changing for Beatrice and Gilbret. Find out more by clicking here: https://www.subscribepage.com/u1v0q5

(It only costs your email address. You will be added to my newsletter and you can unsubscribe at any time. Although I'm planning on keeping you there with the lure of books, and bonus material. Oh, and my phenomenal wit!!)

A new series is on its way … **THE KING'S BARONS** is set in Northumbria twenty years after the Brides of Northumbria series. King Henry's son is trying to wrestle the throne from him and the barons must choose which side they will fight on.

Follow Geifroi, Olivier, Warin and Joss as they navigate the perils of war in twelfth-century Northumbria.

And yes you will recognize their names as they are the squires of Ranulf, Guyon and Gilbret!

The first in the series is available. Click here to preorder Book #1, *The Baron's Prisoner* https://www.amazon.com/dp/B0BK2ZJYP9

He saved her life on the battlefield. Now she is his prisoner.
What happens when war makes an enemy of the woman you have vowed to protect?
In twelfth-century England, honor, not duty can make even the hardest knight question his loyalties.
Follow Gefroi d'Umfraville, Baron Prudhoe, as he fights for his honor in this exciting new medieval romance.

Acknowledgments

A great many people make a book a reality. Foremost among them is my developmental editor, Angela James, but I also owe many thanks to my copyeditor, Maria Fairchild. And of course my amazing book cover designer, Graziana. I am so fortunate to work with such wonderfully talented and encouraging women.

I also want to thank the Otago chapter of RWNZ. Without your support and encouragement, this would never have seen the light of day.

And of course, my own Scottish hero, you have been tireless in your encouragement and I love you.

Thank you!

About the Author

Cate Melville is an emerging author of historical romance. This is Cate's third and final book in the series, **The Brides of Northumbria**.

Set in 12th century Northumbria, the trilogy is full of richly researched historical settings, where her flawed heroes, and the strong woman who defy convention to win their happy ending, transport readers to a time when honor and chivalry really were something to fight, and die, for.

When Cate is not writing, she is busy reading, or re-reading, her favorite authors, cooking for friends, and enjoying the best of Central Otago's Pinot varieties of wine, and taking long walks with her own Scottish hero, and their dogs, Poppy and Lily. She lives in New Zealand's gorgeous South Island.

You can contact Cate at:
  Web: catemelvilleauthor.com
  Email: contact@catemelvilleauthor.com

Also by Cate Melville

<u>Brides of Northumbria series</u>

Born in Deception

Drawn to the Beast

Tempted by Beauty

<u>The King's Barons series</u>

The Baron's Prisoner

(Coming late 2023)